The
Only Ones

ALSO BY AARON STARMER

DWEEB

The
Only Ones

AARON STARMER

DELACORTE PRESS

Text copyright © 2011 by Aaron Starmer
Jacket art copyright © 2011 by Lisa Ericson

Visit us on the Web! www.randomhouse.com/kids
Educators and librarians, for a variety of teaching tools, visit us at
www.randomhouse.com/teachers

Library of Congress Cataloging-in-Publication Data
Starmer, Aaron.
    The only ones / Aaron Starmer. — 1st ed.
        p. cm.
    Summary: After setting off from the island where he has been leading a solitary existence, thirteen-year-old Martin discovers a village with other children who have been living similarly without any adults, after the grown-ups have all been spirited away.
    ISBN 978-0-385-74043-2 (hc : alk. paper) — ISBN 978-0-375-89919-5 (ebook)
ISBN 978-0-385-90839-9 (glb : alk. paper) [1. Supernatural—Fiction.] I. Title.
    PZ.S7972On 2011   [Fic]—dc22   2010040383

The text of this book is set in 11¾-point Baskerville.
Book design by Vikki Sheatsley
Printed in the United States of America
10 9 8 7 6 5 4 3 2 1
First Edition

For William and Randi

The
Only Ones

"The yeas have it. The Council has made its decision. He lives."

"But he knows too much, Crawford."

"That's precisely why he should live."

"What about the other one? The little weakling? We could get the information from him too."

"They lost track of him, somewhere west of the mountains. Few people know what he looks like, anyway. He never let anyone inside with him."

"How long will it take the apprentices to learn?"

"Hard to say. Why don't we call in the expert and ask?"

"He'll bring his security."

"So? Let him. The decision's made. Nobody lays a finger on him or any of his people, at least not for now. You do realize we're still talking about a child, don't you?"

"This is different. It's Martin Maple."

The Summer People

MARTIN MAPLE lived on an island, in a gray-shingled cabin perched on a scrub-choked cliff that plunged down into the ocean. He lived there with his father and a machine. His father was a gentle man who never yelled but also never hugged his boy. The machine was an elaborate bundle of knobs, levers, gears, motors, and propellers, and when it was turned on, it sang out with a comforting whir, but it didn't do much else, because it wasn't finished.

Next to the cabin was a ladder that led down the cliff to mussel-encrusted rocks and a crooked but sturdy dock, where Martin and his father kept a skiff for fishing. They had a small garden that gave them root vegetables and greens, and at the end of a small path was a bigger field for grains and corn. The soil was rocky, but Martin's father understood how to tame it. There were deer on the island, and Martin and his father set traps for them and ate them. From the sea, they pulled mackerel and cod and lobster, though they were careful not to steal from lobster pots.

"They might shoot you without a thought," Martin's father would say as he pointed to the raincoat-clad men piloting the trawlers that bobbed along the frosty horizon. Not stealing from lobster pots was one of Martin's father's rules. He had many rules.

The air on the island smelled of salt and seaweed and firs, but as far as Martin was concerned, that was how the air smelled everywhere. He had never left the island. His father had never allowed it. When he asked his father what lay beyond the island, the answer was always the same: "Not what we're looking for."

In the cabin they had one book, a dog-eared paperback that Martin's father had passed along after he had witnessed his son puzzling over the markings that decorated the sterns of boats. The cover was missing, so Martin didn't know its title, but it was a collection of stories about men traveling to other planets, meeting aliens and doing fantastically strange things. Martin's father had used this book to teach Martin how to read. When Martin asked if this was what it was like beyond the island, his father said, "No, someone just had an active imagination."

The book was about men, but there was one story that featured the line *They piled aboard the vessel, fathers and mothers, and all of the children.* Martin knew what women were, but he had never heard of mothers.

"What are mothers?" he asked his father.

So his father sat him down and had that talk fathers have about men and women and falling in love and playing soft music and turning off the lights.

"Who is my mother?" Martin asked.

His father smiled at this and took a moment to himself. When he finally responded, he said, "Your mother doesn't exist."

"She's dead?" Martin asked.

His father shook his head and said, "Have you ever seen a bubble taken up by the air from the foam of the sea?"

"Yes."

"You know how it seems perfect? How it floats? You know how all the colors of the world seem to be dancing on its skin?"

"Yes."

"That was your mother. But like a bubble . . ." He flicked his fingers out as if to pantomime something bursting into nothingness. He left it at that.

The summer people arrived every year when the days were at their longest. They stayed in tall houses on the other side of the island and came and went on shiny boats with steering wheels and hulking motors or blindingly white sails that reminded Martin of heron wings.

When the summer people were on the island, there was a special set of rules. You never spoke to them. You didn't trap the deer. You stayed close to home. And you never let the summer people see the machine. You would tuck it in the cramped back room of the cabin and you would pull the blinds. You wouldn't touch it at all for months.

They seemed like reasonable rules, and Martin followed them as much as a boy could. When he wasn't fishing or tending the garden with his father, he would hide among the pines and rocks and he would watch the people from a distance, though he was much too scared to approach them. The island had no shops or restaurants, or even roads. The summer people brought their supplies by boat and kept to the trails and rocky shores near their houses. There was never any reason for paths to cross, and Martin's life went on without incident. That is, until the inevitable showed its face.

The inevitable was named George.

Martin was nine years old when he met George. George was nine too, but Martin didn't know that then. He only knew that George was a summer person and he had long blond bangs and a few large freckles on his face and he stayed in a maroon house with a rowboat in the backyard and a flagpole in the front that rattled when the wind blew.

"You live here year-round, don'tcha?" George asked Martin when he snuck up on him in a thick patch of blueberry bushes.

"I'm not supposed to talk to people like you," Martin whispered.

"And I'm not supposed to talk to people like you," George said.

"What sort of person am I like?" Martin asked.

"Stranger," George said.

"Stranger than what?"

"Than anyone I've ever met." George laughed.

It was easy to like George. He was kind and curious and loved dirt and nonsense. It wasn't easy to see him, though. Martin couldn't tell his father about this new friendship. It had to be a secret, and the guilt such secrets carried was nearly unbearable. The thrill, however, was unbearable too. And the thrill inevitably won out.

Late at night, Martin would sneak from his room and

make his way across the island until he found himself at his friend's flagpole. If George had raised a flag that he called the Jolly Roger, it was okay to knock on his window and rouse him from his sleep. Then the two would take off into the woods together.

Martin introduced George to all the mysterious ways of the island. He showed him the hollow tree where he hid things. He brought him to the rock outcropping where he would climb up and look at stars and watch boats come and go. He taught him how to trap animals.

In return, George told Martin stories. Martin desperately wanted to know what life was like off the island, and George always satisfied with tales of chaotic schoolrooms and bicycle stunts and older kids who did scandalous things, like smoking cigarettes and kissing with open mouths. There were a million questions Martin could have asked, but staying up late was exhausting, and their time together lasted only an hour or two each night. So he simply let George talk about the things that were happening in his world, and that was more than enough for Martin.

"Why doesn't your father let you leave the island?" George once asked.

"He says there's nothing for us out there," Martin responded. "Our destiny is here."

"Why doesn't he let you talk to people? He doesn't even let you have pets, does he?" George shook his head in disbelief.

"Losing a pet will break your heart, and you're bound to lose them all," Martin said, echoing his father's words. "And people? People leave. They always have."

"Does he lie to you?" George asked gently.

"Do your parents?" Martin shot back.

"Where's your mom?"

Martin could have told him that he didn't know, that his father was hiding the truth about her in metaphors and silence. But he wasn't ready for that yet. "It doesn't matter," he said defensively. "Just tell me more of your stories."

George and his family left the island at the end of the summer, but he promised Martin he would be back the next year. That autumn, after the last boat of summer people took to the water, Martin celebrated his tenth birthday. Then he and his father pulled the machine out into the yard, where there was room to get at its insides. Like every year since Martin could remember, they went back to work on it.

All day, every day.

It was school for Martin. Through the machine, he learned about physics and engineering, electricity, and everything his father had the ability to explain. It wasn't a particularly big machine. A man and a boy could fit in it, but not much else. Inside, next to a control panel, was a glass door that opened up to a tall and hollow chamber with a small shelf and a round basin at the back. His father said the chamber was the machine's heart. All the while, the purpose of the machine remained a mystery.

"It's our destiny, right?" Martin once asked. "But what does it do?"

"The less you understand, the better," his father explained. "For your own protection. It's a powerful thing, and if it's misused, the results could be devastating."

"I promise I won't misuse it," Martin assured him. "And I would never tell anyone about it."

"Magic, then," his father said. "It's going to help us start over. That's all you need to know. Life is a path, Martin, and you follow it. Sometimes you follow it blind. Maps are for doubters, and I raised a believer."

It was a typical answer from his father, astoundingly elusive, but to a boy of ten, it seemed like wisdom from a life lived. Martin knew only a few details about his father's days before the island. He knew his name was Glen. He knew he had owned a farmhouse. He knew he had even lived with a circus for a time. "It's funny," his father told him with a smile. "I didn't run away *to* it. I ran away *from* it."

"Is that where you learned to build the machine?" Martin asked.

"It's where I learned about it," his father said. "It was my father's circus. There were carnival rides there. Not many, but we had a carousel and a Ferris wheel. Basically things to spin you in a circle. I always helped the mechanic when the rides needed fixing. One day, he gave me a piece of paper. It had small ink sketches of the machine. Showed the inside, showed the outside, not much else."

"Did he tell you what it did?" Martin asked.

"He didn't know," his father said. "He'd found the paper folded and jammed in the gears of the Ferris wheel. There was one word written on it. *Hope.* That didn't explain much, so he gave it to me, thinking a smart kid with fresh eyes and loads of imagination would figure it out. I gave it a close look, but I didn't have all that much interest. A few days later, I ran away. I threw the sketches in a trash can somewhere."

"But you *did* figure it out?" Martin asked.

"Eventually. But not for a long time, not until I'd almost completely forgotten about it. You were just a baby then. We lived in a farmhouse, far away from the island. And I—it's sad to say—was a desperate person. Completely lost, full of regret. The only thing that saved me from going over the edge was a knock on our door one evening. The mechanic, by that time an old man, had found me. He asked if I still had the sketches. I told him I'd thrown them out. It didn't upset him, but he gave me a pat on the shoulder and said, 'I think about that machine every day. I guess it's better to just imagine what it might have done.' Then he left."

"But you didn't just imagine, did you?"

"No I didn't. The realization hit me like a fist to the jaw: the machine could give us exactly what the paper had advertised and exactly what we needed—hope. I started building it from scraps of my memory."

"Where did you get the pieces?" Martin asked.

"I bought some. Stole others. I started the construction in the farmhouse, but it was trial and error. People thought I was crazy. I was a bit crazy, I suppose. I was also careless. There was a fire. I managed to save you and the pieces, but that's all. Not the house, not all the other things. We moved to this island, where I could take my time, be safe and deliberate. It was also a place where no one would bother us."

"And we have everything?"

"Almost."

Almost was the problem. They had almost everything. But on a rainy spring morning, about a month before the summer people were scheduled to arrive, Martin's father put on his coat and told him that he had to leave for a while. He had to get the final piece for the machine.

"Can I come with you?" Martin asked.

"Someone has to stay with the machine."

"How long will you be gone?"

"Hard to say," his father said. "Could be a few days. Could be longer. No matter what, I'll be back for your eleventh birthday. In the meantime, it's your job to carry on."

A few hours later, his father got into the skiff and set out onto the spitting ocean, heading to where the trawlers bobbed.

Days passed. Martin climbed up to the rock outcropping and watched the horizon. The skiff didn't return.

He wasn't too worried, but as the days became weeks and there was still no sign of his father, seeds of doubt were planted in his mind. How far did he have to travel to find this final piece? Was it a dangerous journey? Could he die along the way?

It was still months until his eleventh birthday, so Martin pushed those concerns aside and did what his father had told him to do. He carried on. He tended the garden and the field. He mended the frayed wires that transmitted electricity from solar panels to their cabin. He trapped deer and caught fish. He kept the machine clean and polished, and every morning he practiced the procedure of turning it on. In the evenings, when the distractions of survival were furthest from his mind, loneliness would take hold. So he would sit by a lantern and read the book his father had given him, over and over again. It provided more comfort, perhaps, than it should have.

Finally, when the summer people arrived, he used levers and fulcrums to lift the machine onto dollies, and he moved it to the back room. He spied the Jolly Roger and tapped on George's window.

He had thought long and hard about what to tell George.

On one hand, George was the only person in the world he could trust, and Martin wanted to express how worried he was about his father. On the other, he couldn't betray his father's wishes. The more he thought about it, the more he began to believe that carrying on had nothing to do with surviving. It was all about the machine. And no one else was ever supposed to know about the machine. So he pretended that nothing had changed. The friendship was treated as a secret, relegated to nighttime meetings in the forest.

It started off as thrilling for Martin as it had ever been, but as the summer went on, he began to wonder what else there was in the world besides what George was telling him about. Martin had no idea what video games were, but they sounded soulless and flat to him. Soccer seemed like an intriguing sport at first, but then he realized that nothing happened. And school? It must be something other than just pranks played on substitute teachers and gossip involving invitations to birthday parties. Martin's father had been out beyond the ocean for over a month. There had to be something bigger keeping him there.

"Do you know anyone else's stories?" Martin asked George.

"What do you mean?" George said. "Like books and stuff?"

"You have books?"

"Sure," George said with a shrug. "I'll bring you one."

So he did. The next night, George presented Martin with a ratty paperback with a picture of a pistol and a pair of broken eyeglasses on the cover. Martin took it home, and over the course of the next day, he read the entire thing.

The plot centered on a police detective who was investigating the kidnapping of a child. It didn't make much sense to Martin, but all the voices of the characters were endlessly fascinating. In this book there were people who grunted and cackled when they talked, who sneered and whispered and said inappropriate things. They were nothing like his father and nothing like George or the people he constantly talked about.

"You have any other books?" Martin asked George.

"I don't read much, but my parents have tons," George said. The next night he gave Martin another.

It became an addiction. At first, he took one book a night from George, but after a couple of weeks, he was demanding three or four. All day he would sit on the rock outcropping and read about pirates and doctors and magicians and lots of people who kissed and lots of people who killed and lots of people whose lives changed in an instant. As far as Martin was concerned, all the books were classics, because they were all full of such surprises. They distracted him from life.

The meetings with George became less about friendship than they were about exchanging books. By the end of the summer, George didn't even bother leaving his yard. He would simply place an old wooden lobster pot full of books next to the flagpole, and Martin would grab what he wanted and return what he had finished.

It didn't even occur to Martin that this arrangement might bother George. After all, George had his own family and his own life full of stories, and if those things bored him, then he could always pull a book off the shelf. Martin had taught him everything he could about the island. What more was in it for George?

One night, Martin got his answer to that question. When he opened the lobster pot in search of books, he found just an envelope with his name written on it. Inside, there was a single sheet of paper. On the paper was an address.

It meant nothing to him, so he quietly made his way to George's window and gave it a tap. Almost immediately, George's face appeared. He had been waiting.

"It's his home," George said.

"Whose home?" Martin asked.

"Your dad's. Before he came here."

Martin stared at the address. It was a simple string of numbers and the names of a street and a town. He assumed it was the farmhouse where he and his father had lived when Martin was a baby. It was impossible to picture a place, though. It was impossible to imagine them anywhere but on the island.

"I told you about the Internet, right?" George went on. "You can find all sorts of things with it."

"Thank you . . . I guess," Martin said.

"He left, didn't he?"

"How do you know that?"

"You taught me the island," George said. "How to watch people. Some of us don't sit around all day reading books, you know."

"Oh."

"I haven't told anyone," George assured him. "People try to ignore you and your dad."

"I know."

"Is that why you try to ignore us?"

"What do you mean?"

"I was your friend, Martin. Your only friend."

"You still are."

14

"We're going home tomorrow. I know it's been a while, but I'm gonna miss telling you stories. Helping you out."

"I'm gonna miss—"

George stopped him right there. "Do you wanna come with us?"

This was the question Martin had dreamt about being asked. Now that he was being asked, it was also the most frightening thing he could imagine. The world he had read about was so big and so strange and so unlike the island he didn't know if he could handle it. Besides, his eleventh birthday hadn't come. His father had promised to be back by then. Together, they would finish the machine.

"No," he told George. "No thank you. But can you do me a favor?"

"Maybe."

"Go to the address," Martin said. "Tell me what you see there."

"It's on the other side of the country," George explained.

"Is that far?"

Then George looked at Martin as if this were the first time he had ever laid eyes on him, and asked, "You gonna be okay here, all by yourself?"

"Of course," Martin said, less than convincingly. "I've already done it for months. Besides, my father will be back and everything will be fine."

"I'll be back too," George assured him. "Next summer. Count on it."

On a morning in early autumn, after the summer people had left, Martin celebrated his eleventh birthday. He did so by climbing up to the rock outcropping and watching the ocean. For the last time, he waited for his father.

It was midday and the tide was high when Martin saw a smudge of white on the horizon. It was his father's skiff, its bow pointed toward the island. A rush of pure joy grabbed Martin, and he hurried down from the outcropping, into the woods, past the cabin, to the ladder. He almost slipped on the ladder's steps, but he made it to the rocks unscathed and just in time to see the boat floating a few hundred yards offshore.

He waved his arms and called for his father, but there was no response. The skiff, flat-bottomed and wooden, with slats for seats, rocked back and forth on the water. There was no cabin, so Martin could see why no one waved or called back: it was empty, except for a leafy branch of a tree that was resting on the seats, as if it had broken off and fallen inside during a storm.

Martin dove into the frigid water. The tide was on its way out, a wind was picking up, and the current was pulling the skiff back to sea. Martin couldn't let it get away. He had to know if there was anything else inside, any clue that his father had recently been aboard. But as hard as he swam, it was not nearly hard enough. Before long, the skiff was near the horizon, disappearing almost as quickly as it had come.

Defeated, wet, and cold, Martin returned to the cabin. He lit a fire in their wood-burning stove. Sadness didn't sit with him. Anger did. To be teased by the skiff! His father was an experienced mariner. Was Martin to believe he had fallen overboard? As soon as Martin was dry and warm, he went to the back room, where the machine was hidden. He hoisted it onto the dollies and brought it out into the yard.

He turned all his attention to the machine. By studying it, he hoped that he would understand what exactly his father was seeking, why it was taking so long to find it, and why the skiff had appeared on Martin's birthday in the guise of a gift when it was merely an empty box. He took the machine apart, and he put it back together. He searched the book his father had given him, underlining passages about machines, hoping they would reveal something. They revealed nothing. The blank spaces in the machine were blank spaces in his mind, and he realized the painful truth: he didn't have the ability to know what might fill them.

Martin fell into a deep depression. Every day he regretted his decision to stay on the island instead of leaving with George. As the winter winds blew in and then blew out, the only thing that kept him going was the knowledge that when the days got long, the boats would show up, and so too would his friend. He would have his second chance.

"Of course I'll go with you," he would tell George. "My father's not coming back. I have this machine, but I don't care about that anymore. You were right. You're always right about everything."

So he waited again, only this time he waited for George. He climbed the rock outcropping and looked for boats. He watched the horizon for a long time, but no one came. It was hot, but there was no music playing across the open water. The sun was high, but there were no families fumbling along the rocks with picnic baskets in their hands. It was summer, but the summer people just weren't there.

The lobster trawlers should have clued him in. He hadn't seen them since before that horrible eleventh birthday. While his father used to tell him that "someday the lobsters will run out and the trawlers will disappear," he'd probably meant they would trickle away, with fewer trawlers appearing every year, until one day there would be none left. He probably hadn't meant it would happen all at once. But that was what happened. One day they were there. The next they weren't.

Now the summer people hadn't come, and this went against everything his father had predicted. "They will keep coming," he had said. "There will be more and more of them, until the place becomes a theme park."

"What's a theme park?"

"It's torture, son. With roller coasters."

His father was wrong. *This* was torture. Alone, clueless, Martin was trapped. His body throbbed with anxiety. He slept very little. As strange and cruel as it might have seemed, the loss of Martin's father paled in comparison to the loss of George. Devastation was worsened by desperation. He needed to know what had happened to everyone. When the summer ended, he had to make a choice. He could go on just as he had been, wallowing in self-pity. Or he could prepare.

He thought about something George had once told him: "There are all sorts of people in the world. With all sorts of ways of seeing stuff."

With this in mind, Martin formulated a plan. He would start breaking into the island's houses. He would search them front to back. He would gather every book he could find. From that point on, he would do little else but read.

So he did. He went from house to house, living in each until he finished every title inside. He continued fishing, gardening, and trapping, but only for a couple of hours a day, only for long enough to keep himself going, to keep himself reading.

From the books, he came to realize that the world had

plenty of joy in it, but also some terrible things. Bombs that wiped out cities. Savage landscapes full of people willing to fight you at the drop of a hat. Diseases and vengeful gods and science gone mad. Whether it was fiction didn't matter. This was how the people out there saw their home. If he was going to survive among them, he needed to speak their language.

Eleven years old became twelve years old. Fall tumbled into winter, and winter raged into spring. Another summer arrived and Martin still hadn't seen a single person, but his head was now rattling with a hoard of stories and dialogues. And when that summer neared its end, he confronted a fateful day. He read the last of the books on the island.

So he returned to his cabin. He grabbed the grubby mass of paper that was the book his father had left him. He found the sheet with the address George had given him and slid it into the pages of the book. He placed it all in a canvas bag, which he slung over his shoulder. And he didn't think much about what he did next. Thinking often leads to second thoughts, and he certainly didn't need those. He simply headed straight across the island.

Martin's body could have withered during his year of bookish solitude, but a recent growth spurt had gifted his muscles with an unexpected bulk and had forced him to scavenge a new wardrobe from cardboard boxes in the summer peoples' closets. It had also granted him the strength to drag the rowboat out from behind George's house and over the rocks. He placed it into the ocean. With oars on his shoulder and the bag on his hip, he climbed inside. He looked up at the sun. He looked back at the island he had called home for as long as he could remember.

"They come from where the sun sets," Martin's father had once said about the summer people. "That's why we do our fishing where the sun rises."

Martin leaned an oar into a rock and pushed off. He would head toward the sunset. If he wasn't ready now, then he never would be.

PART 1

———————————— •⚷— ————————————

"They were frozen stiff. I think we mighta killed 'em. There was that blondie, layin' out past those stupid palm trees. I don't think she was breathin'."

"Don't worry about that. Keep running."

"We need to go back for it. We need to check on them."

"You're done with that bunch. We'll find other folks. People we can trust."

"I keep tellin' you. There's nobody else."

"Nonsense. Lies."

"He wasn't lyin' 'bout that. In the mornin', you'll see. It's a totally different world out there."

"Well, if that's true, then . . . it's our world. Isn't it?"

— 1 —

The Mainland

The stars melted away. Martin had rowed through the night. The next time I see stars, he thought, it won't be from the island and it won't be from the ocean.

For through the first spits of morning sunlight, he spied the mainland only a few hundred yards ahead of him. The island had ten houses, while the mainland had hundreds. Dozens of docks lined the water's edge, and countless boats bobbed quietly in a harbor. Many of the boats were half submerged. A few were almost entirely covered in water. Broken masts stuck up through the froth like stubborn little birch trees.

Seagulls circled above him as Martin guided the boat up to a dock. He climbed out and scanned the surroundings. Streets and paths wound their way through the town and into hills in the distance. Cars were strewn everywhere—along the streets, *in* the streets, even in the grass, which was as high as Martin's shoulder. Martin had never seen a car before, but he knew that they were "boats with wheels and windshield wipers," as his father put it, and in nearly every book Martin had read, they were the preferred manner of transportation.

Many of the buildings near the dock were decorated with signs announcing things like THE COLDEST BEER IN TOWN or FINE DINING FOR FINE FOLKS. Martin hadn't eaten in a day, and while he was accustomed to going without a meal or two, the row from the island had left him ravenous.

He made his way down the dock and entered the first building he came upon, a modest construction with a hand-carved sign above the door that read THE BARNACLED BUTCHER.

The first things he noticed were the red stains on the floor. Then a scattering of meat- and marrow-picked bones. Lingering scents of rot and feces hit him next. It had seemed a reasonable place to find a meal, but he had read far too many books about murderers and monsters. He wasn't going to risk meeting such things.

For now, he would explore the rest of the town. Perhaps he would meet someone. Perhaps someone would know where to find George. It had been almost two years since he had seen a soul, and he desperately needed to see one now.

But there wasn't anyone anywhere he looked.

Without even a sliver of warning, a fog hustled in. Martin became blind to everything more than a few yards away. So he kept to the winding streets, hiking for more than a mile and dodging car after car—some with their windows open and their seat cushions torn into tidy little nests; all abandoned and splattered white with gull guano.

If there's not *someone*, he thought, then there must be *something* that can tell me where I am and where I should go.

For now, the best the world could give Martin was a pile

of waterlogged books, pouring out onto the street. He stepped over them and onto a wild, dewy lawn, where he found a series of plastic tables overturned on the ground, their legs sticking up and hugged by weeds. Next to one table, he found a sign. He lifted it, wiped away the mud, and read: GENTLY USED BOOKS—SUPPORT OUR RENOVATIONS THIS SATURDAY AND SUNDAY.

He placed the sign down and squinted through the fog at a building across the lawn. He could barely make out a line of steel letters on the brick entryway.

LIBRARY

It was chillier inside. And dark—so dark that Martin had to let his eyes adjust for a minute before taking a step beyond the doorway. There was an odor, a mustiness, but nothing like in the butcher shop. The floors were relatively free of debris, and as he made his way past a large wooden desk, Martin drew in a breath of relief.

Thousands of books filled dozens of shelves. A few books lay open on the floor, but for the most part, everything seemed in good shape. Martin placed his hand on a line of bindings, then ran his fingers down the row, releasing flurries of dust and listening to the beautiful *thwap, thwap, thwap.*

He lifted a book off a shelf and stared at its glossy cover, adorned with a photograph of the moon. It would take a lifetime to read every book in the library, and Martin began to wonder if maybe it wasn't such a bad way to spend his days. Maybe he wasn't ready to go on. Maybe he was meant to see the world through the filter of books.

Something in the world had changed, though. It couldn't always have been like this, and the books couldn't answer the most important questions.

What happened?

Where is everyone?

Why is something pressing against my knee?

Martin looked down to see a dark mass at his feet. A black nose rubbed gently against his right knee, then moved down his shin until it came to his sock, where it tried to work itself inside with an inquisitive snuff.

Instinctively, Martin reached his hand down to pet the animal at his feet. Its fur was thick and course, like slightly damp hay. He had petted dogs on the island but had never felt one like this. As he pulled his hand away, the nose followed his fingers. Martin got a closer look. It had a snout like a dog's, but its head was rounder and its ears were stiffer. It raised a paw and placed it in the bend of Martin's elbow. Its claws were as thick as Martin's fingers. The pads of its feet were as big as his hands.

"Hello," Martin said softly.

The creature let out a low rumbling sound—soothing at first, then more anxious.

"I'm Martin Maple. From the island. I'm here for a visit. To have a look around."

The creature answered by pulling its head away from Martin. It opened its mouth in what looked like a yawn. Small daggers for teeth, hot breath. It lifted itself until it was standing on two feet. Even standing straight up, it was shorter than Martin by a good foot and a half, but Martin's body still tensed in recognition.

"You're a bear."

The bear blinked.

"I've read about you. You're smaller than I expected. You don't seem *so* mean."

Martin eased his hand back toward the bear, planning to calm it by petting its head. But just as his hand reached the snout, he felt a warm, damp breeze blow onto the top of his neck.

Then he heard a rumble.

It was similar to the rumble the bear had made, but it was coming from behind Martin. It was also deeper and louder. Vibrations crept across Martin's scalp.

He turned around in time to see another bear moving slowly toward him. It was three times as big as the first and had a fox dangling from its jaws. The fox was jerking violently, but the bear didn't seem to notice. Its eyes were locked on Martin.

All at once came a flash of teeth and nostrils as the bigger bear tossed the fox into the darkness and lunged at Martin. Martin threw himself against the bookshelf. A cascade of hardcovers raged out, and the entire thing crashed to the ground.

Martin looked up from the pile of wood and paper. The smaller bear was smiling down at him, and the larger one was rising to its feet, recovering from its failed lunge. Martin's legs flew into a fit of kicking. Books launched into the faces of both bears. They turned their heads, but their backs still blocked the entrance to the library. Martin scrambled to his feet and began to run. Weaving in and out of the aisles, he searched for any sign of sunlight. He would kick and claw a hole in the wall if need be. He had to get out of there.

Then he saw an orange dot in front of him. He zeroed in on it. He didn't dare slow down or turn his head and look back. The dot was moving. It was going somewhere. He was going to follow it.

The orange dot darted purposefully across the floor, at a speed Martin could match but couldn't beat. He followed it through aisles of books, down a hallway, through a wide-open room, all the way to a staircase. Then, without any warning, it stopped. Martin closed in.

At the foot of the staircase sat the fox that had been dangling from the bear's mouth. Its orange fur was shifting to red as blood plotted a slow and insidious takeover. One of the fox's legs was bent, and stuck out uselessly to the side. Exhausted, the animal looked up at Martin. It looked at the stairs it had to climb. It curled into a ball.

Without thinking, Martin snatched the fox, tucked it under his arm, and raced up the stairs. At the top, he saw a pane of glass as big as a door. It was damp with the fog but also glowing with the small bit of sunlight that had found its way through. He lowered his shoulder, held the fox behind his back, and plowed into the glass.

Instead of breaking, the glass heaved. Then it popped from the wall like a head off a dandelion and fluttered down into the grass. Martin's body swayed in the hole for a moment, and his canvas bag dangled and tried to pull his shoulder down with its weight. Behind him was the sound of the bears thundering up the stairway. Below him was the mist-soaked backyard of the library. He looked out to a tight line of trees where a forest began. Gravity and momentum finally took over and Martin closed his eyes as he and the fox tumbled down into a patch of hardy bushes below.

It had been dark for hours. The forest beyond the library was thick, and for now, that was where Martin planned to stay, shielded by the protective glow of a fire. Cradling the dying fox in one hand, he stoked the fire with a stick he held in the other. He wasn't ready, not by a long shot. Towns and cars and library beasts? He knew nothing of these things. What he knew was how to survive in the forest.

His heart was still pounding. His hunger had retreated, but his mind was now a riot of worry. Instead of sleeping, he would tend the fire. When the sun came up, he would hurry back to the rowboat and return to the island.

The fox was breathing, but barely. With his hand on its chest, Martin spoke to it. "Sleep. The pain will go away if you sleep."

The fire was cracking and popping, so Martin didn't hear the footsteps in the pine needles. He heard the voice, though, throaty and high-pitched as it floated out from the darkness.

"Share it with me?"

— 2 —

The Boy

A bone-thin boy stepped into the glow of the fire. He wore a T-shirt and jeans and a tattered red cloak that hung over his shoulders and reached down to his knees and was attached around his chest with a silver bird-shaped medallion. His face was all cheekbones and eyeballs. When he smiled, he revealed a mouth of crooked and brown teeth.

"Would you share?" the boy asked. "Half of it?"

"Wha . . . ?" was the only sound Martin could muster.

"The fox," the boy said. "Or are you just singing it lullabies?"

"It's not dead yet," Martin whispered.

"Seems dead."

Martin looked down at the lump of fur in his hand. His father had always stressed the rules about killing animals: Only when you're hungry. Only if you don't let them suffer.

Martin set the stick down, then placed one hand on the

fox's torso and the other on its head. With a swift motion he turned the head and broke the animal's neck.

"Yikes," the boy said. "Either you've done that before, or you're into horror movies."

"I've never seen a movie," Martin said.

"Sure you haven't," the boy said as he eased himself down onto a rock near the fire. "Can you cook it too?"

"Yes," Martin said, resting the fox in his lap. "I have to skin it first, though."

"Of course," the boy said. "Henry always did the skinning. He had a talent for it. Not my idea of fun."

Martin bent over and unearthed a half-buried piece of limestone. He struck it against a larger rock, chipping away layers until he had a sharp tool. The boy watched with fascination as Martin fastidiously took to the task.

"I don't recognize you from Xibalba," the boy said.

"What's Xibalba?" Martin asked. "Is it a place?"

"It's *the* place. You know that."

"I don't know much," Martin confessed. "I should apologize. I have limited experience talking . . . to people . . ."

"To foxes, then?" the boy asked. "Oh God, don't tell me you're like him."

"Like who?"

"Never mind," the boy said, shaking his head. "So if you never made it to Xibalba, then whatcha been doing since *the Day*?"

"Which day?"

"Which day? Very funny. *The Day!*"

Martin shrugged sheepishly.

"The day they all left us?" the boy said, as if it were the most obvious thing in the world.

31

"Who left us?" Martin asked.

"What island you from, buddy?"

Martin pointed east. "You can't see it from here."

"Priceless." The boy shook his head. "Glad there's someone left with a sense of humor."

"I'm not being humorous," Martin stated. "I *do* come from an island, and everything I know is on that island. I've read some books . . . but when you talk about the people who left us, I'm being honest when I say I don't know who that is. Do you mean my dad? George and his family?"

As the boy considered this, Martin noticed how dark the shadows were on his neck. It was like there were ridges in it. This boy was starving.

"Sorry, kid," the boy said. "I'm also not so good at talking . . . to people. Grandpa was a miner, and Marjorie thinks he left a bit of coal in our hearts. It's been a while since I've even seen anyone. I thought they'd all made it to Xibalba."

"I've made it this far," Martin said as he examined the sharp edge on his hunk of limestone.

"Others came from a lot farther, that's for sure."

"So who left us?" Martin wedged the fox between his knees and ran the stone carefully along its belly.

"Our . . . our moms," the boy said, turning away from the gore. "Our teachers. Our . . . classmates. Everyone. You knew other people on your island, didn't you?"

"I knew my father. I knew George."

"No mom?"

"She doesn't exist."

"Like she's dead?"

"I don't know. I'm not sure if she ever existed. I guess that makes me an immaculate conception," Martin said as he peeled the fox's skin up and over its head. He'd read the term but was a little foggy on the definition.

The boy turned back and flashed his piano-tooth smile. "You—are—astounding. You do know what that means, I assume? Man, they'll have a field day with you in Xibalba. Tell 'em you walk on water, they'll dig you a pond and throw you in."

"Where'd everyone else go, everyone who left us?"

"That's the question, right?" the boy sighed. "Tons of theories, of course. When I saw the smoke from your fire, I thought maybe you were the kid with the answers."

Martin shrugged and gave the skin a last tug until it detached from the body in one solid piece.

"But you're just a fox-skinning messiah from the sea, now, aren't you?" the boy went on.

"My name is Martin."

The boy chuckled. "Good to know you, Marty. I'm Kelvin."

Martin and Kelvin roasted the fox and they ate it together. Martin insisted that Kelvin eat the lion's share, but the boy could hardly finish his half. "My stomach's gotten too small," Kelvin sighed.

After they ate, they sat in silence by the fire. Martin wanted to learn more from him, but Kelvin looked exhausted. His eyes were glazed over and all he did was stare at the flames. So Martin let him stare.

When Kelvin finally wrapped himself up in his cloak and fell asleep, Martin found a perch on a nearby rock and watched him. It felt odd to be so close to another person. Kelvin looked a bit like George with his sharp blond eyebrows and his dimpled chin, but George had never seemed so desperate. After several minutes, Martin walked a few paces away, laid himself down on a bed of pine needles, and closed his eyes. It took a while, but eventually, he fell asleep.

Morning came and Martin felt a tap on his shoulder. He rolled over to see Kelvin hovering above him.

"I'm leaving," Kelvin said.

"Where are you going?"

Kelvin made a visor with his hand to his forehead. "Looking for something."

"I can go with you."

"I'm not made for pals, if you know what I mean."

"I don't."

"I'm better without you." Kelvin's tone was unapologetic.

George never would have said such a thing, or at least not in such a way. It seemed that not all other people were going to be like George, even the ones who looked like him. Kelvin had been nice enough to provide some information. Maybe that was the most Martin could ask for. Still, he had to try.

"How do I find it?" Martin asked. "Shi . . . ?"

"Xibalba?" Kelvin said. "You know it's actually spelled with an 'X,' but sounds like an 'Sh,' as in 'Who gives a Xibalba?' You just find it. Like the rest of them did. You'll know you're close when you smell the nuts."

"Yes, but for me—"

"You'll do fine," Kelvin assured him. "They'll help you, as much as they help anyone, anyway. 'Cause you're the kinda kid they like. Capable. Honest."

Martin nodded. He could tell that his time with Kelvin was up. He reached down, picked the fox skin off the ground, and held it out.

"In case you get cold."

Kelvin took it, held it against his chest. "Ain't exactly Sunday's best," he said, handing it back. "Keep it. A memento. And keep this too." From within his cloak, Kelvin pulled a tiny glass bottle, about the size of his pinkie finger.

Martin took it. "What am I supposed to do with this?"

"It'll bring you luck with the ladies," Kelvin joked.

"Okay."

"When you get there," Kelvin went on, "tell 'em you saw me and tell 'em I looked fantastic."

"I can do that," Martin said.

Kelvin placed his bony hand on Martin's shoulder and gave it a squeeze. He paused, looked Martin up and down, nodded, and withdrew. Then he turned toward town and set off into the forest. His cloak caught the breeze and trembled gently behind him.

"Watch out for the library bears," Martin called out.

"Should be all right," Kelvin called back. "I don't have anything overdue."

As Martin watched the boy disappear into the maze of firs, he wondered if this had all been a put-on, if Kelvin was like some of the people he had read about in books. Were his tales a game he played with the green and gullible? Maybe. Then again, Kelvin's skinny body didn't seem a big enough place for lies.

So Martin chose to trust him, and he decided, right there in the forest, that he wasn't going back to the island. He was going forward. He would find this Xibalba place. He would meet these other people. He would trust them too. Maybe that would make him a bit too curious, a bit too much a fool. It was better than being suspicious and alone.

— 3 —

The Trail

Rain christened Martin's new journey. Trapping was infinitely harder in the rain, so he scavenged in cars for his breakfast and lunch: candy, soda, chips—anything with enough packaging and preservatives to keep it edible. He had no idea which way to go, but he figured if he followed the roads away from the ocean, he'd end up somewhere. Kelvin's confidence in him was hard to believe, but it kept him moving.

That night he slept in a van, where he could stretch out his entire body. He noticed that almost all the vehicles he came across had keys in the ignition, but even if Martin had known how to drive, it wouldn't have been worth the effort to steer around all the other cars that were on the pavement, in the grass, or wrapped around and crushed under trees. It was easier to walk.

Over the next few days, he passed through several towns with vacant, dust-frosted stores and weather-beaten homes.

In each place, animals came and went as they pleased, but once Martin saw that there were no people, he never bothered to stay long. He felt safer away from buildings. The road offered a clear future and a clear past, so he followed it forward.

For eight days he walked. He hadn't given up hope, but he was beginning to wonder how he would ever know if he was headed in the right direction. Signs told him it was ten miles to this place, and twenty miles to that place, two hundred miles to some other place. But not a single sign mentioned Xibalba.

The closest he found was the sign he ultimately chose to follow. It marked a trail. It was small, rectangular, and brown and decorated with a simple silhouette of two people, both carrying walking sticks and wearing backpacks. In the bottom corner of the sign, someone had placed a sticker. It was the same picture as on George's Jolly Roger: a skull, crisscrossing bones, a background of black.

"It can't be a coincidence," Martin whispered to the skull as he stepped off the road and onto the dirt.

It was rougher going. The trail carved its way through damp, mossy forests, over thickly wooded mountains, and along the shores of dark, still lakes. There were plants and animals Martin had never seen, and he would sit next to his campfire at night imagining what else might be out there. Were things like dragons and horses and duck-billed platypuses real, or were they just fanciful embellishments in the books he had read? Could he hike this trail for years, around the entire circumference of the earth? Would it ever lead to Xibalba?

Martin spent his thirteenth birthday at a campsite in the

forest. Memories of other birthdays consumed him. His eleventh birthday still haunted. The sight of the skiff, appearing like a ghost on the sea, was something he would never shake. He had seen inside. He knew his father wasn't there. All he could make out was that branch. Yet the reason he swam after it was to check if something else might be there too, hidden in the crook of the bow. A gift. Another birthday memory.

It was from when Martin had turned eight.

There had been no celebration, only a simple dinner and an evening spent by the fire. Just before heading off to bed, his father had handed Martin a small round alarm clock with two bells that stuck up from the top like ears.

"It doesn't work, but I want you to have it," his father said.

"It's a clock," Martin said, and held it in his lap and stared at the two hands. The big hand was stuck just past the four, the small hand just past the twelve.

"It's the moment I learned you were born," his father told him. "I received a call. In my excitement, I knocked the clock off a nightstand, and it stopped. It was the happiest moment of my life."

His father rarely said things like that, so Martin cherished the gift, and he took extra-special care of it. He wrapped it in a piece of silk and kept it in the dresser next to his bed. On most days, he would take it out and clean its glass face and shine its bells. His father told him that he must never fix it. He wanted it frozen on that moment.

On the day his father set out to find the final piece to the machine, Martin pulled the alarm clock from the drawer. He wasn't worried that his father wouldn't come back, but in the book of stories about men traveling to other planets, there were always scenes in which the space travelers were presented gifts. Martin had never given his father a gift. Then again, Martin's father had never left on a journey.

So as his father prepared the skiff, Martin handed him the clock. "For good luck," Martin said.

In the stories, the men who received the gifts would always say things like "Don't worry, I'll be back in a jiff," and then they would cluck their tongues and snap their fingers and graciously hand the items back. That was what Martin hoped would happen. Instead, his father cupped the clock in his hands and looked at it as if it were the most precious thing on earth.

"Thank you," he said quietly. "By giving me this, a part of you will always be with me." Then he carefully placed the clock in a tackle box at the stern of the boat.

"I just wanted to make you happy," Martin said.

"You did," his father said. "More than you could imagine."

He smiled at his son. They said their goodbyes. He promised to be back by Martin's eleventh birthday. Then he pushed off from the dock.

The clock, and Martin's father, had set off into the world.

The day after his thirteenth birthday, Martin reached the stony peak of a mountain. Along the trail, there had been peaks to summit almost daily. Most of the time they were covered in trees, or shrouded in cool fingers of fog, so Martin was rarely treated to views. On this morning, he could see for miles.

A large range of mountains was behind him, and another,

even bigger one was ahead of him. In the valley between was a thick, unbending river. An imposing brick building studded with lines of dark, rectangular windows sat along the edge of the river, and Martin could just make out the roofs of houses and the white steeple of a church farther downstream. By the looks of it, he would be able to make this town by sunset.

A few paces away from the peak, where views of the river were at their best, Martin came upon a circle of rocks stacked neatly, as if to form a pen. It was only about three feet high and ten feet in diameter. On first examination, it appeared to be completely empty. But after climbing inside, Martin found some smaller stones stacked in the middle and arranged in a series of letters, forming a cryptic message.

A G F L K A Y D C M E M
I'M SO SORRY

What was it supposed to mean? Who was sorry? And for what? Were the letters some sort of code? Martin climbed out of the stone ring and got back on the trail. Another sign, he thought. Like the Jolly Roger, it means this is the right direction.

At the base of the mountain, Martin walked through a lupine-specked field toward the setting sun. A whiff of peanuts lingered in the grassy air. A hunger-born and odorous mirage, he thought. He was simply craving those addictive snacks he had found in the cars at the beginning of his journey. However, the smell got stronger as the sky got darker, and by the time Martin had reached the other side of the field, his nose was nothing but peanuts.

He followed the scent through a small patch of trees, until

he found himself in the studiously clipped backyard of a modest farmhouse with a wraparound porch. In the middle of the porch, blanketed in a gauzy glow, something was moving. He stopped for a moment to be sure.

No, it wasn't a bear.

It wasn't a deer.

It was quite clearly a person.

Martin hurried through the grass toward the house. It didn't matter who it was. It was someone. He was finally someplace.

A portly boy dressed entirely in soft gray fabrics was gently rocking in a wooden rocking chair on the porch. A burning lantern was set on a table nearby. At the boy's side, a barrel was sending off ripples of steam. Each time he rocked forward, the boy reached into the barrel and pulled out roasted peanuts. And as he cracked them open with his teeth, shells fell over his chest.

"Howdy," Martin called out, because books had taught him it was best to be friendly with the natives. It was a moonless night, and Martin had managed to come within fifty feet of the porch without being noticed.

The boy planted his feet, lowered his hand into the barrel, and dropped his uneaten peanuts back inside. "Kelvin?" he asked softly.

"No, it's not Kelvin. It's Martin."

The boy stood up. He brushed the shells from his chest and reached over to the table to grab the lantern. "Martin?" he said. "We don't have a Martin here."

"I'm new," Martin said, moving closer so that he could be seen.

"No kiddin', dude," the boy said, his eyes ablaze. With

41

that, he turned and just about tore the screen door off the house as he bolted inside.

"I come in peace," Martin called as he followed through the door. "Kelvin has sent me. This is the land of Xibalba, right?"

A few mangled candles flickered, revealing a cramped and cluttered abode, but Martin couldn't make out much detail. The lantern's steady glow appeared to bounce around the house, and what Martin couldn't see, he could imagine from the sounds of the boy crashing his way through the bric-a-brac.

Martin followed the lantern and the sounds, carefully tightroping the few bare bits of floor through what he assumed was a dining room, until he reached a door that was swinging wide open.

As Martin moved outside onto the front steps, the boy stopped about forty feet ahead of him, in the middle of a wide street that led away from the house. He turned to look back.

"Stay put, hoss," he said nervously. In one hand, he held the lantern; in the other, a large bell.

"Sure," Martin said, and he buried his hands in the pockets of his pants.

The boy raised the bell over his head and gave it a steady shake. Its clang pattered down the dark street. It was followed by a long silence.

Lines etched a picture of worry in the boy's face. Martin stayed put, but he too was getting nervous.

When it seemed nothing else would happen, the bell was answered with the sound of a higher-pitched and faster bell. It rattled off a frantic *ding-a-ling*.

Moments later, a powerful gong.

Then, almost immediately, the quiet of night was shoved aside by a cacophony of instruments. Martin had never heard such a racket. It wasn't music. It was madness.

Soon globes of light began appearing along the street, like a school of fish reflecting the moon. Martin couldn't stand still any longer. He crept down the steps and into the yard to get a better look.

The boy didn't stop him. He appeared less worried now, but sweat had burst through at his temples, and he was panting heavily. He set his bell on the ground. Taking in a deep breath, he placed his hand to his mouth, then hollered, "A Forgotten! A Forgotten!"

The rest of the instruments faded away and were replaced by a series of kids' voices, all echoing the same thing.

"A Forgotten. A Forgotten. A Forgotten . . ."

— 4 —

The Church

"It's been about a year since we've done one of these," a girl who had introduced herself as Darla said. "Forgive us, Martin, if we're a bit rusty."

Martin sat on a wooden stool, in the middle of a church. The pews had been removed, and in a haphazard circle around him, a group of approximately forty kids reclined on sofas and plush chairs. A stocky boy with a mess of curly red hair circled the room with a large candle, lighting smaller candles that had melted into the ledges next to the soot-caked windows. Yawns were contagious in there, but Martin's pulsing blood had no interest in sleep.

"I'm just happy to have made it," Martin said.

Darla swept her sandy bangs away from her face and gave him a tight-lipped smile. She straightened her back and scooted herself closer to Martin. The wheels on her chair squeaked as they slid across the wood floor.

"And we're delighted you could join us," she said. "How it usually goes is this: you tell your story and then we all go around and tell our stories and then you get to pick your house. Don't worry, there are still plenty of good ones left."

"Okay," Martin said. "But I don't know if I have much of a story."

"Just tell us about your life before the Day," Darla said. "And tell us how you got here."

"I don't think I know when the Day was," Martin admitted.

"Yesterday," the redheaded boy said, turning accusingly from a candle. "Two years ago, yesterday. How couldja not know that?"

"I'm from an island," Martin explained. "I've been living there alone."

"Really?" Darla said, and as her mouth opened in wonder, Martin saw a flash of metal on her two top front teeth.

"Yes," Martin confirmed. "I lived on the island my entire life. Just me and my father. He left more than two years ago. You're some of the first people I've spoken to since."

"Fascinating," Darla said.

The redheaded boy grumbled and grabbed a chair. As he sat, he cradled the burning candle in his lap. It made Martin more than a bit nervous.

"I—that's—how I—I am," Martin stammered. "I came to the mainland about a month back. I saw some bears. I followed a trail and ended up here, just like Kelvin thought I would."

"Kelvin?" Darla craned her neck forward. "You met Kelvin?"

The other kids perked up. They traded whispers.

"Yes," Martin said. "Near the ocean. He looked good. Fantastic. He looked fantastic."

Darla gave a single satisfied nod. "Good," she said. "I'm happy for him, then."

The rest of the kids continued to whisper.

An olive-skinned boy scribbled something down on a block of wood that rested on his knee.

"Where was he going?" a girl stretched out on a sofa asked. Her hair was long and straight and black, and her body was shaped like a pear. But Martin was struck most by her eyes, which, in the flickering candlelight, appeared to be silver.

"I'm not sure," Martin answered. "I don't think he wanted me to know."

"Sounds like our Kelvin," Darla said. "So is that it, then? Your story? That all?"

"Yes. That's it, mostly."

"You're a Forgotten, all right," Darla said. "But my story, if you don't mind me telling it, is a bit more interesting."

The girl on the sofa rolled her eyes, but Martin didn't know why. Stories were food to him. The more interesting, the more nourishing.

"Please," he said. "Tell."

Darla scooted her chair closer to the center of the church and wiggled her body, as if she were shaking dust off it. Then she began.

"I'm a West Coast girl, Martin. Sunshine and sand instead of snow. That's my blood. So it's kinda crazy that I made it all the way here. But as we all know, you find your way. Somehow.

"Anyhow, on the Day, I was sitting by the pool and all the

dogs in the neighborhood began barking up a storm. Howling and yapping, and even my pup, Dr. Fuzzbucket, was going crazy, and he was the sweetest, quietest thing. That must have been the exact moment they left, but I didn't know it till later. Mommy and Daddy were at the lake house, where they usually go on weekends, and I was gonna sit by the pool and eat honeydew and maybe write in my diary. But when the barking finally ended, I opted for a nap instead. Fell asleep in the pool chair. It was the middle of the night when I woke up and smelled the smoke.

"Now, I'd seen forest fires before, driving with Daddy into the mountains. So I thought that maybe that's all it was. But I could totally feel the heat on my skin and I knew it was so much closer than the mountains. I coulda jumped in the pool, but I'm a pretty selfless person, so I decided to save Fuzzy-B first. I ran into the house and found him whimpering in Mommy's closet. Grabbed him and decided to head to the street, 'cause firemen were probably there and they would toss me on their truck and get the sirens spinning.

"By the time I was in the driveway, the fire had gotten to my house, and it was all over the roof. I'm telling you, the whole block was in flames. Houses and trees burning everywhere. And there was absolutely no one around. Not even voices. Only the sounds of explosions and car alarms and roofs caving in and I didn't have the time to cry or even scream. I got into Daddy's pickup, which he kept in the driveway 'cause he thought it made the neighbors think we were regular even though we definitely weren't regular. I dug the extra keys from the visor, where Mommy kept them hidden, and I started it up.

"Eleven years old, Martin, and I'm driving. Can you

believe that? Mommy had let me do it in parking lots before, but this was prime time. I was swerving around cars that were exploding and sizzling in the middle of the road, and I was like a pro out there. The stereo was blasting and I had to keep the AC pumping 'cause it was crazy hot. . . ."

Darla stopped for a moment. A tear escaped from her eye. She looked around the church, nodded confidently, and went on.

"But I was alone. Even when I escaped from the neighborhood and it wasn't fire everywhere, I was still alone. It was a ghost town for miles and miles. Everyone was gone, and if it had been a dream, then I would have known it was a dream and pinched myself awake 'cause it was all so crazy. But I was awake and afraid and alone."

Darla stopped again. She closed her eyes and smiled. "Four days later, after getting practically nowhere because of all the stuff in the streets, I found Kid Godzilla."

"Her monster truck," the girl with silver eyes explained with a sigh. It didn't mean much to Martin, though. He knew monsters. He knew trucks. He didn't associate the two.

"You gotta see the wheels," Darla said excitedly. "Big as a moose, Martin! Kid Godzilla was parked at a burger joint and the keys were in it. So I ditched the pickup and I rode that beast straight across the country. Three weeks. Twenty tanks of gas. Rolling over and crushing everything! Until I got here."

"You knew to come here?" Martin asked.

"I checked the lake house and my parents weren't there. I had family on the East Coast and thought there was a chance that maybe *they* were still around. I passed through this place on the way. I haven't left since. Deep down, we all knew to come here."

"We all ended up here," the boy with olive skin corrected her.

"Call it coincidence, call it fate," Darla said. "This is the place you come. There's nowhere else. There's no *one* else. Martin, this is the entire world."

Looking around the church, Martin was greeted with a chorus of nods.

"It seems like a nice place" was all he could think to say.

Laughter echoed through the room.

"Shhh!" Darla chided. "Stories! There are many to get through. Henry is next. Henry."

The redheaded boy nodded and scooted his chair toward the center.

"Didja have a tree house on your island?" he barked at Martin.

"No. I don't believe I did."

"I had two," Henry said firmly. "Parents had a hundred acres. In the back, two tree houses. Had a telescope. I could watch the stars, but from the taller tree house, I could see town too. It was a small town, but things happened. Could watch people comin' and goin' from the hardware store and the grocery store. I would know what they were buyin'. I would know who they were talkin' to. I would know where they were goin'. I would know . . . *everything.*

"On the mornin' of the Day, I was in town with my dad, and Mr. Henkles was at the hardware store, and that ol' lady that stinks like mouthwash was sellin' banana bread or some garbage on the corner, and it was sunny and there was a whole lotta other crap happenin' too. But when I went home, and went out to my scope, I looked back and everything changed. A car was smashed through the front winda of the hardware store, which was pretty awesome.

Grocery bags were tipped over and on the street. Dogs were wrestlin' around on the lawns. And nobody was there. Nobody.

"I went back to the house to tell my brother. But he was gone too. And my parents were gone and my neighbors were gone and everyone—"

"Jeez Louise!" the olive-skinned boy butted in. "Do we have to go through all these stories again?"

Henry scowled at him.

"It's what we do, Felix," Darla said diplomatically.

"It's what we used to do," Felix said. He held up the block of wood he had been scribbling on. "We can think for ourselves now. We have the Internet now. He can read it all there."

"I know," Darla said. "And we all appreciate the Internet. But this is a tradition."

Felix shook his head. "Does anyone here really give a hoot about tradition?"

A few hands shot up in the crowd, but the question was mostly met with tired indifference.

"That doesn't mean—" Darla started.

"I'm going home," Felix said, standing from his chair and bowing graciously to Martin. "Welcome, Martin. Hope you enjoy your stay." Then he turned to the door.

"Thank you," Martin called to him.

Following Felix's lead, all the other kids popped up from their chairs and headed for the exit.

"Well," Darla said with a deep breath. "That didn't go as planned."

"I rode a bike here," Henry told Martin. "That's what happened next in the story. On the highway. Cool, right? I thought I might see dead people, but I didn't see any dead people."

"That's good," Martin said.

"Eh," Henry squawked with a shrug.

Darla gave Martin a quick pat on his knee. "Let's get you a house," she said. "What type would you like?"

— 5 —

The House

They walked down the main street of town, Martin in the middle, with Henry and Darla on either side of him, lanterns in their hands. The other kids retreated to houses along the street or down the leafy lanes that splintered off. Their lanterns bobbed along with them and then disappeared.

"Books, I guess," Martin told Darla and Henry. "One with a lot of books in it."

"Most of 'em got books," Henry said.

"Electricity?" Martin asked, looking down at the lanterns.

"We have batteries and a few generators," Darla said, "but only for special occasions."

"What about solar panels?" Martin asked.

"Not any we know how to use," Henry said.

"I could help with that," Martin said.

"You can?" Darla exclaimed. "That must be your thing!"

"My thing?"

"We all have a thing here," Darla explained. "Like Henry

is the guy who hunts and protects us. And I'm the girl who drives and . . . decides. So you're the guy who knows about solar panels. That's why you're here. Don't you see?"

"Okay," Martin agreed. It sounded fine to him. After all, people were supposed to have jobs.

They walked quietly for a while as Martin surveyed the houses and storefronts. Even in the dark, he could tell this town was different from the others he'd visited. The shutters and signs were straight. Displays in windows, consisting of pumpkins and corn husks and mason jars, were all clean and orderly. The roads were clear. The grass was cut. This was a home, or as close to one as he had ever encountered.

"That's the Smash Factory there," Henry said, pointing to a storefront with a giant hammer painted on the window. "Raul did it up a while back. If you're angry, or just plain bored, you can go on in there and bust things up. TVs, flower vases, car windshields, that sort of stuff. It's good for a laugh."

"And that's Gina's Joint," Darla said, pointing to a house painted with swirls of neon green and pink. "It's all kaleido-scopes and tie-dye and glow-in-the-dark hippy garbage. Avoid it if you get dizzy, but if you ever want any Roman candles or bottle rockets, then Gina's your girl."

Perched on top of a small hill, overlooking the town square, was a tall yellow house with a sharply slanted slate roof. A boy on its front steps caught Martin's eye. A burning torch was in his left hand. His right hand was petting some sort of striped animal that was sitting patiently by his side. Martin didn't recognize the boy from the church.

"What about him?" Martin asked, pointing. "What's his thing?"

"That's Nigel," Henry said, grabbing Martin's hand and

lowering it. "His thing is he does whatever the heck he wants and we give him whatever he wants. It's 'cause he talks to animals. Probably talking to that stupid tiger right now."

"Do the animals talk back?" Martin asked.

"Well . . . ," Darla said, cocking her chin.

The house Martin picked reminded him of the houses on the island. It had gray shingles and a matching pair of gables. The ocean was miles off, but there was a creek that ran through the backyard with a calming whoosh.

"A bold choice," Darla told him.

"How so?" Martin asked.

"You'll find out soon enough," she said with a sly smile. "I don't know. Maybe it means something. A fresh beginning."

Henry snorted, as if he couldn't care less, and Darla let out a quick, jabbing laugh. They left Martin standing alone at the front door.

In almost every room of Martin's new home, there were shelves full of books. In the garage, there were tools, covered in a thin film of dust. In the kitchen, there were canned goods stocking the cupboards. What Martin found most intriguing, however, was in the basement.

The basement consisted of one scanty low-ceilinged room with brick walls and a concrete floor. Candles in glass vases decorated ledges, and trunks, and wooden crates. A Ping-Pong table, with a stack of boxes on it, was pushed into the corner. From the pictures on the boxes, Martin could see they held kits for model cars and boats and trains. Against one wall was a grimy plaid sofa with a woven wool blanket hanging over its arm. On a coffee table, in front of the sofa, was a miniature house, cut in half to show its innards.

It was a dollhouse, or that was what Martin assumed. Only it didn't look like the dollhouses he had imagined. The rooms inside weren't reproductions of kitchens or bedrooms or parlors. They were all the same room, decorated in the same way, over and over, three floors of three, nine rooms in all. They had minuscule candles in glass vases, baby Ping-Pong tables pushed into their corners, grimy toy sofas. They were shrunken duplicates of the room Martin was standing in now. The only difference was that in every room except for one, there was a single glass bottle on the coffee table rather than a shrunken dollhouse. In that odd room out, the coffee table was empty.

Martin still had the bottle Kelvin had given him. Gingerly, he eased his fingers over the toy furniture and set it in its rightful place on the tiny table.

Martin slept in a giant bed on the top floor of the house, and he woke when the sun angled through an octagonal window just above the headboard. Downstairs, he opened a can of beans and then went out to the back porch and ate them for breakfast as he watched the creek. He had expected Darla or Henry or someone to stop by, but after a couple of hours and no visitors, he slipped on some shoes and headed to the front door to go for a walk.

Two large plastic jugs, each filled to the top with water, were waiting on the front step. A note sandwiched between the jugs read:

To get you started—Trent

In the distance, a boy pedaled a bicycle down the street, towing behind him a small red wagon filled with more jugs. Martin couldn't catch up with the bike, so he opted to walk in the opposite direction, toward the town square.

The next person he came upon was a lanky girl with cropped blond hair and a tight outfit made from synthetic fabrics. She was jogging at a steady clip, heading straight for Martin.

As she approached, Martin waved. "Top of the morning," he said.

Maybe that wasn't the thing to say in this neck of the woods, because the girl didn't slow her pace. As she blew by him, she raised four fingers.

"Four miles to go," she grunted.

Four miles to go? Figuring out local phrases was sure to be a chore, Martin thought, but there was no point in stressing over these things. Martin was the new guy, and it was the new guy's job to make mistakes, to learn. So he simply chose to move on.

He paused only when the yellow house from the night before came into view. Nigel wasn't anywhere to be seen, but there was a collection of animals grazing and lounging in the yard. There were chickens and goats and cats and a few other creatures that Martin couldn't figure out. He wondered why they weren't scurrying off, as animals tended to do in the wild.

In the corner of the yard, a group of dogs were collected around a giant replica of an ice cream cone. It was at least eight feet tall, the sheen of it indicating fiberglass construction. The cone had a waffle-print design, and the ice cream was three scoops of three different colors—red, white, and brown. Martin had seen pictures of ice cream cones in a cookbook before, but he had never realized that dogs had such an interest in them. Their noses were glued to the thing.

"Git!" Henry commanded as he stepped out of some

bushes, waving a stick. The dogs scattered, and Henry tossed the stick at the biggest one to make sure he didn't contemplate turning back. Reaching into the bushes, he then pulled out a long nylon duffel bag, which he set next to the ice cream cone. He gave the scoops of ice cream a push from underneath. They detached from the cone and flopped backward on a hinge. It made sense to Martin now. This was a container.

Henry bent down and unzipped the duffel. From inside, he started pulling body parts of an animal: legs, torso, head. It was a deer, a moderately sized doe. Unaware or unconcerned that he was being watched, Henry deposited each piece into the cone, and when the bag was empty, he circled around and pushed the scoops of ice cream up. The hinges creaked. The scoops fell back on the cone. The container was shut. Henry grabbed the duffel and slipped back through the bushes and headed toward the town square.

Martin decided to avoid Henry and continue his explorations by turning down a narrow side street. It was quiet and pleasant, and the only other person around was a boy walking purposefully toward a narrow dirt trail that led into a thick patch of trees. Martin followed. It was easy to catch up, but he thought it best to keep his distance.

About a quarter mile down the trail, the boy angled off through a thicket of bushes, then stopped next to a rocky ledge. In the side of the ledge was a dark rectangular hole, framed with wood. The boy set something down next to the hole and bowed his head. After a minute or so, he turned back around.

"Oh, it's you," he said to Martin. "I thought I heard some sort of a ruckus."

"I'm so sorry." Martin started to back away.

"No, no, stay," the boy yelled. "I want to yak it up for a sec."

Martin recognized him as he got closer. It was the olive-skinned boy named Felix, the one who had been jotting down notes in the church. The night before, in the dark, Martin hadn't gotten a good look at most of the kids. For instance, he hadn't noticed that Felix's hair had been cut away in the front, and that he wore a dark band around his forehead where his bangs might have hung. Sticking out from that band were spools of string, screwdrivers, pens, and tiny light-bulbs.

When Felix reached Martin, he grabbed him by the wrist and said, "Wanna see what I've been working on?"

Martin shrugged.

Felix started pulling him back toward town. "Yes, oh yes! You will most definitely want to see this. Let's log on. What do you say? We'll log on and I'll show you the finest Internet the world knows."

— 6 —

The Web

The door to Felix's house was painted black. Near the top, there was a heavy iron knocker in the shape of a field mouse. Below the mouse, two words were written in green paint.

Username
Password

"You'll need to choose a username first," Felix explained. "It could be anything. Last name and first initial. Maybe people call you Scooter or something. Who am I to judge?"

"Will Martin work?" Martin asked.

"Well, it isn't exactly original, but it also isn't taken," Felix said with a thumbs-up. "What about a password?"

"Alarm clock," Martin said without thinking.

"Spell it so I get it right."

"A-L-A-R-M C-L-O-C-K."

"All as one word?"

"Two words."

"Any capitals? Do you use a zero for the 'o'? You can never be too careful."

"Just alarm clock," Martin said. "As it's spelled."

"Okeydoke. Can't say I didn't warn you." Felix retrieved a nub of a pencil and a key from his headband and pulled a small block of wood from his pocket. He hurried off a few quick notes. Then he placed the key in the door and pointed at Martin. "Try it," he said.

"Try what?"

"Knock on the door."

"But you're out here with me."

"Just knock."

So Martin lifted the mouse and struck it against the door three times.

"Username?" Felix said in a deep voice.

"Excuse me?"

"Username?" he said again.

"Oh, yes . . . Martin."

"Password?"

"Alarm clock."

"Logged in," Felix said, turning the key and shouldering the door open.

Felix's home wasn't a home at all. There was no furniture or decorations or anything to make one think this was a place to burrow, to sleep, to live. Thousands of strings created jagged checkerboards and drooping nets and twisted vines that covered the bare hallways and rooms. Each string was connected at both sides to blocks of wood that were either set on the floor or hung on the walls. Writing was scribbled all over each block.

"We only have about five hundred websites," Felix explained, "but I'm adding more every day."

"I thought the Internet was something for computers," Martin said.

"Well, duh," Felix said. "But do you know any servers that are still operating? Plenty of laptops out there with batteries, but it isn't like you can go to the café for some Wi-Fi."

Admittedly, computers were an abstract concept for Martin. He'd read about them. George had told him about them. He imagined picture frames filled with constantly changing text and images, and he imagined the Internet to be the source of all that visual chatter. He never thought it could be something so organic.

"What's written on the blocks?" Martin asked.

"Ah, more to the point at hand," Felix said. Then he led Martin into a vast room with a large block positioned in the center of it. Hundreds of strings sprouted from the block, like hairs from a giant square head. Only about one quarter of the block was covered with writing. In the biggest letters, the word *Xibalba* was written.

"Think of this as your default home page," Felix said. "You have the story of Xibalba here, and there are screws on any word where I made a hyperlink. The string tied to the screw is the link. So if you want to know about . . . ohh, I don't know, the peanut roaster . . . then you grab the string and follow it to another block. In other words, the peanut roaster's web page. Then that block might have links to lots of other blocks and on and on and on and on."

"The Internet was once used to find missing people, right?" Martin asked.

"It was used to find naked ladies too," Felix said, "but this version isn't advanced enough for either. Apologies if I got your hopes up."

"That's all right," Martin said. "I'm okay with this version."

"Well, then try it out, why don'tcha?" Felix insisted.

Leaning over the large block, Martin began to read. The writing was small but clear. It appeared to be rendered in black pen, but there were chunks of the wood that had been sanded or shaved away and rewritten on in fresh red ink. Martin ran his finger over the indentations.

"Edits," Felix explained. "No web page should be static. Certainly not. Certainly not."

"Of course," Martin said as he resumed his reading.

XIBALBA
The town of Xibalba was founded on *the Day.* It is believed to be the only place where humans currently live. Its name comes from the Mayan people. The founder and first resident was a boy named Kelvin Rice. . . .

The word *was* appeared freshly written in a sanded dent in the wood. There was a screw in the middle of the name Kelvin Rice.

"Is there more about him?" Martin asked.

"Use the string," Felix said.

Placing the string between his finger and thumb, Martin began to follow its path. It required a bit of patience, as the string twisted its way around and over and under other strings, but Martin was in no hurry. When he finally reached the block, he found it hanging by a hook on the wall. He took it down and looked at it closely. It was about the size of a fisherman's tackle box. Three sides of the block were covered in writing. The fourth side was basically a door, with a small handle and keyhole. He began reading.

KELVIN RICE

Kelvin Rice was the founder of Xibalba. He lived here on and before the Day, but he never told anyone what Xibalba was called before the Day. By the time everyone else got here, its signs had been destroyed, and evidence of its past removed. Kelvin was the only person in Xibalba who didn't have an Arrival Story, but he began the tradition of sharing Arrival Stories whenever a Forgotten appeared. He also created the Ring of Penance and it is believed that he had kissed upward of fourteen girls. He loved eating peanuts, and Chet Buckley cooked them for him in a peanut roaster near his greenhouse. In the days following the Collapse, it was decided that Kelvin should be banished for two months to the Ring of Penance. Many loved the irony of it, but Kelvin

A knock on the door interrupted Martin's reading. "Excuse me for a sec." Felix made his way around the

63

strings until he reached the door. He turned the lock slowly. "Username?" he said.

A voice came back: "You know who."

"Username!" Felix insisted.

"You got island boy in there?"

"Yes I do," Felix said, "but I will require a username and password. Rules are rules."

The door flew open, knocking Felix to the ground. Henry stood there with a rifle slung over his back.

"Forgot my username and password," Henry said. "How 'bout you email 'em to me?"

— 7 —

The Marble

"Martin!" Darla exclaimed, stepping into the room from behind Henry. "You're out and about and surfing the web. Good for you."

"Good morning, Darla," Martin said as he hung Kelvin Rice's block back on its hook.

"That Kelvin's page?" Henry asked.

"It is," Martin said.

"Beautiful," Darla said. "Exactly what we came for."

Henry hurried around the strings, his rifle dangerously close to getting snagged. Darla put a hand out to Felix and helped him to his feet.

"I cannot let any joker in off the street. Passwords are a requirement," Felix told her.

"This is important, Fee," Darla crooned. "Gotta understand that."

"It's always important with you, Darla," Felix moaned.

"I'm an important girl," Darla chirped.

"And, Henry," Felix went on, "I've told you time and again, no guns in the Internet."

"No guns in the Internet," Henry mimicked in a high-pitched voice. He stepped past Martin and pulled Kelvin Rice's block off its hook.

"We'll need to get into Kelvin's personal page," Darla said. "With Martin showing up outta nowhere, we gotta see if this is another thing he kept to himself."

"No can doozy," Felix said. "Need a password and authentication in the form of a signed note. You know this."

"He's gone, and he isn't coming back," Darla said. "Besides, he gave up his rights to privacy when he lied to us."

"Yeah! And like you're not peekin' inside all the personal pages when you're here all alone." Henry snorted. "Puh-lease."

"It's called a code of ethics," Felix said. "Something I work hard to maintain."

No one had been watching Martin this whole time, but Martin had been watching Henry's rifle. Its muzzle was nearly brushing against Martin's cheek as it angled from Henry's back. Martin knew what was happening here. He had read about this type of situation. A gun was in the room. Before they left the room, that gun was going to be fired. It was inevitable. He surely didn't want anyone to be hurt. With the exception of Henry, whom he was beginning to wonder about, they seemed like reasonable people. So he did what he thought was the best thing to do.

Martin punched Henry in the face.

Henry wobbled, stunned into submission. Martin grabbed for the rifle. When he yanked it away, it sent Henry spinning and the block of wood sailing across the room.

Felix and Darla watched, speechless, as Henry fell into a web of strings and Martin pointed the gun to the ceiling and fired off five rounds.

Blam, blam, blam, blam, blam, click . . .

The rifle was empty. Holes the diameter of Martin's fingers decorated the ceiling, and debris flurried down. As the echoes from the gunshots faded away, Martin sighed in relief. Of course, no one could hear the sigh over Henry's screams.

"Don't kill me! Please don't kill me!" The pits of Henry's elbows shielded his eyes, and his stubby hands covered his ears.

"It's okay," Martin said calmly. "I was making sure we were all safe."

Felix stared at him. His right eye held the stare for a moment, then seemed to lose its nerve, turning away. His left eye, however, stayed fixed in place.

"We do not hit!" Darla stepped forward and yelled. "We. Do. Not. Hit! And we do not shoot! We do not. Shoot. Guns. Near people! What kind of place do you think this is?"

"I—"

"What were you thinking?" Darla said.

"I— He had a gun. I wanted to make sure nobody was shot," Martin said.

"Turkeys," Darla barked. "Deer. Rabbits. He uses it to shoot animals. I was going to cook you dinner tonight, Martin."

"Oh," Martin said. "I guess I misunderstood."

"Friggin' right you did," Henry grumbled as he pulled himself up and quickly ran his sleeve across his cheek.

"Sorry," Martin whispered as he handed the rifle back to Henry.

Darla tilted her head and pursed her lips. Then she

flicked her fingers out like she was displaying claws, held them there for a moment, and slowly lowered them to her sides. "We will accept your apology," she said through her teeth, "because I honestly think that island folk such as yourself probably have different rules. But here, in civilization, we act civilized."

"I understand," Martin said softly.

"Goody," Darla said, then rescued the block from the floor and flipped it over to reveal the small door and keyhole on the back. She gave Felix a playful but insistent push on the shoulder, knocking him back to attention. "Gonna need that key, lazy eye," she said. "High time we get inside Kelvin's mind."

Felix closed his eyes and nodded. He was not going to fight this fight. He reached into his headband. From inside he pulled a tiny key with a series of intricate teeth. He handed it to Darla.

"Thank you very much, sir," she said. "The honorable choice."

Bracing herself with her free hand, she carefully got down on the floor and sat cross-legged with the block in her lap. She wielded the key. The slip, the turn, the click, the creak of the door hinges came next. Then she reached inside.

She held a small green marble up in the air for all to see.

"That's it?" Henry asked.

"That is indeed it," Darla said with a crooked smile.

"Don't let Lane have it," Henry sniped. "She'll send it rollin' in one of her whirligigs."

"Lane does not worry me," Darla said, sliding the marble into the front pocket of her jeans.

"Who's Lane?" Martin asked.

"Pudgy girl," Darla said. "No consequence."

"Is that really necessary?" Felix said.

"What?" Darla giggled. "Lane's *zaftig*. That's a *thing* for some people, apparently. And I'm being truthful. I think Martin is the type of guy who appreciates the truth."

"I am," Martin said.

"See?" Darla closed and locked the little door, stood up, and handed the block and key back to Felix.

"What are you going to do with it?" Felix asked.

"I'm not sure," Darla said with a shrug. "But it's gotta be important if Kelvin was hiding it, right?"

"People hide plenty of things for plenty of reasons that I don't understand," Felix said.

"And you're so good at helping them, aren't you?" Darla teased, thumbing Felix on the cheek.

"We all do what we do," Felix said plainly.

"Ah!" Darla remarked. "Speaking of which, let's get Henry some bullets and Martin some solar panels. We'll be eating rabbit and watching DVDs before the night is out!"

She threw her arm around Martin and pulled him in close. Then she grabbed Henry by the collar of his T-shirt. Reluctantly, he sidled over to her, and she threw her other arm around him.

Squeezed tightly against her, Martin could feel the curves of Darla's body. It wasn't entirely uncomfortable. Yet pressing into his thigh was the marble in her pocket. Its round, hard coldness had penetrated her jeans and Martin's pant leg.

— 8 —

The Declaration

Darla's house, a stately four-story Victorian in the middle of town, would be the first one wired for electricity. It took Martin all day, but it was relatively easy. With Henry's and Felix's help, he mounted some solar panels on her roof and created an electrical hub in her pantry from which she could run extension cords.

"You're only going to be able to use a few things at a time," Martin told Darla. "Some lights at night. Maybe a toaster oven."

"I want hot water, a fridge, and surround sound, Martin," she said, pouting.

"How many houses are there left to do?" he asked.

"Well, there are now forty-one kids in town, including you," Felix told him.

"Do they all have to live in their own houses?" Martin asked. "I mean, couldn't everyone move in together and—"

Henry stopped him with a shake of his head and a look that said, "Don't even think about thinking that."

"Fine," Martin responded. "But with the number of solar panels we have here, we have to ration."

"Rationing is for lifeboats, silly," Darla said. "The world is ours to take. We can siphon some gas from cars on the highway, fuel up Kid Godzilla, and go looting. I do it all the time."

"For now, don't you think it's fair if we simply distribute what we have?" Martin said.

"Fair is fair," Darla said. "Everyone gets their share. That island you came from, it wasn't Cuba, was it?"

"No, I don't believe so," Martin said.

"She's teasing you, Martin," Felix explained.

"Oh," Martin said.

"Cuba's full of Mexicans," Henry added.

"It is?"

"Ignore him," Felix said. "Geography's not his strong suit. Let's decide whose house is next. You can skip mine for now. I have big plans to revamp the entire Internet. Electrify it. Spread it through town. But I need to set up the main-frame. Much work to be done. Plenty, plenty of work."

"I don't need no electricity," Henry said. "Do fine with-out it."

"Okeydoke," Felix said. "So then I guess you should just start from one end of town and make your way across."

A question had been festering in Martin's mind since the moment he had arrived in Xibalba. It was a long shot, but he had to ask.

"Is there a guy named George who lives here?"

The others thought about it for a moment.

"There's a Greg," Henry said.

"Gabe," Felix said. "You mean Gabe."

"No, we don't have a George," Darla assured him. "Quite sure of it."

"That's fine," Martin said, trying to hide his disappointment. "Thought I'd ask."

"What's done is done and who's gone is gone," Darla said with a wink. *"C'est la vie."*

The portly, peanut-eating boy's name was Chet, and he was the first on the list. Chet lived on the edge of town, in a farmhouse that might as well have been a junkyard. The boy was a pack rat, and his home was a nest of clutter—broken toys, piles of rusty farm equipment, swords and helmets, and Lord knew what else. As Martin surveyed the house to determine where to feed the electricity, he could hardly tell where the walls were.

"Rather use them sunlight suckers for the greenhouse, anyway," Chet told him. Then he led Martin out and down a short path to a small dome made almost exclusively of wooden dowels and clear plastic sheeting. Chet peeled back a few layers of the plastic, creating a door, and he ushered Martin inside.

Rows of plants were lined up in rectangular trays suspended above the ground. White plastic pipes created a latticework ceiling, formed frames around the trays, and angled down like beams into the soft earth.

"You did all this without electricity?" Martin asked, amazed by the complexity.

"Wasn't easy. Still isn't." Chet thrust his greasy fingers through his wavy hair as he spoke. "But folks want tomatoes outta season. King Kelvin wanted those darn fine peanuts."

"How did you do it?"

"Hydroponics," Chet told him. "I may be a slob, but I'm no doofus. And you want someone to get their knuckles in the dirt, you're gonna need a slob."

"Can you—"

"Don't even ask. I don't harvest that junk."

"No. Can you tell me how you built it?" Martin said.

"What's this? A little friendly competition? Haven't you learned the deal? You do somethin' for me; I do somethin' for you. You hook up the panels; I keep you in the taters. I don't have time for a price war."

"I'm curious is all," Martin said, bending over to run his hand across a patch of beet greens.

Chet swatted his hand away. "Chet's Farmer's Market is Friday in town square. Tickle the veggies then."

"Sorry."

"You're really just curious how it's built?" Chet asked. "You'd be the first."

"Did Felix and Henry help?"

"The geek and the mouth breather?" Chet laughed. "I wanted this thing to work, didn't I? No, Lane was the only one."

"She's the pudgy girl?"

Chet furrowed his brow and pointed to his own round belly. "How 'bout some sensitivity, dude?"

"Sorry, but I'm still learning who everyone is," Martin said.

"Good luck with that," Chet said. "Lane's cool and all, but . . ."

"But?"

"But she has a way about her."

"What's that supposed to mean?"

73

"Just sayin'." Chet shrugged. "Be careful. Everybody's got an angle."

"What about that guy Nigel?" Martin asked. "He has a tiger."

"He most certainly does," Chet said with a nod. "You know, you look a bit like him."

"Really?"

"In the eyes," Chet said. "Same intensity. But that dude . . . that dude is the real McCoy."

"The real McCoy?"

"Genuine issue, bona fide. A prophet. I kid you not. The one thing King Kelvin should have respected."

"I see."

"Tell you what," Chet said, peeling open the plastic door. "Electrify this place, and you get veggies for a year. Heck, I'll even let you touch the Declaration of Independence."

"The real McCoy?" Martin asked, hoping he was using the term correctly.

"Straight from Independence Hall," Chet said with a grin. "Swiped it on my way up here. I signed it too. Right next to Ben Franklin. Chet Friggin' Buckley. Sweet, right?"

Martin smiled nervously and stepped under the plastic to escape the boggy humidity.

— 9 —

The Treadmill

At each house he visited, Martin met one of Xibalba's residents. They were all either thirteen or fourteen years old. Most were welcoming, if a bit suspicious. A few were surly, like Chet. All were thoroughly disinterested in what Martin was doing. The only thing they cared about was that he was giving them electricity. They were willing to trade almost anything for it.

A girl named Riley offered to tailor any clothes Martin had, as long as he got her sewing machine working. "Ninja gear, a superhero suit, a cowboy getup," she told him. "Whatever you fancy, Martin. I'm just sick of hand-stitching everything."

A boy named Hal promised to mow Martin's lawn, rake his leaves, and shovel his driveway in exchange for enough power to play video games. "It's certainly a good deal for you. I may even let you come over and sit in sometime, assuming you know how to undo a paralysis spell on a level seventy-one druid."

Martin had no idea how to do anything on a level seventy-one druid, but he soon understood that this was how things were accomplished in Xibalba. Give and you shall receive.

What Martin wanted more than anything was their stories. So he would make up excuses to have them join him on their roofs or at their fuse boxes. He'd say he needed their help, and when they would begrudgingly join him, he'd press them for the details of their lives.

They recited their Arrival Stories, the tales of how they'd come to Xibalba. They told of months-long journeys along highways or up the coast, of hiding in flooded and fire-eaten cities, in spookily deserted villages. Some had traveled by bike. Others by boat. None could really explain why they ended up where they did. They were looking for someone, trying to make it somewhere, or just keeping on the move. Xibalba got in the way.

The common strain in all the stories was that none of the kids ever actually saw anyone disappear. They had all been hiding away somewhere, too consumed in their own private lives to notice what was happening . . . until it had already happened.

One of the more fascinating tales came from Sigrid Hansen. Sigrid was Xibalba's resident messenger, a one-girl postal system who ferried messages throughout town in addition to maintaining a rigorous jogging regimen. A world-class junior-division runner, she had been born and raised in Norway but had been invited to an international cross-country meet in the United States. Because of her fear of flying, Sigrid traveled with her parents on a transatlantic cruise that would take them from Oslo to Scotland to New York and on to Florida, where the race was to be held. They arrived in New York on the Day.

Rather than go sightseeing, like everyone else from the ship, Sigrid stayed aboard, put on a pair of headphones, and dedicated two hours to the treadmill. When she finally left the ship's gym, she noticed that everyone was gone. And when they didn't come back, she walked down the gangplank and into an empty Manhattan.

"It should have been my day off, you know? I did not need to train that day," Sigrid told Martin, throwing her hands in the air. "New York City was out there. My first time to visit it. And I choose to be in a room without a porthole. It is a cruel trick, yeah? Like an . . . irony, I think. I am staying in place for once, and it is everyone else who is now running away."

"Do you really think they were running away?" Martin asked.

She shrugged and choked back some tears. "There is a hospital in this town. On rainy days, that was where I used to train. Kelvin never liked me going there, but who cares, yeah? It has long hallways, good for a stride. I kept the doors closed, because I didn't like to see empty beds. The sheets still messy, you know? Made me sad. Still makes me sad, thinking about it. An empty hospital should be a good thing, yeah? I don't go there anymore, of course. You don't have to see ghosts, you know, to believe in them. You only have to feel them."

Martin thought it might be appropriate to hug her, but he didn't. He was beginning to wonder if when people reached out to him, it was only an act. It was because he, quite literally, held the power. Sigrid had asked him to provide electricity to, of all things, a treadmill.

At night, Martin would go to Felix's house and log on to the Internet. The house was still without electricity, but Felix was up at all hours, working alone in his kitchen, wiring together circuit boards and getting his mainframe prepared for its launch. He did it all by the dim illumination from a series of tiny lightbulbs tucked into his headband. The bulbs weren't attached to batteries of any sort, and Martin couldn't figure out how they worked.

Felix proudly revealed his secret. "Fireflies," he said. "Extract their luminescent chemicals and use them to fill Christmas lights. Voila."

The solution astounded Martin. Fireflies were thick on the island every summer, yet he had never thought to harness their abilities. Felix, and every other kid in Xibalba, seemed to possess a unique ingenuity. Yet almost all of them lacked curiosity beyond their own insular interests. They were clever but guarded. They were relentlessly suspicious. They had little to no interest in playing games together or telling stories, in discovering anything new. These kids were so different from George.

As Martin searched the Internet, learning all he could about Xibalba and its inhabitants, he watched kids come and go from Felix's house. Of all of them, Darla was the most frequent visitor. Every time she entered, she slipped a piece of paper in a mailbox marked *Updates & New Page Requests*. Then she would touch her fingers to her lips and blow Martin a kiss. He never knew how to react. Most of the time, he gave her a wave and she let out a loud, knowing laugh, then headed for the door.

The rest of the kids ignored Martin. Mostly they came in and asked Felix for access to their personal pages. Using his master key, Felix would unlock the pages and lead his guests into empty closets, where they could be alone with the contents, sometimes for seconds, sometimes for hours.

Martin wasn't sure why these children needed to keep things locked away from each other, but he decided that if he was going to be one of them, then he needed a personal page too. So he approached Felix one evening, and the two had a look at the block in the Internet that featured Martin's brief biography:

MARTIN MAPLE
Martin is from an island. He came to
Xibalba more than a year after all the
other Forgottens arrived. He met Kelvin
Rice near the ocean. He is quite good
at installing solar panels. Other than that,
he doesn't do much. He asks a lot of
questions.

"Who wrote this?" Martin asked.

"Anonymity," Felix said. "Essential in the process. It's all fact-checked, of course. On occasion, I reject slanderous entries. And there are some things from our past that some of us would rather forget about. For better or worse, we keep that sorta noise out of it."

"Can I add anything?" Martin asked.

"Not to your biography, but you can spruce up your personal page all you like," Felix said. "Put whatever you want in there."

He unlocked Martin's block and handed it to him. "I've set you to private access, okay?"

Alone in an empty closet, Martin opened the door on the back of the piece of wood. Into the hollowed-out interior, he inserted the mottled and muddy pages of the book his father had given him. Beneath them, he hid the address from George. He had yet to tell anyone about these two valuable items. Chances were they wouldn't care.

The block was nearly full, so Martin closed it and returned it to its spot hanging from a hook in a cluttered corner of the former living room.

Felix was waiting there for him. "Can I have your ear for a sec?" he asked. "Security is important. Passwords and locks are great, but I can't get that day from a couple weeks ago out of my noggin. Darla and Henry shouldn't just barge in here and do what they want. And I have my suspicions about others and their monkeyshines. You're good at building things, Martin. Is there some way you could offer a smidge of help on this?"

"I could set a trap," Martin told him.

"We don't need a pit of alligators or anything, but I like the idea," Felix said. "Yes. Yes. I like the idea a lot."

"A snare or something," Martin offered.

"Exactly," Felix said excitedly. "Snag them in the act. I had proposed something similar to Lane last year, but all she cares about these days are her contraptions. I mean, it's top-notch entertainment and the last one I saw was a marvel, but odd, very odd."

"I don't know Lane," Martin admitted. "I mean, I've heard about her, of course."

"Really?" Felix said. "You've never seen one of her . . . thingamajigs?"

Martin shook his head.

"Grab your coat."

A chill had settled on the town. Martin and Felix hurried through the darkness, hands in pockets. They passed Henry patrolling Town Square, but didn't bother to stop and say hello. The show could be starting at any moment. When they reached Lane's house, an unusually large and modern construction, given its humble neighborhood, Felix rang the bell.

Lane opened the door. She was dressed entirely in black, except for a blue-and-white-striped railroad conductor's hat, which sat atop her head and kept her avalanche of dark hair at bay.

"Give them all electricity and they all stay home," she said, her silver eyes narrowing. "Starting to think no one would show tonight. Starts in two minutes. Payment?"

"When the new Internet is up, free installation," Felix said.

"I work with solar panels," Martin added.

"I know what you do," she said.

"You're next in line," Martin said to sweeten the deal.

"That doesn't concern me," she said. "What does concern me is your choice of lodging. But we can chat about that later. Tell you what. Consider this show on the house. For both of you."

"A freebie?" Felix said. "Well, isn't that something? This one a dud?"

"Hardly," Lane said. "Sometimes, the most important art is free." With that, she rotated on one heel and led the way inside. Stepping through the door, Martin was confronted with a sight as strange as any he had seen. Felix's house was nothing compared to this.

— 10 —

The Rube

Walls had been knocked down or chopped apart until the support beams were all that remained. Floors had been removed so that the ceilings reached to the heavens. They had to. With everything piled inside, ten feet of vertical space wouldn't do. Neither would twenty.

Glass lanterns mounted on the beams provided an eggy glow. White plastic pipes, sliced in half lengthwise, cut twisting paths through the open air. Bunches of shoes were hung by their laces like wind chimes or mobiles. A green plastic swimming pool filled with water was suspended in the air by tight metal cords. Wooden tables were stacked on top of each other to form pyramids. Bells, each a different size, descended diagonally above the tables. Ropes and pulleys. Record players. Doves in cages. A tepee of paper and wood, sitting on the floor, in the middle of it all.

Every color and shape imaginable was vying for Martin's attention, but he chose to watch Lane. She lumbered around and over everything in her way until she was standing at the foot of a long steel ladder that leaned against the highest of the pipes. For some reason, Martin had expected her to be more graceful, but there was still something fluid about the way she moved. As she began to climb, her hips swung from side to side and her arms and legs made large swooping movements and attacked each rung. Her awkward, swaying confidence reminded him of twisted fronds of kelp floating on the ocean.

When she reached the top of the ladder, she stopped for a moment to catch her breath, then turned the top half of her body around and steadied herself by grabbing the pipe.

"Gentlemen," she called out. "Are you ready to be dazzled?"

Felix raised his fist and called back, "You betcha!"

"Are you ready to be shocked?" she yelled.

"Why the heck not!" Felix was clearly swept up in the moment. Martin didn't have a clue what any of this was about, but he nodded and smiled just the same.

"Welcome to the world premiere of Lane Ruez's brand-new masterpiece. I call it . . . *The Rube!*"

With that, she thrust a hand up in the air and grabbed a thin chain that was dangling next to her ear. She gave it a violent yank.

Ropes and pulleys let loose with whines and squeaks, which were followed by a quick smack of darkness. Somehow, all but one of the lanterns had been extinguished.

Martin looked up at the sole lantern that remained lit. It had a small door in its glass shell that eased open. The flame inside grew larger. Then an orb of fire fell through the opening, as if it were a freshly laid egg.

The orb plummeted through the darkness, giving off a

wisp of sparks. It landed in the open curve of one of the white plastic pipes. Having been sliced in half, the pipe now served as a track. The orb rolled, slowly at first, along its twisting path. As its momentum built, so did the flames, illuminating more and more of the surroundings. Martin could see that there was a break in the track. Surely a mistake?

When the orb reached the break, it sailed through the air until it struck one of the hanging shoes. Flames shot out from the bottom of the shoe, the sole of which must have been packed with something highly combustible. The thrust of the flames sent the shoe into motion. It kicked forward until it struck another shoe, which was dangling in front of it. That shoe struck another. And so on and so forth. Soon there were pinwheels of spinning, flaming shoes everywhere.

Meanwhile, the orb had fallen into the pool of water and had been extinguished. But from a hole in the toe of another shoe, another flaming orb emerged. This one landed on the pyramid of tables. As it bounced its way down from table to table, it struck the series of bells.

Dong dong, dong dong, dong dong, ding . . .

Martin recognized the melody. It was a song his father used to hum on especially clear nights.

When the orb reached the bottom of the tables, it spiraled through a giant funnel, landed on another track, slalomed along, and struck a line of spoons in its way. The spoons were attached to the turntables of antique record players, each with an ornate amplifying horn. Records began to spin. Voices, garbled and slow, sang or spoke the following phrases in near perfect succession:

There once was a . . . noble . . . white . . . savage . . .
. . . his fate . . . deemed . . . grander . . . than average . . .

85

. . . our box . . . lost its hope . . .
. . . and was filled . . . with this . . . dope
. . . with a brain . . . quite as . . . plain . . . as a cabbage . . .

The flaming orb then shot off the track and skipped its way along the floor. Its journey ended when it struck the tepee of wood and paper in the middle of the room. A bonfire roared to life.

The heat was intense and immediate. Martin's eyes dried out as he watched the flames leap up and touch the bottom of the plastic swimming pool. Doves fluttered wildly in cages that hung in a circle around the pool. Wax, which was holding the doors to the cages closed, began to melt and release its grip. The doors swung open. The doves took flight.

The sound of the flapping wings engulfed the space. Attached to the birds' legs were tiny prisms that took the light from the fire and projected it as rainbows on the walls. The rainbows danced. The flames pummeled the air.

Then, all at once, the bottom of the pool gave out. A mass of water dumped on the bonfire, snuffing it. Smoke and steam raced up from the smoldering wood. The rainbows disappeared and the sound of the wings retreated as the birds found their way to perches.

The dark, smoky room was now silent except for the faint and haunting sound of a staticky record. Martin couldn't understand the words being sung. It sounded like *"Vu or nut rar seevor. Vu or nut rar seevor."* Perhaps it was another language?

Lane stepped through the smoke, holding a record player in her arm. The horn was propped up on her right shoulder, and she was rotating the record counterclockwise with her left hand.

"Get out," she said plainly.

Felix grabbed Martin by the arm.

"Get out," she said again.

Martin was frozen. Staring at Lane, listening to the odd sounds from the record player, he was transfixed. Love, whatever that was, might not have felt like this, but this, this was definitely something.

"Out," she said once more, raising her finger but not her voice.

Felix pulled Martin to the doorway and then out into the cold. The door to Lane's house slammed, but the lingering smell of smoke served as a reminder of what they had witnessed.

"Holy shmoly, was that a strange one," Felix said. "Last time she threw canned sardines at us, but it was nowhere near as spectacular as that!"

Martin didn't respond. He stepped closer to the door and placed a hand on it. It was warm. He wondered if this was all part of the show.

"Time to go," Felix said, spinning him around. "Lane doesn't take kindly to loitering."

Facing the street, Martin saw a splotch of color in the distance. An enormous pink pig with an arched back and a twitching snout was prancing directly at them.

"Oh jeepers!" Felix exclaimed as the pig got closer. "Remington. Of course. Of course this was coming."

In the pig's mouth was a small stone statue of a bear balancing on a ball. As soon as the pig reached them, it dropped the statue at Martin's feet. Martin bent over to pick it up.

There was a message etched onto the ball.

YOU HAVE BEEN SUMMONED

— 11 —

The Head

The chair used to be Kelvin Rice's. Or so Martin assumed. After all, Kelvin's name was scratched in the wood that framed its plush red back. It had a regal air—ornate oak arms, flecks of gold in the fabric. In any case, Martin found it comfortable.

Felix had gone home. "He's only ever summoned a couple people," he had told Martin with a dismissive shake of his head. "Be careful, that's all I can say."

Martin was alone in Nigel's living room. Well, not alone exactly. There were the goats and the dogs and the sheep that huddled around him, sniffing at his feet and rubbing their necks against the chair's legs. Nigel hadn't appeared yet. There had simply been a note on the front door that said:

Greetings, Martin! Come in.
Have a seat in the living room.
You will find the red chair to be lovely.

Nigel's home was actually a home. The living room had a love seat flanked by end tables. A fireplace had a stack of wood next to it. An intricate rug with swirling floral designs covered most of the wood floor. Books and magazines were spread neatly across the coffee table. There were the animals, of course, but otherwise, this place seemed like any of the homes Martin had visited on the island.

A voice came from another room: "Would you like tea?"

"No thank you," Martin answered.

"Fair enough. I'm having orange pekoe."

Moments later, a boy appeared in the doorway, cupping a steaming mug in both hands. This was the first time Martin had seen Nigel up close. Since the night Martin had arrived in town, Nigel had remained out of sight, which, judging from his Internet page, was not surprising.

NIGEL MOON

Nigel Moon arrived in Xibalba with a tiger and a Komodo dragon. Since his arrival, Nigel has been rounding up any and every animal he can find and they all live together in his house. The animals apparently provide Nigel with prophecies. Nigel summoned Kelvin Rice to his house regularly, to inform him of these prophecies. Since the Collapse, and since Kelvin's departure, Nigel has summoned only one person: Lane Ruez. She refuses to reveal what he told her. Nigel has predicted the following things: The plague of swallows. The infection of Tammy Green. The Collapse.

There was something familiar about Nigel that Martin couldn't place, but he didn't appear particularly special. His eyelids seemed thick, saggy. His hair was dense and puffy. A few large freckles lived around his slightly fat, slightly flat nose. Otherwise, a kid.

Nigel didn't come any closer. Rather, he stood in the doorway, sipping his tea and examining Martin. The animals shifted their attention to their master, and even though he didn't look at them, his presence had a calming effect on them. They all lowered themselves to the ground, surrounding his feet.

"I don't care about solar panels," Nigel said plainly.

"That's okay," Martin said. "Not everyone does. I'm just happy to have finally met you."

"And I you." Nigel smiled warmly. "Comfy?"

"Yes, very."

"Good," Nigel said as he leaned against the doorjamb. For some reason, he wasn't entering the room. "Now, I've been told about you," he went on. "I'm sure you've heard things about me too. And the truth, well, it's not nearly as interesting as you might hope. But that's why you're here, right? To learn the truth? To ask me questions?"

"Okay," Martin said with a bit of hesitation. "But you summoned *me*."

"I did. And you're here to ask me questions." Nigel's voice was a boy's voice, tuneless and fresh, yet Martin felt as though it had been living inside his head forever, whispering suggestions and giving orders.

"Okay," Martin said. "That's fine."

"I'm not a god." Nigel chuckled. "I have a gift. The animals are the gods. And they see and hear all. Then they tell me. And then I tell you. But only if you ask."

"So you do talk to animals?"

"We communicate, yes."

"That's amazing," Martin said. "I've read about things like that, but I wasn't sure if it was real."

"Faith," Nigel said. "The word gets too mixed up in religion. It's really about trust, isn't it?"

"I suppose so."

"*You* can't hear the things that *I* can. If you don't have faith in that premise, then what do you have? You can't exactly trust my answers to your questions, can you?"

"I suppose not," Martin said.

"You want a comfortable life here?" Nigel asked. "I can make sure you get that."

"I just want answers," Martin told him. "Information."

Nigel paused. He patted the doorjamb with his hand in a slow, steady beat. "I've been told that you're a hunter," he said.

Martin considered his response for a moment. "I . . . I . . . trap animals, but only for survival."

"Animals eat animals!" Nigel announced with a final, triumphant drum to the wood. "That's nature. Animals are delicious. I eat animals. Not friends, of course."

Martin wasn't sure whether to laugh. He chose to nod.

"Wait here," Nigel said. He ducked around the doorway for a moment.

Leaving was an option. Martin thought of calling out that he was feeling ill, and heading for the door. It wasn't that Nigel wasn't acting perfectly nice. He was. Something was just weird.

Before Martin could say a word, Nigel appeared in the doorway again. Instead of his mug of tea, he had the head of a deer in his hands. The head was not connected to a body.

"Dismemberment bothers some," Nigel said, finally stepping into the room. "Let the squeamish starve. Can't kill or dress an animal? Perhaps you shouldn't be eating it."

Noses took to the air as Nigel walked toward Martin. Blood dripped from the head and left a trail across the floor. Some of the dogs were quick to lick it up. Nigel presented the head to Martin, who took it because he figured he didn't have any other choice. It was still warm.

"Thank you," Martin whispered.

"Boris!" Nigel yelled.

The dogs stopped licking the blood and all the animals' heads shot up in attention. Their ears stiffened. They sniffed the air. In the other room, there was a steady click that was building to a crescendo.

Like that, the animals were on their feet. Behind Martin, there was another doorway. A mad rush to that exit ensued. Within a couple of seconds, the only ones left in the room were Nigel, Martin, and the head of a recently departed deer.

Until Boris joined them.

Boris's face peeked through under Nigel's armpit and Nigel gave him a squeeze around the neck and a healthy pat on his furry chest. Boris snorted through his giant black nose in appreciation.

"A Russian circus bear," Nigel said proudly. "He *can* balance on a ball, but he would prefer not to."

"Are you joking?" Martin said nervously, looking down at the deer's head in his arms. His lap was now soaked with blood.

"What?" Nigel said. "I don't joke about circuses. They're too insulting to the dignity of these majestic beasts."

"He's dangerous, Nigel," Martin pleaded.

"Only to you," Nigel said, raising his arm and letting Boris go. Boris sat down on the floor next to him, but he didn't take his eyes off Martin.

Martin thought of tossing the head across the room, then making a dash to the back exit and joining the other animals, but his luck with racing bears was sure to run out sooner rather than later.

"Do you have faith in me?" Nigel asked.

"I . . . ?"

"Boris and I have a deal," Nigel went on. "As long as you sit in that chair, he won't lay a paw on you. Then, at the end of our session, Boris gets that tasty head. But if you get up . . ."

"He . . . ?"

"Do you have faith in me?" Nigel said again, his voice now serious. He took a step to the side, leaving Boris to his own devices. Boris remained still.

"I do," Martin said. Regret choked every inch of him. What had he agreed to?

"Fantastic, then. Everything will be fine," Nigel said, flopping himself down on the love seat opposite Martin. "Ask away."

Martin assumed that if he didn't look at Boris, this would be easier. So he concentrated on Nigel, who had planted his hands behind his head and appeared the picture of comfort on the love seat.

"What should I ask you?"

"Anything," Nigel said.

"Okay, then. Ummmm . . . what happened on the Day?"

Nigel sighed. "Always the first question. Answer's obvious. They all left."

"Where'd they go?"

"Where they ended up."

"Where did they end up?"

"Where we'll meet them."

"We'll see them again?"

"Well, yes. Though not all of us will."

"Why are you being so vague?"

"Your questions are vague."

"Are they dead?"

"No."

"How do we find them?"

"I think you know that."

"I don't think I do. Why don't you tell me?"

"You'll use your machine," Nigel said without missing a beat.

Martin just about dropped the head. Boris reared back to pounce.

"Careful there," Nigel warned.

"I—I . . . How . . . ," Martin stuttered, gathering himself and getting a firmer grip on the head. "How did you know about the machine?"

"A little bird told me," Nigel said, and he clucked his tongue.

"And the address? Do you know about that too?" Martin asked. He hadn't thought it was possible, but he was now even more scared than he'd been when Boris entered the room. Boris seemed to sense it too and let the tip of his tongue peep out between his teeth.

Nigel nodded. "I know about the address. But you're not going to find what you're looking for there."

Martin paused. His sinuses began to throb, and he

reached up to rub his eyes, but he stopped when he realized his fingers were covered in deer blood.

"Faith," Nigel said. "It gives back, doesn't it?"

"It . . ." Martin lowered his hands.

"Time to go," Nigel said.

"I have more questions," Martin said quickly.

"Didn't you learn enough for today? Besides, Boris is hungry."

Martin turned his gaze back to Boris. The bear lifted himself from his sitting position and opened his mouth. The low rumbling growl, a sound Martin had last heard in the library, made the room shiver.

Martin tried to joke. "I think I would have preferred it if you'd brought the tiger."

Nigel smiled and shook his head. "No you wouldn't. There's no bargaining with that tiger. Now give Boris the head. He kept his promise."

With that, Martin flung the head to the bear. Boris was quick, springing to his feet and catching the head in his jaws. As the bear tore into the flesh, Nigel motioned with his chin, coaxing Martin to stand up.

Slowly, he did. Careful not to slip on the blood and flesh that were now being strewn violently across the floor by the overly enthusiastic Boris, Martin tiptoed to the exit.

PART 11

"Give him a push? We're still talking about intergalactic travel, right? Or is it swing sets?"

"You can joke if you want. I'm simply telling you what needs to happen."

"And I'm simply reminding you that a girl with a quick wit is a girl who gets things done. Nothing to worry your furry little heads about."

"We don't worry."

"Of course you don't. So tell me. Is this the guy right here?"

"The guy?"

"Who bit the doctor? Poisoned my B?"

"It is."

"Relay a message for me. He's a real snake."

"Not exactly. See the legs?"

"Whatever."

"Anything else?"

"As a matter of fact, there is. What do you make of this? Do you know what it does?"

"Of course."

"So? What does it do?"

"Whatever you want it to do."

— 12 —

The Diary

It was impossible to sleep. Martin threw out his bloody clothes, wrapped himself in covers, and searched the house for a pencil and paper. Something had been roused in him. He couldn't fathom how Nigel knew about the machine, but honestly, he didn't care. The machine suddenly mattered again, to one person at least. That person was a slightly sadistic boy who got his information from animals, but he was also a boy who looked to the future. So few in Xibalba did.

Martin quickly found a sketchbook in an upstairs bedroom, but he couldn't locate a pencil anywhere. Sparked by a memory, he descended into the basement. He hadn't been down there much. It was the dollhouse that bothered him most. It imbued the basement with a strange, almost holy significance, though the exact nature of it was impossible to decipher. Of course, Martin knew whose basement this had once been, whose house in which he had chosen to live. The others reminded him of it daily. Some shrugged it off as coincidence, but most seemed committed to a cautious unease. Whenever he told one of them his address, eyes sent him the same message: *Who the heck do you think you are?*

Martin thought he was a person who would change things. At least, that was what he thought now. He needed a pencil to prove it.

The coffee table in the basement had a thin drawer. Martin pulled it open. Just as he'd remembered from the last time he'd snuck a peek inside, there was a pencil sitting atop an instruction booklet about how to build an ant farm. When he snagged the pencil, he knocked the instructions to the side, revealing a book beneath them.

Martin set the pencil down on the table and fished the book out. It was a small leather-bound book, not much bigger than a pack of cards. It had no title on the cover, but what it did have was a sticker, the same sticker Martin had seen on the trail on his way to Xibalba. Skull, crossbones—the Jolly Roger. Martin opened it to the first page, where he found an inscription, written in ghostly graphite.

The Life and Times of Kelvin Rice

He nearly dropped the book. This was a diary. This was *Kelvin's* diary! Outside of the Internet, it was nearly impossible to find information about Kelvin. People rarely wanted to talk about him. Yet here was an unedited view into his mind.

Doodles of knights, monsters, curvy women, and aliens dominated the opening pages. The first entry was only a couple of sentences.

> Tyler said that diaries are for girls. I
> don't think that's true, but I'm still going
> to keep this one to myself.

After that, the entries were longer, but not by much. And there were no indications of when they were written. They were simply a series of thoughts and observations, scribbled out dusty and quick.

> Skipped school today. Aunt Bonnie
> doesn't care. She's got her mysteries and
> "a bottle to get to the bottom of."
> Spent most of my time in the basement
> carving a talisman out of wood. A
> talisman is like something that keeps
> demons out. Hang it up and scare them
> off. People have been doing it for tons
> of years, so it's got to work.

> I'm killing myself over what I could have
> done today, cuz Tyler was smoking behind
> the shed after last bell and he didn't
> know I was hiding in the bushes and I really
> wanted to get some dog crap on a stick
> and jab him with it, but I knew he would
> pummel me. I bite the side of my lip
> sometimes cuz I get so angry and even
> if it bleeds at least it's something.

> Marjorie still treats me like a kid, like
> we're in the Land of Neverseens or

whatever. Sometimes she says, "The hole beneath the quarry leads to the heart of the world and it's where we should meet if we get split up." It makes me know her meds are low. I think she says it cuz her dad got lost and died in there and that kind of stuff sticks with you forever. Anyway, I've checked it out. It's blocked up with bricks and wood, but I bet a pickax would do. I don't believe her, you know, but I think it's cool that one of the entrances to the Mayan underworld was a cave, and it's sort of like a cave in there, and so I wonder if it might hold something. Secrets. The stuff they don't tell you about in books.

There are girls in my classes who I look at and I wonder how it is that someone kissed them or that someone will kiss them someday. I know you only have to have a party and invite them and play those stupid bottle and closet games. There have to be other ways. I don't write poetry. I don't throw baseballs. If I die and I haven't kissed a girl, is there a place they send guys like me? Ha!

In submarines? Through caves? By rocket ship? Somehow...

That was where it ended. Martin checked the binding for remnant bits of paper. He ran his fingers across the blank pages, feeling for indentations. He searched for anything that might indicate there had once been more to the diary. It was a worthless endeavor. This was all there was. A few pages of writing and nothing else. Still, the last entry, the last words, struck him hard.

When the morning arrived, it found Martin sitting at the kitchen table, sketching. He hardly left his chair that day. By evening, his notebook was full, and he began tearing pages out of it and stuffing them in large envelopes. With a Magic Marker, he wrote a name on each envelope. Then, weary and a little nervous, he put the envelopes under his arm and left the house.

He went straight to Sigrid's. When she opened the door, she was wiping sweat from the back of her neck with a hand towel.

"Sorry to bother you," Martin said.

"No worries," Sigrid said. "I am enjoying my new treadmill, that is all. Thanks to you, of course."

"Can you deliver some messages for me?" Martin asked, presenting the envelopes.

"It will be my pleasure," Sigrid said, grabbing them and looking at the names.

"They're . . . top . . . secret," Martin explained. "And urgent."

"Then I must go now, yeah?" she said with a smile.

Martin thanked her and returned home and slept for more than twelve hours.

— 13 —

The Team

The next morning, Martin entered the church. He hadn't been inside since the night he'd arrived in Xibalba. It looked as though no one else had either. All the chairs and sofas were in the same places as before. The stool was still positioned in the center of the room.

To make things more inviting, he removed the stool and began to rearrange some of the furniture into a tight circle. He found a small table tucked away in the corner and made it the centerpiece. He tossed his notebook on it.

During his quick redecorating, he also found a cloth bag filled with dozens of Bibles. Martin had read the Bible, both the Old and New Testaments. Even though he thought they were a bit monotonous and repetitive, he knew they were beloved books, because he'd seen them in almost every house on the island.

To pass the time, he eased back in a chair and cracked

one of the Bibles open. He remembered the stories almost immediately. They were an endless string of life and death and lessons handed down from the heavens. Reading them now, Martin found himself surprisingly engrossed. They were ancient tales, true, but they were also things to which he could relate.

"Hate to spoil it for you, dude, but he comes back in three days, good as new."

Martin looked up from the book to see Chet standing in the doorway, holding one of the envelopes.

"Old Testament," Martin said, showing him the book.

"That the one with the boat?"

"It is," Martin said, setting the book down.

"So, you angling to be the new Kelvin Rice?"

"I don't think so," Martin said. "Why do you say that?"

"I dunno. Living in his house. Delivering doodles. Calling secret meetings." Chet heaved his bulk down into a chair.

"Kelvin was your leader?" Martin asked.

"He liked to think he was. Hard to take your leader seriously when he insists on wearing a cloak and playing spin the bottle all the time."

"I'm not trying to be a leader," Martin said. "I'm only looking for help."

A voice came from the doorway. "Martin's a Spacer, that's what he is." Lane had entered the church, her own envelope in hand.

"Oh man, a Spacer?" Chet said. "That's what this is about?"

"Hello, Lane," Martin said carefully. "I'm delighted you could make it."

Lane sauntered across the room. Her outfit of all black

from two nights before had been replaced by a blue police uniform. On her head, she wore a madras bandana. She reclined on a sofa.

"Why do you think he's a Spacer?" Chet asked.

"Did he give you the same drawings?" Lane took the notebook pages out of her envelope and tossed them on the table.

"I gave everyone the same thing," Martin said.

"Expecting more people?" Chet asked.

"One more," Martin said.

"And we'll all wear moon boots, eat freeze-dried ice cream, and have a big Spacer party, is that right?" Lane said. "I don't know why I bothered to leave the house."

"You came here because I wanted your help," Martin said. "As for being a Spacer, I don't know what that is."

"You think the answers are in the stars," Lane said. "So you drew a friggin' spaceship."

"I thought it was a popcorn popper," Chet joked.

In all the years of working on the machine, there had been plenty of times when Martin wanted to believe that it was a spacecraft. His father would never confirm or deny what it was meant to do, but he would often say, "There's a different world for us than this one, Martin, and you'll see it soon."

"Do you think it will work?" Martin asked Lane as he nudged the drawings to her side of the table.

"Beats me," she said. "I'm not a Spacer. Never will be."

"She's a Vaporist, like me," Chet said.

Martin's silence revealed his ignorance.

"There are the Spacers, of course," Chet explained. "And there are, or were, the Diggers. You know, kids who think everyone went underground. And the Parallelodorks, like

106

Felix. Believe in alternate dimensions and all that junk. There are the Reapers. Think we're all dead and dancin' the limbo or something. Then there are the Vaporists. Vaporists believe what they see. Everyone is gone, gone, gone. Vaporized."

"They're definitely not on Venus, having a picnic and waiting for us," Lane said.

This didn't deter Martin. He couldn't ignore what he was feeling. "I believe we need this machine," he told Lane. "I believe it more than anything."

Lane didn't answer. Instead, she shoved the drawings back across the table.

"Lane. Tell him what Nigel told you," Chet blurted out.

"What? No," Lane said quickly.

"That's why you're here, isn't it?" Chet badgered her. "Didn't Nigel tell you that someone was coming to town and it wasn't gonna be Santa? You thought it'd be Kelvin, and you—"

"Shut your mouth," Lane snarled. "I never should have told you that."

"You understand how to build things, both of you do," Martin said calmly. "That's all I care about. That's why I need your help."

Lane turned away.

"This is complex stuff, dude," Chet said, pointing at the papers. "How do you know we can build it?"

"'Cause I've built it before," Martin said. "I spent my whole life building it. Now we just need to build it bigger."

The floor began to vibrate ever so slightly. Across the room, someone's throat cleared.

"Him?" Lane exclaimed. She sat up and shot an accusatory finger toward the door. "He's the other one?"

107

Henry took a few steps toward them, his rifle slung over his shoulder.

"Can we help you, Henry?" Martin asked.

"She's ready," was all Henry would say. Then he walked back outside.

Kid Godzilla was painted green with curls of silver to produce the illusion of scales. A series of glossy white metallic teeth made up the front grill. A jagged tail fin stuck out from the back. The tires, thick and black, were at least five feet tall. Taller than Henry, in any case. When Martin, Lane, and Chet came out of the church, they saw the squat boy standing next to the monster truck, which was vibrating and spitting exhaust from its curling green tailpipe.

Darla shoved her head and a fist out the driver's-side window. "A Spacer! An honest-to-goodness Spacer!" she hooted. She gave the fist an overly celebratory pump.

"She gets excited sometimes," Henry explained.

"Of course I do." Darla laughed. "I'm psyched. Climb aboard, one and all. Three Vaporists and a Spacer. Makin' a spaceship. Who woulda thunk it?"

Henry began to hoist himself up to the passenger-side seat when Darla waved him off. "Shoo, boy. That seat is reserved for Mr. Maple."

Head down, Henry shuffled over to the extended cab in the back.

"Thank you," Martin whispered as he climbed up and into the truck.

"And make sure you sit *squirrel*," Darla commanded Henry. "We got a coupla huskies that deserve window seats."

Henry moved to the center of the cramped back cab, squeezed his legs together, lifted his knees, and brought his hands in close to his chin. His rifle stuck up behind him like a tail.

"Whatcha waiting on?" Darla said to Chet and Lane, who hadn't made a move from their spots along the edge of the church parking lot. By the looks on their faces, it was easy to tell they weren't happy with the situation.

"Flying pigs," Lane deadpanned.

"I'm sure Nigel could arrange something," Darla said. "Come on and get in, ya bums."

"Yes," Martin said. "I think it's important that we all work together. Where are we going, anyway, Darla?"

In response, she smiled, revved the engine, then pulled a small lever on the dashboard. Fire shot out from two nostril-shaped holes in the hood of Kid Godzilla, and the laugh Darla set free from her lungs was only a tad short of maniacal.

— 14 —

The Island

They spotted the Ferris wheel first. It rose through the trees like the skeleton of a giant flower. As the truck got closer, they saw the sign.

"What's Impossible Island?" Chet asked from the backseat.

"You're looking at it," Darla said. "Finest theme park within fifty miles of Xibalba."

"Theme parks are torture," Martin blurted out.

"What?" Henry said.

"It's something . . . someone told me once," Martin said.

"Well, someone was a real wet blanket," Darla said. "Theme parks are all kinds of awesome. Even if abandoned ones have the occasional raccoon problem. Hope y'all had your rabies shots."

Darla parked Kid Godzilla next to the gate and Henry took the lead, hopping a turnstile with his rifle at the ready.

He checked all sides, then motioned with two fingers for everyone to follow.

The park wasn't particularly big, but Martin didn't realize that. To him it appeared to be an entire city. Lines of miniature houses, torn from the pages of storybooks, made up the downtown. Colorful insectlike rides lorded over the borderlands.

Lane was in awe. She stepped on a slat of a fence and hoisted herself up to get a closer look at a Tilt-A-Whirl. "All right. This place is pretty rad," she admitted.

"Kelvin told me about it once," Darla said. "I always figured it'd be a perfect site for a secret project."

Lane circled the fence, found the controls to the ride, and gave them a closer look. Chet occupied himself with a taffy machine, knocking away hardened braids of sugar so he could give the arms a spin. Henry kept busy scouting for raccoons, kicking open any door he saw and thrusting his rifle inside. While next to a food cart, Martin stood with Darla. She opened a silver cooler and plunged her hand in. It emerged holding an orange soda.

"When we got in the truck, you said we had three Vaporists and a Spacer," Martin said to her. "So you're a Vaporist?"

"Used to be," Darla said, cracking the soda open. She took a big slug from it and gave Martin a quick nudge to the ribs with her elbow. "I'm on your team now. Your drawings officially converted me into a Spacer."

She lifted the can in a toast, then took another drink.

"What about Henry? What's he?" Martin asked.

"He's an idiot, Martin. But he's eager, and he's loyal. He told me once that he thought the Day happened because of all the bad things he did when he was a kid. Yikes! Right? He can't help it, though, I guess."

"I never asked him to be a part of this," Martin said.

"He would've found out eventually," Darla said. "Spying is his biggest talent."

"Well, it's probably best if he stays with you in the truck," Martin said.

"What's that supposed to mean? We're all working together, right?"

"Well . . ." Martin paused for a moment. He'd thought the distribution of labor would be obvious. "Lane, Chet, and I are going to do the actual building. I figured you, and Henry, could get us the supplies we need. You know, with the truck?"

"Oh, yeah, sure," Darla said quickly. "That makes perfect sense." As if plugging up her mouth to stave off a snide comment, she immediately put the can back to her lips. When she was finished taking a long swig, she presented it to Martin.

"Thank you," he said. He reached for it, but she yanked it away.

"No way, wild child," she said with a half laugh, half snarl. "Gonna have to be faster than that if you want to keep up with me."

With that, she turned and skittered away, joining Chet, who was rummaging around in a wooden shack that bore a sign reading UNCLE SCHMITTY'S SHOOTING GALLERY.

Chet pulled out a plastic toy rifle. He pointed it at Henry, who was prowling in the distance. "Lookie here, Darla," Chet joked. "It's me, Henry. I'm gonna win you a panda bear by shootin' this here fire stick at a Mongoloid."

Darla giggled guiltily. Martin was too far away to be positive, but he was pretty sure he saw Henry's lips trembling, as if he was muttering something under his breath.

Impossible Island was the perfect place to build the machine. Not only did it provide an ample amount of hardware in the form of roller coasters and other amusements, it was also far from the prying eyes of Xibalba. Lane, Chet, Darla, and Henry were in agreement that the project was best kept a secret. For whatever their reasons, they believed in Martin's designs, but they weren't sure the other kids would be enamored.

"They'll think they got another Kelvin on their hands," Chet said. "And we all know how that ended."

Actually, Martin didn't know how that ended. The information on the Internet about Kelvin's exile was limited at best, and kids always changed the subject when asked about it. All he knew was that it had ended badly and that Nigel had been involved. That compelled Martin to keep quiet about his meeting with Nigel as well. There was a good chance that in some minds, Nigel was a lunatic.

So as not to arouse suspicion, every evening for the next month, the team gathered in the parking lot of the large brick hospital on the edge of town, about as desolate a place as you could find in Xibalba, due to rumors that it was haunted. Unseen, all five would pile into Kid Godzilla. Darla would drop Martin, Lane, and Chet off at Impossible Island, and she and Henry, armed with the latest list of supplies, would go searching nearby communities. Around midnight, Kid Godzilla would return, full of the latest take. They would unload the gear; then they would all get back in the truck and go home together.

Their mornings and afternoons were still dedicated to their various "day jobs." Martin tended to solar panels and installed a security system for Felix's Internet. Chet worked his greenhouse. Henry guarded the town's streets and hunted turkeys and rabbits and the occasional deer, which he traded for other goods and services. When she wasn't driving Kid Godzilla, Darla made submissions to the Internet and sat on her front steps, doling out orders in the form of advice to anyone who happened to pass by.

"Hey, Wendy," Martin once heard Darla holler from the steps. "A girl with your complexion should stick to the earth tones. Calls less attention to the acne, don't you think?"

Only Lane, whose spectacular shows used to be Xibalba's nightly entertainment, gave up the work of her former life. "Thanks to your solar panels," she told Martin, "no one cares about live entertainment anymore. Video games and DVDs. The wave of the future."

Martin felt guilty, of course, but he didn't know what to do. Every time he tried to reach out to Lane, she gave him the cold shoulder. Other than contributing to the conversations that building the machine required, she remained silent on most evenings. It was strange that she even wanted to help. Still, she was always there. She always worked hard.

The plan was to make the machine twenty times as big as the one Martin had built with his father. It seemed ludicrous when Martin first thought of it, but when they put it into action, he saw how achievable it was. He was not limited by materials. The colossal rides at Impossible Island provided more than enough gears and knobs and metallic casings. He was also not slowed by the constant need for redesign. In all the years that Martin's father had been working on the machine, he had tinkered and adjusted and rebuilt over and over again. But by the time of his departure, the machine had basically been completed. That was the machine Martin had studied, the machine that was only missing that final piece.

That final piece. That was another thing Martin kept to himself: he still didn't know what it was. He had hoped either Lane or Chet would naturally figure out what it might be, but as both of them were willing to admit, they didn't understand the machine beyond what Martin told them.

"Hey, chief, I'm far from a rocket scientist, but I'm still curious as to how this birdy's gonna fly," Chet once joked.

Martin was curious too. The machine looked like a giant bullet, and he could picture it ripping and flaming through the atmosphere. The only problems were it didn't seem suited to the harsh environment of outer space and there wasn't any logical place to put fuel. Martin tried to push these worries aside. His father had told him the machine was magic. After all Martin had experienced, after all the world had experienced, he was willing to believe in a little magic.

— 15 —

The Skyway

It was late in the fall. The fireworks of color that were the autumnal forest had finished their show. The trees were now bare, and the air crisp. Snow hadn't taken to the ground yet, but Martin would occasionally feel tiny swarms of cold crystals against his cheek. The shell of the machine was complete. When the winter did come, which it would, they'd be sheltered. It would be cold, but they could work.

It was warm on the evening Darla dropped them off at Impossible Island and set out on a mission to find blowtorches. When she left, she was her chatty self, and if asked, Martin wouldn't have been able to recall what she had said. It was probably no different from any other evening.

The big project of the night involved attaching the interior door. There were two doors in the machine. There was the exterior one, which was constructed from sturdy sheets of steel sandwiched into multiple layers and bolted together to keep the weather out. There was also the interior one, which went next to the control panel and divided the machine into two chambers. In the original version of the machine, the interior door was only three feet high and a couple of feet wide, but it was an essential piece. Martin's father had always said it opened the machine's heart. For the supersized edition, they were going with a massive fifteen-foot-tall slab of glass that had served as the entrance to the park's cafeteria.

"Not sure why you sent the fattest one," Chet joked as he climbed onto the roof of the cafeteria and got down on his hands and knees so he could remove the last set of screws that held the hinges near the top of the door. Dangling a few feet above him was an oval gondola that was part of the Skyway, the park's cable-supported transportation system. Twenty feet below him were Lane and Martin, holding the door steady.

"It's almost out," Chet announced, one hand on top of the door, the other manning a screwdriver. "Careful now."

As the door came off the top hinge, Martin could feel its immense weight pressing against him. His shoulder began to ache, and he figured that Lane needed to get in a better position so she could bear more of the weight. "Don't let it go yet," he told Chet. "We're not ready."

Martin motioned with his head for Lane to move around to the other side. She nodded and let the door go.

The moment her fingers released the glass, it became apparent that Lane had been holding up more than her share. The door began to tip. Its bottom began to slide along the gravelly ground and emit the awful shriek that comes from scratching glass.

"Mutha!" Chet bellowed. He lost his grip. The door was

sure to fall on Martin. Chet dove forward, snagging the corner just in time and leaving the front half of his body hanging precariously over the edge. He reached his free hand up and grabbed a rail that ran along the bottom of the gondola. The gondola tipped. Its door flew open. From inside, a nasty snarl escaped.

A raccoon jumped out from the gondola and down onto Chet's back.

"Get it off me! Get it off me!" Chet screamed, letting go of the door and swatting at the raccoon. The raccoon hissed and swatted back. Its fangs were drawn and its head was cocked, ready to strike.

Martin couldn't hold the entire weight of the door and jumped away. The glass struck the ground, let out a monumental boom, and shattered into hundreds of sharp little cubes.

The sound stole the raccoon's attention for a moment. It was enough time for Chet to deliver the decisive blow, knocking the animal with his elbow down into the pile of glass. The momentum from the melee might have sent Chet down into the glass too, but his grip on the gondola was firm, even as the cable that held it dipped, then sprang back, causing the gondola to jump away from the roof.

The raccoon, its fur now decorated with bits of glass, locked eyes with Lane. She didn't hesitate. Lane lunged at the creature—fingers poised, chest unleashing a primal scream. The raccoon did the smart thing. It scurried into the darkness.

Chet, on the other hand, remained where he was, hanging from the gondola, twenty feet off the ground. "Sonuva . . . ," he panted as he got both hands on the rail and rocked back and forth in the air.

"Holy cow, are you okay?" Lane asked.

"I . . . think . . . so," Chet said between breaths. "Dirty rascal was going . . . was going for the throat."

"He's gone now," Martin assured him.

The gondola was swinging like a pendulum, but its arc was gradually getting smaller. Chet looked down over his shoulder and saw the twinkling galaxy of glass that had once been the door.

"Sorry, pals," he called down. "Didn't mean to wreck it."

"It's okay," Martin said. "There are plenty of other doors out there."

"Gonna have to say, *did not* see that one coming," Chet said, chuckling.

"You were lucky," Lane replied. "I guess Henry isn't so crazy, always out there on coon patrol."

"Am I too high to jump down?" Chet asked.

"Probably," Martin said. "Let me get the ladder. It's over by the Gravitron."

"No rush," Chet joked. "Enjoying the view up here."

Afterward, Martin would play the next moment over in his head countless times. It was a quick succession of events, but he was sure he could have done something differently.

It started when he turned. That was when he heard the creaking sound. He thought nothing of it. He took a few steps away. Next came the snap and the ghostly howl whipping through the air. That was when he turned back. That was when he looked up. The cable had broken.

Instead of trying to break Chet's fall, Martin went straight for Lane, knocking her from the path of the falling gondola. As his shoulder drove into her, he felt a rush of air behind him. Then he was lying on top of her.

At the same moment, Chet landed on his back, right in the glass. There wasn't time for him even to blink his eyes, let alone sit up or slide over. Because the gondola landed square on Chet. As it crushed his chest, it forced all the wind from his lungs. "Pffffaaaa . . ." was the only sound that came out of his mouth. Then there was silence.

"Chet. Chet. Chet," Lane said softly, her mouth right next to Martin's ear. It sounded less like she was calling for him than it did like she was trying to calm herself down. Her heart was pounding ferociously; Martin could feel it against his shoulder.

Martin rolled off her and onto his back. He sat bolt upright. Chet's head was just inches from his feet. His face was turned toward Martin.

"Chet. Chet. Chet."

Blood was leaking from Chet's mouth onto the cubes of glass. His eyes were open, and they were blinking. He was still conscious, but he wasn't saying anything.

As Martin reached forward to touch him, a glob of snowflakes, plump and wet, landed on his hand.

/

— 16 —

The Tarp

The invasion of snow came fast. It was like a switch had been turned, shutting off the world's thermostat and opening up the clouds. There was no wind, only a downward tirade of flakes.

However much the gondola weighed was too much. Martin and Lane couldn't move it an inch. Even with a lever, fashioned from some two-by-fours, they couldn't begin to lift it off Chet. They couldn't get access to his hands or feet. They could touch only his face.

"Hang in there," Lane said as she ran her hand across his cheek. The snow was piling up, and Lane was doing her best to keep Chet from getting covered. He was still conscious, but only barely. His lips were a straight line. His eyes were struggling to stay open.

"I found these shovels and a tarp," Martin said. "But there's nothing to warm him up quickly. We already used all the propane."

"Darla should be here any minute," Lane said, checking her watch.

"Right, good," Martin said, and he busied himself with clearing all the snow that had collected on the ground around them.

"He's so cold, Martin," Lane whispered, as if Chet couldn't hear her. Both of her hands were now petting his cheeks.

"Keep doing what you're doing," Martin said as he shoveled. It was the best advice he could give. After all, what he was doing certainly wasn't making much of a difference. Each time he turned around, the spot he had just shoveled was already covered in a skin of snow.

The snow was at least two feet high on the gondola, and every so often a hunk would slide down and land on Lane's back or, worse, Chet's face. Martin was tempted to knock some of it off the other side, but it had the potential to cause an avalanche and only make matters worse. He contemplated building some sort of a shelter around them, but the snow was coming fast and he didn't want to leave Lane and Chet alone while he was collecting supplies.

Instead, he set the shovel down. He sat next to Lane. He took the blue plastic tarp he had found and pulled it over them.

"I'm here," he said, placing his hand on Chet's forehead. Chet's eyes had finally closed. Lane waved her palm in front of his nose.

"He's still breathing," she said.

"Huddle in close," Martin said.

The two curled up shoulder to shoulder to create more shelter with their bodies. They switched back and forth: one would rub both hands together while the other placed warm fingers on Chet's face.

"We should keep talking. Give him something to listen to," Martin suggested.

"What do you want to talk about?" Lane asked.

"I don't know," Martin said. "Books. Do you read books?"

"I've read books."

"What type do you like? Mystery? Comedy? Sometimes I can't tell the difference," Martin said.

"Is that supposed to be a joke?"

"I guess so."

"You're not funny, Martin," Lane said delicately. "That's one thing about you. You've never been funny."

"Oh."

"It's not your fault. Being funny takes experience."

"I've read a lot of books."

"And you've built a lot of machines, evidently," Lane said. "Not the same as living."

"Just one other," Martin admitted.

"What?"

"I've only built one other machine."

"Okay," Lane said. "And did that one work?"

Martin didn't answer.

Lane filled in the blank by saying, "And this one won't either."

Until that point, Martin had only been annoyed by Lane's cynicism. Now he found himself legitimately angry.

"Then why are you helping me?" he asked.

"Have you ever wondered why we're the only ones left?" she responded.

"All the time."

"But you haven't figured it out?"

"'Cause we're lucky?"

"No. 'Cause we're awful," Lane said plainly. "None of us really care that everyone is gone. We only care about ourselves."

"I wouldn't go that far," Martin said, though he did understand her point.

"And you're different," Lane said. "That's why I'm helping. You're the only kid in the world who wants to do something big. There must be a reason why that is. If I hitch myself to your post, things will happen to me. Things I can't do for myself. Even when this machine doesn't work."

Martin blew into his hands and rubbed them together. As he placed them on Chet's face, Lane took her hands away. Their eyes met for a moment. Over the last couple of months, Martin had gotten better at reading people. While he couldn't tell for sure if Lane was lying, he could see in those brilliant silver eyes that she wasn't telling him everything.

"I had one friend on the island," Martin said. "His name was George. And I had my father. All I want to do is see them again. Maybe I'm as selfish as everyone else."

"Maybe," she said.

The tarp began to sag under the weight of the snow, so the two huddled even closer.

Chet died sometime around five a.m. His breathing slowed, then stopped, and no matter how much they rubbed their hands, they couldn't bring the warmth back to his face. A couple more feet of snow had collected on the tarp and the gondola. From the outside, they must have seemed like nothing but a few bumps along the wintery landscape. Lane and Martin didn't say anything to each other. They just took their hands off Chet's face and stood up. The cocoon of white broke open.

Silently, they trudged through the snow as best they could, but they were wearing only sneakers, jeans, and thin jackets. The going was tough, and the sensation in their hands and feet was starting to shift from pinpricks to numbness. What should have been a five-minute walk back to the machine stretched out to over half an hour. When they finally reached it, they knocked snow from the door and tumbled inside.

They lay down on their backs next to each other. It was cold in there, but not nearly as cold as it was outside. Martin turned his head to look up at the empty spot near the control panel where the glass door was to have been mounted, where it was to have divided the machine into its two chambers. Then he turned back and looked at Lane. Her face was damp and red.

"It shouldn't have been Chet. It should've been me," she said.

Martin didn't respond.

"This is when people say, 'Don't talk like that.' This is when people cry, Martin."

"I know," he said, but he really didn't. He had no idea what a person did with death, and he didn't feel like crying. His mind buzzed with images of himself, alone in the world once again.

"This is also when people hold each other."

Before he could respond, Lane was pushing her hand underneath Martin's back and reaching around to his side.

As she pulled herself closer to him, he felt her cold fingers on his ribs. He shivered.

"Sorry," she said, snaking her head under his arm and onto his chest.

"It's okay."

Her long black hair spread over him like oil. He leaned his head forward until his nose was touching her scalp. It smelled vaguely smoky and rusty, but in an appealing way. His mind wandered to passages in books about first kisses. They always described how a girl's hair smelled. Like dew, like heather, like the ocean, like nutmeg. Like clouds, like childhood, like dreams. Like all sorts of things, but never like this.

He kissed a spot on her scalp where the hair sprouted in different directions.

"Thank you," Lane said, not moving.

Then Martin closed his eyes. The sun would be up soon. He was hungry. He was cold. He wanted to sleep. More than anything, he wanted to sleep.

The growl of Kid Godzilla woke him. Lane stood at the exterior door of the machine. As she pushed it open, sunlight raced in. Martin pulled himself up and followed her outside.

The snow had stopped falling, but it was piled nearly four feet high in some places. It wasn't enough to deter Kid Godzilla, though. The truck was cutting through the snow slowly, but easily. It came to a stop a few yards from the machine. The door opened and down hopped Darla, fully outfitted in a brand-new lavender snowmobile suit.

"Check it out, squares," she chirped. "Ready for a new winter."

Before Darla could take a step, Lane chucked a snowball

at her. Darla dodged and stumbled backward, as it barely missed her shoulder. From the other side of the truck, Henry hopped down. He was wearing a white camouflage jumpsuit. He didn't appear to notice the snowball assault. His face was uncharacteristically cheery.

"What the what?" Darla said, checking herself to see if she had been hit.

"Where were you?" Lane screamed.

"Settle down, you spaz," Darla said. "We got distracted. Don't worry, when the snow started, we went on a shopping spree. Got everyone new scarves and cute mittens and everything. People's outfits from last winter are so . . . last winter."

"It started snowing hours ago," Martin said.

"Figured you'd be laughing it up by the fire, roasting marshmallows," Darla said.

"Making s'mores," Henry added.

"Speaking of marshmallows," Darla said, chuckling, "where's Chet?"

No one answered.

"Chet?" Darla pressed. "You know? Tons o' fun?"

Lane formed another snowball as if she were crushing the life out of it. This one hit Darla square in the nose.

— 17 —

The Supermarket

Martin had never seen a dead body before. In those days following the appearance of the skiff, he had imagined one. He had imagined his father dead on the bottom of the ocean. Dead on a dock on the mainland, the skiff drifting away from him. Dead somewhere, anywhere, maybe even on the island, crushed and hidden beneath a tree. Dead. Rotting. Dead.

But his father wasn't dead. It had become clear to Martin that he had left, along with everyone else. It made little sense, yet all the evidence seemed to indicate that it was true. What frustrated Martin most was what had always frustrated him: his father had never told him why. It was not only cruel, but it was the height of hypocrisy. For on the night before he'd set out on his journey, he had asked Martin a huge question.

"Have you ever thought of leaving me?"

"No," Martin said. "Never." This was the truth, too. As curious as he was about the world off the island, he never wanted to leave his father.

"It's okay if you think it," his father said. "It's natural."

"I never think it."

"*Never* is a word that only boys use," his father said. "If you do decide to leave, and not to come back, I just ask you this: tell me why."

"I'll never leave you," Martin stated firmly.

His father smiled. He didn't say anything else.

Martin's father was a stickler for his own rules. Never had he been known to break one. Yet he hadn't held himself to a promise to which he had held his son. He never told him why.

A funeral service for Chet was held in the supermarket. The church had always been a place for meetings and Arrival Stories, but when it came to events like this, no one could agree on which religious tone to strike, and no one bothered to learn about anyone else's religious beliefs. So they held it in the supermarket. Because Chet liked food. Because Chet provided food. Because Chet was fat.

There were still cans of beets and yams and Vienna sausages populating the shelves. Pineapples and tuna fish and other canned goodies had been gobbled up in the early days of Xibalba, but the kids never had to resort to opening the strange stuff. Between Henry's hunting, Chet's farming, and everyone else's scavenging, no one ever came close to starving.

The produce section had been cleared out long before, leaving a wide-open space near the entrance of the store. They brought in comfy chairs and a lectern borrowed from the school. Chet's body, packed to the chin with snow, was placed in a coffin-shaped shelf that used to hold tomatoes. Cameron, a virtuoso on guitar, played a selection of solemn acoustic tunes.

The plan was to have kids speak at the lectern, to tell stories and talk about their impressions of Chet. The best that most of them could come up with was a few phrases: he grew good vegetables; he roasted tasty peanuts; he said "dude" a lot.

Felix went the furthest simply by reading Chet's recently updated Internet page aloud.

CHET BUCKLEY

Chet Buckley was from a small town in an Appalachian Mountain valley. His mother was a scientist. His father owned a store. He came to Xibalba by following railroad tracks. On his way, he collected a few items of note, including the Declaration of Independence, a painting that looks like blobs of color but is supposedly really famous, and a bunch of Civil War stuff. He stored it all among the junk he kept crammed in his house. Despite his outward appearance, and the appearance of his house, Chet was a talented farmer. He used the word *dude* quite often.

When Felix finished reading, he returned to his seat. Everyone except for Nigel was there, but no one else bothered to stand, and no more than five minutes passed before was basically over. Martin felt bad about that, so

d up to the lectern. He didn't have anything pre-

ut he spoke anyway.

et was a good friend to me," Martin said. "He was

and loyal and helpful. He died courageously and I . . .

guess that's what I can say about Chet."

Iartin was about to return to his seat when Ryan

ated, "How'd it happen?"

"Yeah." Felix joined in. "What shenanigans were you

iys up to?"

"We were . . . ," Martin began, then stopped. The machine was far from finished. They needed more time. Still, he
wasn't comfortable with lying. "We were at a theme park."

"Like with bumper cars?" Felix said.

"What crushed him?" Cameron added sarcastically, looking up from her guitar. "A giant teacup?"

"Gondola," Martin stated, and he moved sideways from
the lectern to avoid any more questions.

"Odd," Felix said. "First big snowstorm of the season.
You're at an amusement park? Doesn't add up."

"Do you have to ruin the surprise, Felix?" Lane jumped in.

"What surprise?" Felix asked.

This is it, Martin thought. She's going to tell them about
the machine—the machine that doesn't work yet and, according to her, probably never will.

"Excitement," Lane said. "Something our lives have all
been lacking. Martin kindly volunteered to power up an
amusement park. Chet and I were helping. It was going to be
our Christmas present to Xibalba. But it might not happen
now, for obvious reasons."

"But wouldn't that be dangerous?" Felix asked.

"Well, sure," Lane said. "We know that now."

"I'm sorry," Felix said, turning away from Chet's body.

"No," Martin told him, "don't be. We weren't cautious enough, and it ended in tragedy."

"Which might not have been the case," Lane said, a little louder than necessary, "if someone actually showed up when they were supposed to."

Darla, who had been sitting quietly in the back, dismissed Lane with a flick of her wrist and said, "I'm not even going to acknowledge that."

"What? Your incompetence or your selfishness?" Lane fired back.

"Shove it, Lane. It was my birthday, okay?" Darla explained. "I was doing something special for myself. No one here ever does anything special for anyone's birthday."

"Cry me a river, princess." Lane's voice was dripping venom.

Even though he agreed with Lane, Martin didn't think Chet's memorial was the right forum for such a confrontation. He moved into the crowd. Putting his hands up, he stepped between the two girls.

"I deserve some sympathy," Darla cried, standing and holding her head aloft. "I'm an orphan!"

Lane was on her feet immediately, pointing a finger at her. "We're all orphans, you idiot!"

Someone started laughing. It was Henry. His hand was over his mouth, but he couldn't conceal his amusement.

"Shut it!" Darla snapped.

"It's funny," Henry said.

"Arrrr," Darla snarled, pulling at her hair as if this were the most frustrating moment of her life. It appeared that at any moment, she would storm out.

132

"Let's calm down and—" Martin said, but he was interrupted by a new guest. Remington the pig had entered the supermarket. A statue of a lizard was in his mouth. Everybody froze. They knew what this meant.

Remington surveyed the crowd and put his nose in the air. He took in a quick batch of snorts. Then he put his nose to the ground and wiggled his way around the chairs until he stopped at a pair of fuzzy camel-colored boots. That was where he dropped the statue.

Darla picked it up and sighed. "About time."

— 18 —

The Prophecy

They all decided to wait outside Nigel's house. This was a special occurrence. With the exception of Kelvin, Nigel had summoned only two people: Lane and Martin. Now there was Darla.

To keep themselves occupied, the kids built snow sculptures, dug tunnels, and had contests to see who could throw a snowball the farthest. The din of chatter and laughter indicated that they all enjoyed it much more than they'd expected. A shame, really, what it took to bring them all together like this.

Martin was giving snowman construction a try—rolling a ball to make a head—when Felix offered him a carrot.

"Traditionally, the nose," Felix said. "Doesn't make much sense to me. Baby eggplant would make a better nose. Or a radish."

Martin nodded his thanks. Carrots and eggplants and

radishes would be hard to come by soon. Did the others recognize this? Did they care? Was there another green thumb among them to pick up where Chet had left off?

Martin was tempted to pose these questions to Felix, but he suspected that his friend would just shrug them off and say that they'd have to do without. It had been a while since the two had spoken one on one, and Martin was starting to learn that it was always better to chat with his neighbors about common interests than problems.

"Our security system," he said with a labored wink. "Snagged anyone yet?"

"Nope," Felix responded.

"That's a good thing, right?"

Felix shrugged. Then, timidly, he asked, "Didn't you want my help? At the amusement park?"

"Oh." Martin stumbled over his response. "I knew you were too . . . busy with your Internet for something silly like that."

This was only part of the answer. Martin also knew that Felix, for all his talk about technology, really didn't have a firm grasp of it. The mainframe he had been working on for the last couple of months was a calamity of wires and circuit boards. Even Martin, who knew nothing about computers, could tell it was all wrong. Felix's genius wasn't for mechanics or electronics. It wasn't for computers. It was conceptual. Firefly lightbulbs. A World Wide Web that was actually a web. These were his gifts to the world, but Martin wasn't going to tell him that. Perhaps he didn't need to be told. He still hadn't asked Martin to hook up the power to his house. Things were obviously not on track.

"And you never mention your session with Nigel. It makes

me wonder, you know? Does that have something to do with all of this?"

The temptation to lie was strong, but Martin owed Felix more than that. "It does," he admitted.

"Did he tell you Chet would die?" Felix asked.

"No."

"They're convenient, his predictions."

"I have reasons to believe them," Martin explained.

"Most people do."

When the door to Nigel's house opened and Darla strutted to the front steps, Gabe, who was perched in a tree, hollered, "She's back!"

Darla placed a hand to her heart, feigning shock. Then she gave a little curtsy to the crowd, even though she wasn't wearing a dress, just a long peacoat and tights. Martin noticed they were spotless. Maybe deer heads weren't always on the menu at Nigel's house.

"Well, well," Darla said with pouty lips, "were y'all waiting for little ol' me?"

Everybody stopped what they were doing.

"What'd Nigel say?" a girl named Tiberia yelled.

"Was it good?" Ryan said.

"Is it a secret?" Henry asked, his eyebrows at full mast.

"A secret? Heavens, no. I don't keep secrets." As she said this, Darla stared at Lane and Martin.

"So what'd he say?"

Darla smiled widely. "He said we should all be Spacers."

"I do not believe it," Sigrid said. "Nigel does not say things like that."

"Okay," Darla admitted. "You got me. Then he *implied* that we should all be Spacers. After all, we've got ourselves a spaceship."

136

The crowd reacted with confused silence, so Darla continued. "Oh, is that a secret? I'm so sorry, but how can we keep secrets if we're expected to rebuild civilization?"

"Out with it, Darla!" Tiberia yelled. "What's this about a spaceship?"

"Remember a few months ago, when Kelvin was banished, and Lane was all weepy and more suicidey than usual? And remember how Nigel summoned her and she was way too cool for school to tell us his prophecy?"

In the shade of a nearby tree, Lane leaned and seethed, but she didn't say a word. Her eyes were injecting poison straight into Darla's jugular.

"Out with it!" Tiberia shouted again.

"Chill, rock star," Darla said, putting a hand up. "I'm getting there. Nigel told Lane that the next person who appeared in Xibalba was gonna have a plan to fix everything. And wouldn't you know it, a few weeks later, Martin Maple comes strolling in, all smiles and sunshine and solar panels. And you know what Martin Maple knows how to build?"

"A spaceship," Martin stated with a humble nod. He thought it best they heard it from him, even if Darla was now running the show.

"Hallelujah!" Darla shouted. "A sky-scorching spaceship! And Nigel told me that you all have to pitch in because we don't have much time. We need to get this thing fired up as soon as possible."

"He said that?" Felix asked, his eyes narrowing in doubt.

"In so many words. You know what he also said?" Darla was truly relishing the moment, punctuating her speech with gestures, winks, and smirks. "He said that Martin doesn't have everything he needs to finish the job. But don't worry, kiddies, Darla does."

It was unbelievable. Nigel had done it again. How could he have known about the missing piece?

"What are you talking about?" Lane finally asked, turning from Darla to Martin, whose hanging head didn't seem to instill any confidence in her.

"Is the rifle loaded, sweetie?" Darla said softly to Henry, who had snuck his way to her side.

Henry gave her the thumbs-up.

"Then you're forgiven for laughing earlier. I'm going to need your protection."

Henry took the rifle off his shoulder and held it at the ready.

"What are you talking about?" Lane asked again.

Darla pushed Henry forward so he would take the lead, and then they both started down the steps. "Kelvin might not have known it, but he had the key to our salvation all along. And now I have it. The fuel to a spaceship."

Darla stopped, put her thumb and forefinger up as if she were holding something very small between them, and looked at Martin. "When you're ready for it, come see me. We'll make a deal."

Martin knew exactly what she meant.

— 19 —

The Sleigh

A braid of extension cords ran from Darla's pantry up two flights of stairs and into the master suite, where the individual cords forked off and joined up with a refrigerator, a TV, a DVD player, a stereo, and a spinning mirror ball. Darla sat on her bed, happily chomping on slices of apples and watching Martin and Felix push the refrigerator against the wall.

"Thank you, boys," she said. "You made quick work of that, didn't you?"

Next to Darla on the bed, Henry sat cross-legged. The butt of his rifle was held firm between his bicep and ribs as he pointed it outward.

"If everyone's going to work on the machine," Martin said carefully, "we're going to need to bring it to Xibalba."

"Sounds about right," Darla said, continuing to munch the apple slices.

"With all the snow out there," Martin went on, "Kid Godzilla is the only truck that can do the job."

"Maybe," Darla said with a shrug. From her nightstand, she grabbed the only set of keys to Kid Godzilla and spun them around on her finger.

"But you're not going to help?" Martin asked.

"Don't you remember?" she said. "It's your job to build the machine. Henry and I were supposed to get supplies. Since we now have the most important supply, we figure our job is done."

"Really, Darla? We're still talking about a marble, aren't we?" Felix asked.

"I prefer to call it the Magic Bean," Darla said. "And I prefer not to tell you where I've hidden it until you meet my conditions."

"Conditions?" Martin said.

"Yes. The first you've met fabulously by setting up my little palace here," Darla said with a wink. "I'll be in communication about the rest. And when all my needs are satisfied, I'll give you the Magic Bean. In the meantime, you'd be smart to figure out on your own how to get the machine here."

"Yeah, you two," Henry teased, "go be smart."

After they left, Darla locked the door to her room. Henry escorted them down the stairs at rifle-point and pushed them out the front door. Lane was waiting in front of the house.

"They want to know what's next," Lane explained.

Martin didn't have a clue. The machine was miles away. The weather hadn't gotten any warmer since the storm, so the snow was still almost four feet high. He turned to Felix for help.

"Santa uses a sleigh," Felix joked.

* * *

140

Impossible Island was broken into four sections: The Weird West, Volcano Jungle, Confederacy of Robots, and Land of the Neverseens. Land of the Neverseens was dedicated entirely to those imaginary entities that kept children up at night. There was the Boogeyman's Closet, a haunted house where kids were whisked along in a bed as animatronic hands grabbed at them. There was a two-acre maze of giant glittering teeth that led to the Tooth Fairy's Carousel. There were spinning pastel eggs in the turf-lined Easter Bunny's Meadow. And there was a massive candy cane that swung back and forth and sometimes upside down as it held a chariot of red fiberglass and dark wood, the main attraction in the Land of the Neverseens, the enormous ride known simply as the Sleigh.

To accomplish the mission Martin had in mind, nearly everyone in town would need to be involved. He approached Felix first.

"I don't think our future should depend on a nutcase, a liar, and a marble," Felix told him.

"I do. And your idea for the sleigh was inspirational," Martin countered.

"It was a joke."

"It was clever. If we're going to succeed, we're going to need clever," Martin told him.

Felix had no choice but to relent. He might not have trusted Darla or Nigel, but he trusted Martin. To add to that, Martin had built the security system for the Internet. In the quid pro quo world of Xibalba, that meant Felix owed him one, and Martin was ready to cash in.

The others didn't require nearly as much convincing. When he told them the plan, everyone except for Darla,

Henry, and Nigel was packed, outfitted with snowshoes and trekking poles, and ready to go by the next morning. Martin suspected that it had less to do with their trust in him than it did with their desire to find something (anything!) that would reunite them with their friends and family. He was the only one currently offering that.

The hike to Impossible Island took two days. As soon as they got there, they split into two teams. Lane's team was tasked with taking the sleigh from its giant candy cane arm and then converting it into something they could use. Martin's team scoured the park, stripping rides of all the materials he thought they might need.

"What are we gonna use that for?" Trent asked as they removed a piston from the bowels of the Tilt-A-Whirl.

"Well," Martin said, handing him the greasy piston, "that's kind of complicated. Do you know much about mechanics?"

It didn't weigh much, but Trent's shoulders sagged as he held the piston. It was no wonder he was known as Tiny Trent. While he wasn't tiny by a kid's standards, he was the definition of meek.

"I'm willing to learn," Trent said.

Martin hadn't spoken to him much. Trent mostly kept to himself. His contribution to their community seemed born more out of necessity than out of interest. He was the kid who purified water. His home was full of carbon filters and iodine and giant cauldrons used for boiling. Kids would leave an empty jug or two on their doorsteps, and Trent would come by and replenish their supplies. He could usually be seen in the morning, riding a bike while towing a little red wagon full of water jugs.

"Wanna learn how to take a gear train out of a log flume?" Martin asked him.

Trent nodded enthusiastically.

Enthusiasm was less evident in the other helpers. The mood was beyond gloomy. They were dutiful, though, and within a couple of days, they had collected the materials they needed. At the same time, Lane's team had detached the sleigh and equipped it with sturdy skis.

Together, using an elaborate rig of ropes and pulleys, all thirty-eight of them hoisted the machine in the air, tied it to nearby trees, and left it dangling. Then they harnessed themselves to the sleigh and guided it underneath. When they lowered the machine, it barely fit, filling up the cavity of the sleigh with only inches to spare on each side. So they stuffed the materials in cracks or bound them to edges and piled on as much weight as the skis could bear.

Exhausted sighs and a small round of applause followed, but the work was hardly over. Lane ordered everyone back into the harnesses, and Martin cried out, "Mush!"

— 20 —

The List

The going was slow but steady. In three days, they made it nearly halfway home. Most of their energy was spent pulling the sleigh around and over obstacles, but when they found flat straightaways, they coordinated their movements—the stronger evened out the weaker; the faster adopted the rhythms of the slower.

Conversation was sparse during the day, and at night, when they sat by a bonfire, it was mostly whispered. Martin could sense he was losing them. He noticed more and more sideways glances at the machine, the type that said, "Really? *This* is our spaceship?"

So he decided to address the issue.

It was the third night of their journey back. With the sleigh as a backdrop, Martin stood on a tree stump near the bonfire and cleared his throat. "I want to thank you all again for your dedication."

They responded with solemn nods. Martin figured he ought to cut to the chase.

"I also want to ask you something. How many of you have doubts that this machine will work?

Almost every hand went up.

"And how many of you are still only here because Nigel said this is what we should do?"

Again, almost every hand went up.

"Okay," Martin said. "I personally believe in Nigel. But I find it hard to believe that everyone is making such an effort just . . . because."

"What? Just because we want to stay alive?" Tiberia shouted out.

"Stay alive? I don't get it," Martin said.

There were murmurs in the crowd, but the only words Martin could make out were *collapse* and *diggers*.

"People who don't do what Nigel says," she responded slowly, "are people who end up dead."

Martin hesitated. "He kills them?"

"No," Sigrid said quickly. "It is more like if he is to warn you of something, it is best for you to listen."

"Kelvin definitely didn't listen," Tiberia added.

"I'm not Kelvin," Martin said firmly. "I need you all to know that."

The crowd reacted with raised eyebrows and contemptuous breaths through their noses.

"All I can say is that if you continue to help, and if you can trust that I can bring you to your families, then you'll be seeing them as soon as we finish this thing," Martin told them. "Count on it."

He stepped down from the tree stump and Felix put a

hand on his shoulder. "Word to the wise: Want to be different than Kelvin? You probably shouldn't stand next to bonfires and give speeches."

It was dusk when they arrived home. An endless necklace of rainbow lights was strung along the main street of Xibalba. From lamppost to lamppost they dipped and twirled and splattered their drops of color on the snow, and on the packed sleigh, and on the pack of weary kids. Smiles, something rare in this crowd, bubbled to the surface of their faces. They were home, and they were surprised. The welcome was a warm one.

As they pulled the sleigh into Town Square, they came upon Henry, who was hard at work on a nativity scene, stuffing a manger with hay.

"I'm shootin' anyone who thinks of laughin'," he told them. Harsh words, but understandable. Henry was dressed from head to toe in green. Little green hat, with a pom-pom on top. Green jacket with big gleaming buttons. Green bloomers. Green tights. Green boots that curled at the toes.

"Did *you* do all this?" Martin asked.

"I did," Henry said cautiously. "'Cept for the costume. That was . . . requested."

"It's beautiful," Martin said. "A wonderful thing to come back to."

"It's Christmas in a couple weeks. Darla likes Christmas," Henry said plainly, and got back to the manger.

They took off the harnesses and began to unload. The machine would be placed where Chet used to set up his farm stand every Friday, at the northeast corner of the square, near the firehouse and the bowling alley.

They were attaching the ropes and pulleys to nearby trees when Darla emerged from the bowling alley. Her outfit was just as festive as Henry's, but much more flattering. Clad in tight red and white velvet with a furry hood and cuffs, she skipped over to greet them.

"Spotted you a few hours ago, chugging up a hill," she said. "Very impressive. So which one of you is Rudolph?"

No one bothered to answer. They kept on with their work.

"Kidding, of course. I've got cocoa brewing and . . . Lookie here. Is this my Christmas list?" she exclaimed as she pulled a folded piece of paper from somewhere deep in her blouse. She handed it to Martin, who moved to pocket it. She grabbed his wrist and rolled her eyes. "Otherwise known as my conditions."

Martin stopped. As he began to unfold the paper, Darla prefaced things. "Now, Henry has *borrowed* some power to make it all possible. Sadly, it means most of you are gonna have to go without for a few days. The price of negotiations."

That was when Martin noticed all the black extension cords slithering from nearby houses through the square and into a few surrounding buildings. He read the paper.

My conditions:
1. Free your schedule for Friday night.
2. Get a haircut.
3. Be at my place by six.

— 21 —

The Alley

"Chocolates," Lane muttered. "And flowers. She's definitely the type of girl who wants flowers."

Noticing a ripple in the front of his shirt, Martin pulled down on the tails and saw that he was off by a button. He started over.

"Am I expected to kiss her?" Martin asked.

"Beats me," Lane said. "We need what she has, though, right?"

"Would you expect a kiss?"

"I wouldn't *not* expect one," Lane said. "But don't ask me to get too deep into Darla's head. Not a place I want to be."

As Martin buttoned the top button on his shirt, Lane reached forward to stop him. Her hands clasped his. "No one does the top one."

* * *

Martin knocked. Darla was there in a flash, opening her door and presenting herself with a quarter twirl. She was dressed in a blue coat with a fur-lined hood, a simple green dress, blue tights, and a pair of fuzzy beige boots. Martin looked down at his attire—sports jacket, plain white shirt, black pants, black shoes.

"Am I overdressed?"

"You look cute," Darla said, liberating the box of chocolates from his hand. "Caramels?"

"Some of them, I think," Martin said. "A bit old, of course."

"Well done anyways, Maple." Darla smiled. "And what's behind your back?"

It was something Lane had told him to do: hide the flowers behind your back, then pull them out as a surprise. Surefire way to melt a silly girl's heart. He wasn't so sure about that now, though. He had managed to find only three wilted daisies, tucked away as keepsakes in a book. When he showed the sad little things to Darla, he saw her face drop; then what he thought was a frown took hold of her lips.

"That's so sweet," Darla said softly. She hugged Martin. He hesitated, but it was impossible not to give in. Her body was much softer than he had imagined. He put his arms around her.

"You're welcome."

"Our chariot awaits," Darla whispered into his ear.

Kid Godzilla pulled up to Darla's house on cue, and Martin and Darla climbed aboard. Martin was happy to see Felix at the wheel. Felix wore a black hat, which he tipped, revealing his trademark headband underneath. "Mr. Maple," he said with almost no enthusiasm. "Ms. Barnes."

"Greetings, Felix," Darla said. "Lovely evening, isn't it?"

"Felix can drive?" Martin asked suspiciously.

"Don't worry," Darla said, patting Martin on the shoulder. "Straight shot. Not far to go."

She wasn't kidding either. They drove approximately one hundred yards and stopped in front of the town's bowling alley.

Every light in the place was on. A catchy melody played over the loudspeaker. It was one that Darla knew well, and she lip-synched and did a little dance as they walked over to a counter where two pairs of shoes were laid out and waiting for them.

"Size eight, if I'm not mistaken," Darla said, handing Martin the larger pair.

Sigrid, wearing a turquoise-and-white waitress's dress, wobbled over to them on a pair of roller skates. "May I take your order for beverages?" she asked.

"How 'bout a beer?" Darla asked. "Might loosen you up."

"No thank you," Martin replied. "I think I'm already plenty loose."

"Come on, Maple," Darla teased. "It's the apocalypse, no one's checking IDs."

"I prefer ginger ale," Martin said. If it got the machine working, he was willing to play along with Darla on most things, but he was also determined to keep his wits about him.

Darla shrugged. "You sure know how to class an evening up, don't you?" she said. Then she pointed at Sigrid. "You heard the man. *Dos* ginger ales. And make them extra gingery."

The table next to their lane was set with candles, lace, china, and crystal. Darla helped Martin off with his sports jacket and she placed it on the back of his chair.

"Beef isn't easy to come by," she explained. "Coyotes took most of the cows two years ago. So I hope you're okay with venison burgers. Dale and Hannah will be the chefs tonight. While they're not as good as me, they aren't half bad."

"Do you have everyone in town helping out?" Martin asked.

"Most," she said. "Not Henry. He's on his evening guard duty, patrolling for chipmunks and all that. But most everyone else is helping out. A good date takes a village, you know?"

"Is that a saying?"

"Could be," Darla said with a smirk. Then she walked over to the rack of bowling balls. She lifted a neon-green one, cupped it in her hands, and centered herself in front of the lane. She took three steps, swung her arm and twirled her wrist, and let the ball loose. It slid along the wood, gently hugging the gutter. Then it changed direction, spinning back toward the center. Darla didn't even bother to watch. She turned back to Martin, held her fist in the air, then gave it a celebratory pump. The ball struck the ten pins, and a satisfying racket erupted and echoed through the alley.

All ten pins lay defeated. From the dark space behind the lane, three sets of hands popped out and began setting the pins back up.

"Two hundred twelve to forty-two," Darla announced as she tallied the final scores.

"So much for beginner's luck," Martin said. Admittedly,

as frustrated as he was by his first attempt at bowling, he was beginning to enjoy it a little. It didn't hurt that Darla was actually entertaining. Hooting and dancing while she plowed down the pins, she was the perfect ambassador for the activity.

Sigrid arrived shakily on skates, fumbling a tray of burgers, fries, and pickles onto their table.

"Careful there, Pippi Longstocking," Darla teased.

"I do not really know how to roller-skate," Sigrid explained.

"Sure you do," Darla said, laughing. "You're Swedish or whatever. Probably ice-skate to school. Same idea."

Sigrid shook her head but didn't say anything. She wobbled away while Martin and Darla took their seats and dug in. While never wanting for food, the kids of Xibalba were rarely treated to such a bounty, and the temptation to overindulge was hard to avoid.

Three whole pickles, two burgers, and a mound of fries later, Martin waved the white flag. He placed his hands down on the table. Gorging had made him slightly dizzy, so he closed his eyes as he methodically chewed his last mouthful. When that made things worse, he chose to focus on something—the cloudy and effervescent soda in Darla's wineglass.

Darla lifted the glass and hid the bottom half of her face behind it and her hand. Peering over the edge, she gave her eyelashes a flutter.

"Tell me about your island," she said.

"Hmmm . . ." He didn't know where to start.

"Actually, scratch that. I don't care about your island. Tell me about your dad."

Martin finally swallowed and then he licked the burger

juice from his hand. "He was my father. What do you want to know?"

"Was he a good person?"

The question was harder to answer than Martin might have anticipated. "He was good to me," he said after some consideration.

"What did he like?"

"What do you mean?"

"Golf? Cooking? That sort of thing."

"I'm not sure if he liked anything, really," Martin said. He paused, surprised he would say such a thing.

Darla jumped in. "My dad liked bowling. He took me on most weekends. He got me my own ball."

"Must be why you're so good."

"He got me braces too." Darla lowered her glass, bit down on her bottom lip, and displayed her front teeth, which shimmered in the candlelight. "But I've forgiven him for that. Everyone else cut their braces off years ago. I kept mine."

"They suit you," Martin said, and he wasn't lying exactly. Darla and sparkly things did tend to go together.

"They do, don't they?" Darla laughed. "I loathed them at first. And Daddy bought me Dr. Fuzzbucket because he felt so bad about torturing me with them."

"That's your dog?"

"You remembered," Darla gushed. "Most people don't. Fuzzy B died almost as soon as I got here. Nigel took him from me. He said that all the animals had to live together or some silliness. A few days later, that stupid Komodo dragon took a bite outta my pooch. Poor guy died with poison racing through his blood."

"I'm sorry, Darla," Martin said. Having never owned a

pet, he didn't know what it was like to lose one. But he could imagine.

"This is a weird place," she said with a hint of sadness. "I don't know if a guy like you can realize how weird it is here. You do what you have to do to get by."

In his head, Martin ran through all the strange and unpleasant things Darla had done since he'd arrived in Xibalba. He wasn't sure he could understand her, but he couldn't deny that there were things about Darla he liked. He liked her energy. He liked her ambition. And he liked this date. It was a pleasant and relaxing respite from everything that had complicated his life thus far. He would see it through to the end.

They sat in the middle of a movie theater. A tub of popcorn was resting in Darla's lap. She tilted it toward Martin. He felt bloated, but the dizziness was gone, and he was willing to find room in his belly for more. Dinner had been the most spectacular meal of his life, and he wanted to keep the glory coming. Half a handful to start. As his teeth crunched into the popcorn, the butter and salt attacked his boggy mouth. He needed more.

"Are you in love with Lane?" Darla asked him matter-of-factly.

Martin's hand returned to the tub. "I don't think so. I mean . . . I don't know what love is."

"Come on, Maple. You have an idea."

Martin thought it over for a moment. Sure, almost every book he knew talked about love and what it meant to different people. And yes, there were times when he looked at Lane and felt his lungs clench into fists, but he wasn't sure that love was a physical thing like that.

"My father told me once that love is something you plant," he finally said. "Like a . . . tree, or something, I guess."

"Sounds kinda . . . perverse," Darla said, taking some popcorn.

"Not really," Martin went on. He tried to channel his father's exact words. "He said . . . he said that someone can give you something that seems so insignificant at first. Then you plant it, and it takes in the water, and it takes in the light, and soon it's so big and so important that you can't imagine life without it. And it doesn't go anywhere. It stays there for you."

"Well, then that sounds like something in a picture book." Darla laughed.

Her flippant attitude annoyed him, but she had a point. After saying it out loud, he did realize it sounded a bit childish. "What's your definition of love?" he asked.

Darla smiled, then pointed up to the screen. "Movies."

The theater went dark, as if she had planned the timing. There was a flickering sound behind them. Martin turned and looked up. Two muddy silhouettes moved behind a thick pane of glass. A bloom of white light burst through and splashed color all over the screen.

The movie was transcendent. For two hours, men and women talked fast and drove fast and jumped out of helicopters only to land on other helicopters. They shot machine guns and rolled around on beds and strapped skis to their feet and raced down mountains as grenades blew snow into geysers. They drank cocktails while swimming, threw their bodies through stained-glass windows, and flicked cigarette butts at crocodiles. There was Tunisia, with its sandstorms and camels. There was the Great Barrier Reef, with its bejeweled aquatic wonders. There was Florence, pulsing and crumbling and chattering. All at once, the world was laid out before Martin's eyes and he understood what Darla meant.

Near the end, when he turned to look at her, he noticed that she wasn't watching the movie at all. She was watching him watch the movie. She lifted a finger up, reached forward, and placed it on the patch of hair just above Martin's temple. Then she twirled it in a tight circle. It felt good, so Martin didn't stop her.

With two fingers from her other hand, she reached across and stroked his knuckles. Martin wasn't completely clueless. The signal was obvious. He turned his hand over so that she could grab hold of it.

But Darla didn't grab hold. Instead, she dropped something into his palm.

Martin looked down. Green. Glass. About the size of a grape. He closed his hand and held the marble tight.

— 22 —

The Dragon

They watched through the closing credits, until the projector spit the film out and the screen was a bright blob of white. Taking his hand, Darla led Martin to the lobby. There was really no need to ask if he liked it. The answer was obvious, painted in the stunned elation of his face.

"Right?" Darla said with a knowing nod.

"Uh-huh," Martin said breathlessly. Remembering to be a gentleman, he stepped forward and put his hand on the door. He pushed it open, letting a ripe winter breeze in and letting Darla duck under his arm to get out.

Felix was supposed to be waiting. Kid Godzilla was supposed to be running, heat pumping. But they weren't. Outside the movie theater, the town was empty except for the Christmas lights, strung like colorful musical scores above the streets.

"Is that him?" Martin asked, pointing up the hill to

Nigel's house. On the snow-crusted lawn was a shadowy mass that could only be Kid Godzilla.

Darla hustled closer to get a better look. "What the heck's he doing up there? He wasn't supposed to move! He knew when the movie ended!"

Martin dropped the marble into the interior pocket of his jacket and followed her along the waffle tracks of Kid Godzilla. As they were nearing Nigel's yard, the door to the house opened, and Felix stepped outside carrying a lantern. He set it down and yelled something back toward the door.

From a distance, the only words Martin could make out were "Never again!"

Felix spun around and marched toward Kid Godzilla. His lantern lit the entrance to the house, and Martin expected to see Nigel step outside or at least close the door. Instead, a small serpentine head inched into the light.

Darla spotted it first. "Felix!" she yelled. "Run!"

Looking back over his shoulder, Felix saw what she saw. Nigel's Komodo dragon, squat and long but fierce and fast, bolted at him. It was unlikely that Felix could make it to the door and open it before the lizard had his leg in its jaws, and Felix seemed to sense this. He made a beeline for the front of the truck, latched a hand on the toothy front grill, and hoisted himself onto the hood.

Undeterred, the dragon reared back on its hind legs and flopped its body against the grill. Felix moved fast, wiggling like a seal up the windshield until he was on the roof.

Martin started forward to help him, but Darla grabbed his shoulder. "Poison saliva. Razor teeth. That thing will kill you."

The dragon wasn't quite long enough to make it onto the

hood, but it also wasn't about to give up. Back on all fours, it scampered to the driver's side of the truck, where it latched its front claws onto the door handle.

Felix looked down from above. He was at a safe distance for now, but to get inside, he would need to think fast. He reached into his headband, grabbed a handful of his firefly lightbulbs, and threw them into the dragon's face. The little pops of light and glass put it onto its back. As the lizard struggled to regain its footing, Felix wielded a tiny screwdriver and frantically pecked the driver's-side window until the glass cracked. Then he hammered it with his fist until it shattered.

"Oh, come on, Fee," Darla cried. "I'm gonna need that window this winter!"

The dragon was back in action just as Felix was pulling himself through the broken window into the front cab of the truck. It leapt, jaws snapping, barely missing Felix's calves.

As he got behind the wheel and started the engine, Felix screamed out, "Reverse?"

"First there's a lever—"

Fire belched forth from the nostrils on Kid Godzilla's hood. It licked the wooden posts at the entryway to the house and set them ablaze. The dragon waddled backward, clearly taken by surprise.

"No, the other—"

The wheels began to spin in place, spitting snow into the air. Then the truck itself began to spin, doing tight doughnuts. The flames were still pouring from the front, birthing rings of light and melting the snow.

It was hard to say exactly what Felix was doing. Because all of a sudden, the truck stopped its spin and lurched forward. As the hood dipped, the flames blasted the dragon full force. It shrieked in pain. Then, as if shot from a cannon, the truck flew backward over the snow.

It struck the giant ice cream cone, which toppled over and opened up. Into the snow, it coughed out its contents— a bounty of dead rabbits and raccoons, ears of corn and bags of sugar, even strange little offerings like glass statues and teddy bears.

The truck plowed through it all as it cut a swerving backward path. When it reached the hill, it skipped down, like a bird landing on water, hit a telephone pole, spun, rolled onto its roof, and slid across the snowy street. The spinning wheels filled the night air with a tinny whine.

Charred and hacking, the dragon walked a few paces and then collapsed. The fire had quickly moved from the front entrance and was now tearing into Nigel's house. Howls and hisses dove from the windows. But Martin and Darla were much more concerned with Felix. They sprinted to the crash site.

Felix crawled through the shattered window. Blood found a path in the part of his hair and was soaked up by his head-band. He plunged his face into the snow. When his face emerged, it possessed a look of cautious relief, but as he climbed to his feet, the relief shifted to dread.

"Hey," Darla said as she and Martin stopped a few yards away. "You're okay, right?"

He didn't respond. He just ran away from them. Darla and Martin would have run too had they seen what Felix now saw.

Nigel's tiger had escaped from the burning house and was galloping after Felix.

The tiger might have been small, but it was unquestion-ably dedicated. The tip of its tail was on fire and resembled a torn orange flag, flapping violently in the wind. It didn't slow the tiger down at all, and had the situation not been so dire, it might have been beautiful. The beast. The flaming tail. The Christmas lights. The starry sky. The dunelike drifts of snow.

But beauty was the last thing on Felix's mind as he struggled to make it back to his house. Every few yards, his foot would sink in the snow and he would fall forward onto his chest. The tiger continued to gain ground. When Felix finally made it to his front door, he bulldozed inside, but the tiger was too quick and too close. It followed him through before Felix had a chance to slam the door.

A few seconds later, the sound of gunshots pierced the heart of the night.

— 23 —

The Rifle

In the largest room of Felix's house, Martin and Darla were confronted with the following scene:

Fire, slowly eating up the thousands of Internet strings as if they were dynamite wicks.

Henry, hanging upside down in a snare, a handful of paper in one fist, his rifle in the other.

Felix, back pressed to the wall, legs spread, standing on two blocks of wood mounted about six feet above the floor.

And the tiger, roaring and jumping and snapping at Felix's feet.

"Shoot again! Shoot again!" Felix screamed.

Henry lifted the rifle with one arm, but being upside down and rocking back and forth made it impossible for him to aim. "I can't risk it. I might hit ya!" Henry responded.

"Drop the papers, you moron!" Felix pleaded. "This is serious business!"

The fire on the tiger's tail had gone out, but the flames were quickly moving through the room, traveling from the strings to the blocks. Henry tossed the papers to the side and got two hands on the rifle. Now Martin could see exactly what Henry had been holding.

It was his book. And it was on fire.

Bam!

The rifle went off and the tiger withdrew. Plaster exploded and left a hole in the wall between Felix's legs.

"Jiminy Christmas!" Felix howled.

"I told you!" Henry screamed back.

At that moment, Martin didn't care about Felix or Henry or anything other than the book. As he raced over to grab it, he heard Darla yelp, "Gimme it," but he paid her no mind. It was as if the chaos around him had melted away.

Pages from the book burned quickly, one after another taking to the air like black and red butterflies. Martin lifted his foot to kick the fire out and end the destruction. Before he could stomp, something walloped his shoe.

Bam! Bam!

Searing pain coursed through Martin's foot as he fell to the ground. Had he been shot? He lifted his leg to see. His shoe had been torn open and blood was bubbling up through the holes. Only they didn't look like bullet holes. They were long and thin, like claw marks.

Hot stale breath caressed his nose. Turning over, Martin was now face to face with the tiger. Its tongue was leaking from its mouth, but the beast was lying on its side, and nothing else in its body was moving, not even its eyes.

Bam! Bam!

Darla emptied the rifle into the tiger's head as she straddled it. Blood splattered upon her blue tights and into Martin's face.

"You got it!" Felix screamed gleefully.

Darla set the rifle down and paced over to Henry. "What are you doing here?"

"Just get me down!" Henry pleaded. "This place is burnin' like crazy."

It was true. The fire was spreading. Nearly every block in the house was now burning and the walls were starting to catch.

Felix jumped from his perch and offered Martin a hand. There was no hope left for the book. It was fully consumed. So he accepted Felix's help. Hobbling his way onto one foot, Martin wiped the tiger blood from his face.

Darla untied the snare, and Henry crashed onto his back. It should have knocked the wind out of him, but adrenaline was more powerful. He was on his feet immediately, snatching the rifle and heading for the exit.

"I guess our trap worked," Martin, coughing, said to Felix as they limped after Henry.

Darla joined them, propping Martin up on the other side. "What was that pile of paper you were so busy with?" she asked.

"Something important to me" was all Martin said.

She turned to Felix. "And what in the half-baked heck was going on at Nigel's?"

"He's a fraud, okay?" Felix said defensively. "Magic? No way, Jose. He's a con man. Where do you think he gets his information? Spies. Which might explain that burglar we caught. And you know what Nigel was doing tonight? He was out there drawing pictures of the machine. Why would he do that? I was sitting in Kid Godzilla, minding my own business, and I saw him through the window. So I followed him back to his house and I told him I was on to him. And I'm gonna tell him again!"

It appeared as though he might have a chance to tell him again. Because when they stepped outside, there was Nigel, standing only a few feet in front of them. Henry was whimpering and fumbling through the snow, trying to escape into town. Nigel had commandeered his rifle.

"Get away, the whole place is about to go up," Darla warned, raising a hand and waving Nigel back.

Nigel's clothes were covered in black ash, and his eyes were ponds of swirling red. He clenched his lips, as if he were holding back a torrent of angry words. A tear slipped over his left cheekbone. He raised the rifle.

"That's no way for them to die," Nigel said.

"Nigel," Felix replied, the iris of his lazy eye retreating to the edge. "Calm down."

"This was our world." Nigel's voice was both steely and sad. "And the only reason you're still here is because we let you be here."

He steadied the rifle.

He clenched his teeth.

Then Nigel shot Felix in the head.

Felix's body crumpled, taking Martin and Darla down with it. And Nigel didn't say a word. He simply turned around and walked back toward his house.

Shock left Martin frozen, until the sharp smell of smoke and burning animal flesh brought him to. Darla was sitting in the snow, Felix's body resting in her lap. There was a hole in his forehead. It was small, dark, and perfectly round.

"He shot him," Darla said, looking over at Martin in disbelief. "Just like that."

By now, Nigel had reached the edge of his lawn. His house was completely engulfed. Flames screamed from the windows and ripped away at the slates. Black smoke hovered over it all as the animals inside continued their horrible racket. A few had escaped to the lawn. A goat, two cats, a massive snake.

Nigel climbed the hill and stopped when he reached the goat. He placed a hand on its back, and the animal's legs shuddered. Nigel petted it and ducked over to whisper something into its ear. The goat unleashed a terrifying bleat and fell forward onto its chest. It rolled over and stopped moving.

Throwing the rifle strap over his shoulder, Nigel was possessed by a sudden jolt of energy. He burst into a run, headed straight to the front door of the house, ducked his head down, and disappeared through a wall of fire.

PART III

―――――――――― ⚷ ――――――――――

"Xibalba welcomes you."

"Thank you. That's mighty swell."

"Mighty swell?"

"I say kooky things sometimes."

"Well, I guess it's understandable. Hard not to be 'kooky' these days, what with all we've gone through. You must be hungry. Hey, Chet! Why don't you fetch our new pal an apple or something? And, Tiberia. Maybe some ointment for that cut on his leg?"

"Thank you, Calvin."

"It's Kelvin, actually. Common mistake. And we've already established that you're Felix. So why don't you tell us how you got here, Felix?"

"Balloons."

"Like a hot-air balloon? Gotta be a first."

"No. Regular birthday balloons. I had a sack of them. And I found a helium tank thingy. I'd fill up a balloon and let it fly. Then I'd follow it. Once I lost it, I'd fill up another and off it'd go and off I'd go."

"An odd way to travel."

"I don't think so. People like balloons. I thought maybe someone would spot one and we'd meet up and have a chat. Ended up here instead."

"Still have that helium tank?"

"Sure do."

"Does it make your voice all squeaky and hilarious?"

"I suppose."

"So you've made yourself useful already. We're gonna have some fun here, Felix."

— 24 —

The Trial

The smoke weaseled in through a window of Sigrid's house and attacked her nostrils as she ran on her treadmill. When she pulled back the curtains and saw the flames, she grabbed her cymbals and took to the streets, running up and down, sounding the alarm. Before long, all of Xibalba was gathered around Felix.

There was nothing they could do. He was quite clearly dead.

The fire spread, marauding from building to building. When it reached Gina's candy-colored home, the fireworks inside kicked things to another level, unleashing whistles and deafening thumps of rainbow explosions. It quickly came to a point where fighting the fire was impossible. Since everyone wanted his or her own house to be saved, no one's could be saved. They could agree on only one thing: they would save the machine.

They surrounded it with walls of snow at least two feet thick. Then they gathered behind the walls with an arsenal of snowballs to pelt back the flames. When morning came, a fresh warm rain accompanied it. The fire had started to peter out on its own, but the rain finished the job. And it provided them with a chance to see the destruction. They went to Nigel's house first.

In the pile of ash and blackened wood, there were too many animal bones to count. Whether Nigel's bones were among them was impossible to say. All they knew was he was gone.

Most of the homes were destroyed or damaged beyond repair. The kids split up in an attempt to recover what they could while Martin stayed back. He said it was to clean his injured foot. It was really to think.

The realization entered him like a piping hot drink, scalded him at first and then overtook his core. Things had changed. Chet's death, while tragic, had been accidental. Felix's murder was something else entirely. In Nigel's cold eyes, Martin had seen pain and rage and desperation. He had seen a human, doing a profoundly human and thoroughly awful thing, all because of events Martin had set in motion.

It was like Lane's contraption, only instead of orbs racing along tracks, these were kids, pushed along by fear and emotion. Martin had started it, so it was his responsibility to end it. He fought the urge to cry. He needed to be decisive and convincing, win over the doubters. And those who couldn't be won over—they would need to be dealt with in other ways. It was a tough stance, but he had to take control, or else they would all career into their doom.

A steel-handled broom played the role of a crutch, and he lifted himself up. He limped through the smoldering town until he reached his former house, where sizzling snow greeted him. Lane happened to be there too. She was walking circles around the foundation, poking at embers with a bent wire coat hanger.

"You already go to your house?" Martin asked.

"It's a smoking pile," Lane said. "Brown plastic icicles and rebar. But, you know, kind of pretty in its way. Like a black-sand beach. Ever seen one of those? The horns from the record players looked like silver seashells."

"I'm sorry," Martin said.

"What for? You didn't do anything. You didn't start the fire. You didn't shoot Felix."

It was true. He was as passive an observer as he could have been. He didn't do a thing. Like so much of his past life, he had let it happen all around him.

"At your house, when you did your show for me, the . . ."

"*The Rube?*"

Martin nodded. "There was a record you were playing. I've been thinking about that. About what the words might have been."

"I was playing it backwards," Lane explained. "Heavy metal. Backwards messages. It's a thing . . . people do."

"And?"

"And yes, it was supposed to sound like a bunch of words." Lane tapped the tip of her shoe against a rippled and broken beam.

"What words?"

Leaning in and pushing with a sole, Lane sent the beam toppling. A flurry of sparks danced through the damp air. She looked down and saw something.

"'You are not our savior,'" she said breathlessly.

"Excuse me?"

"You. Are. Not. Our. Savior. Those were the words, or those were supposed to be the words. The atheist in me isn't exactly a perfectionist." She lowered herself to her knees and poked the hanger through the rubble. Then she grabbed a handful of snow and plunged it into the smoldering mess.

"I . . . could be . . . our savior," Martin offered hesitantly.

"Oh boy," Lane said. "Don't even start with that." With a sneer and a grunt, she pulled her hand back.

Why not? Martin thought. After all, there were far too many coincidences. He'd heard enough Arrival Stories to know that his eleventh birthday had happened at the same time as the Day. Exactly two years later, he arrived in Xibalba. Nigel had predicted someone would come and save them all. Martin had to be that person. There was no con here. This was fate. And the machine? It was more than a hunk of metal. It was, quite simply, all that was left of Martin's father—his headaches, his sleepless nights, his pulsing green eyes staring out at the sea. It was an essential part in all this, and it had to be protected. Nothing could stand in the way of its completion.

"Think what you want about me," Martin said, "but I'm going to make things right. It's what I was destined to do."

"Okay." Lane shrugged, still grasping what she had rescued from the rubble. "Then tell me exactly how you're gonna pull that off."

Henry was out there somewhere, hiding. By breaking into the Internet, by stealing Martin's book, by letting it burn, Henry had done something wrong and he knew it. But it was far worse than he might have imagined. Martin didn't care what Henry's motives were. He only knew that he was a danger and a liability, that he couldn't be trusted. He only knew that this angry kid had destroyed one of Martin's last links to his former life.

"I'll start by finding Henry," Martin said. "It's because of him that this happened. He needs to be punished. And with him out of the way, and with everyone pitching in, we'll finish the machine. Now more than ever we need the machine."

As she brushed snow from her hand onto the ground, Lane revealed what she had found. It was one of the bottles from the dollhouse. "You know, Felix told me about the marble," she said. "Does everyone else know Darla was hiding a marble? That a *marble* is supposed to complete the machine?"

"I don't think so," Martin admitted. "They don't have to."

"Why a marble? Why not anything? Why not a bottle, like this?"

"It was Kelvin Rice's marble," Martin said. "Without Kelvin, I would never have found Xibalba. The machine never would have been built."

"You ever play spin the bottle?"

"No."

"Neither have I," Lane said. "It was Kelvin's idea of romance. Messages in a bottle too. He loved those. Sometimes he'd place a tiny bottle on my doorstep with a note in it, inviting me to hang out with him in his basement. I never told him, but I thought it was the cheesiest thing in the world."

"Are you upset that I was living in his house?"

Lane shook her head and tossed the bottle back into the blackened remains, and it knocked pollen-thin ash into the air. "It doesn't matter now," she sighed. "It was just a place and

Kelvin was just a kid. He had marbles and bottles and model airplanes and stuff that kids have. Stuff, that's all it is. It burns, or you lose it, or you forget about it. If you want to tie it in to some grand plan of fate and destiny, be my guest. But believing in that sort of thing means you have to believe in the good and the bad, the victories and the disasters. It's all equally profound. It's all equally meaningless."

"I know that," Martin said.

"Fair enough. So first we find Henry. Then punish him. How?" she asked.

There would be a trial. Outside, during the day, by the machine, where everyone could watch. Chairs and couches were to be planted in what remained of the snow, and a large oak table was to be positioned center stage. The search for Henry didn't take long. He was found sleeping in the police station, of all places. He was given two days to prepare his defense.

A precedent had been set. Kelvin had been given a trial too.

"He called it a kangaroo court," Darla told Martin.

"What's that?" Martin asked.

"Beats me. Never been to Australia."

Apparently, since the kids knew legal proceedings only from television, there never had been much actual law. Their courtroom had simply been a collection of odd clichés. A croquet mallet served as a gavel, and even though no one was officially appointed judge, Ryan took it upon himself to bang it every once in a while and holler, "Objection! Overruled!" Riley fashioned a series of mops into ridiculous British court wigs, which a few kids donned to class up proceedings. Felix, of course, was the stenographer, jotting down notes on pieces of wood. There was almost nothing to write, however. Kelvin had been found guilty in a matter of minutes, and his defense had amounted to "Yes, I did it, but I thought it was the right thing to do."

"What did he do?" Martin asked.

"He betrayed us" was Darla's answer.

"Like Henry did?" Martin said.

"What's Henry's crime, really?" Darla asked. "He was caught up in the craziness with us. I hardly think he deserves a trial."

"He was sabotaging our mission," Martin explained. Then Martin did something he had never done in his life. He told a flat-out lie. "Those papers he had, the ones he burned. He stole them from my personal page. They contained important coordinates we need to enter into the machine."

"Really?" Darla asked. "They looked a bit more like a novel or something, from a distance, at least."

"Why would Henry break in to steal a novel?" Martin asked.

Darla shrugged. "The guy is loopy. You should go easy on him."

Henry's trial would be a more restrained affair than Kelvin's. Light on pomp and circumstance, heavy on accusations. On the day of the trial, Henry arrived, escorted by Tiberia. Stern and muscular and proud of it, Tiberia was a girl, but she was the closest thing Xibalba had to a man. She was six foot one, and she shaved her scalp every day, to show off her head's perfect roundness. Her contribution to their community was simple. Tiberia was the muscle. Need to move a rock, tighten a bolt, swing an ax? Call Tiberia. Her passion wasn't manual labor, however. It was, in some ways, quite the opposite.

She spent most of her free time in the kitchen, mixing vitamins and powders she found at drugstores. She was trying to devise the perfect protein shake, one that, in her words, would make "gettin' buff as easy as having breakfast." In the process, she had acquired all the town's narcotics and antibiotics, which she locked in a massive fireproof safe. "No one here has a PhD, so I'm the closest thing to a person who knows a thing or two about a thing or two. If you need some, you'll get some, but only if you need some," she told kids.

Two days before, when Martin had asked Tiberia to guard Henry until the trial, she wasn't surprised. "Send a brat to his room, you're gonna want the biggest, baddest babysitter," she said.

When Tiberia showed Henry to his seat at the oak table, she stood behind him, her massive hands on the back of the chair, ready for any move. The eyes of the crowd practically spat at him. Details about the night of the fire were hard to come by. Darla and Martin had agreed to remain tight-lipped until the trial. Everyone just assumed it was all Henry's fault.

Darla spoke first. She was dressed in a business suit for the occasion, and her hair was held together in an elaborate bun by a pair of glass chopsticks. Taking a seat next to Martin at the table, she launched into her version of events.

"First of all, I'd like to thank everyone for helping me organize an evening to remember. A truly magical time, until, well, you know. . . ."

She went on to describe everything in lavish detail. The bowling. The meal. The movie. When she came to Felix and Henry and Nigel, she didn't slow down one bit. She talked

176

about the oily smell of Kid Godzilla, the phlegmy hack of the dying Komodo dragon, the warmth of tiger blood on her stockinged legs. And she didn't lie or exaggerate. The only things she neglected to relate were Felix's accusations regarding Nigel. She said the two of them were having an argument, and she left it at that. It was a curious omission, but Martin assumed she was simply trying to help Henry by not implicating him in some larger conspiracy.

Everything else she said was accurate, or at least seemed to be to Martin. Yet with all the facts laid bare, it was hard for the kids to take her seriously. As she left the table and took a seat in the crowd, there were more than a few snickers and whispers along the lines of "The day I believe that girl . . ."

Martin came next. His strategy was simple. Rather than confirm or deny what Darla had said, he would focus on Henry, and Henry alone.

"What exactly were you doing in the Internet, by yourself, without Felix's permission?" Martin asked.

Henry leaned forward, and as if he had been rehearsing his response, he said, "I'd rather not answer that question."

"Were you only sneaking into my personal page, or were you sneaking into everyone's personal pages?"

"I'd rather not answer that question."

"When you burned the book that contained the coordinates for the machine, were you trying to doom us all?"

"I'd rather not—"

"And when you should have been protecting us, when you should have been doing your job, the one that provides you with your food, and your health, and your entertainment, when you should have been doing that, why were you letting this town burn and two boys die?"

"I wasn't lettin' no one do nothin'. They did it all by

177

themselves," Henry said in a voice only a bit louder than a whisper.

"Right. With your gun. On your watch," Martin said. It was a nice touch. He had read enough courtroom novels to know that simple and understated worked best. No reason to linger too long on theatrics.

A yell came from the crowd: "What do you have to say for yourself?"

"Nothin'," Henry said. "'Cept for sorry, I guess. For whatever it is ya think I did."

Martin took it upon himself to speak for the crowd. "We think that you tried to sabotage us. We think you don't care about the future. We think you should be sentenced to six months in the Ring of Penance."

Darla leapt from her seat and to his defense. "A bit harsh, huh? I mean, Kelvin only got two months."

"Who here thinks six months is too harsh for trying to steal our hope and letting our home burn?" Martin asked.

Darla's hand was the only one to go up. Not even Henry budged. At first, her arm was rigid, its stubbornness doing its darndest to inspire a mass conversion. It wasn't working, though, and as she lowered it, she raised her eyes and looked around, feigning innocent ignorance.

Martin pounded a fist on the table. "Xibalba has spoken!"

Tiberia reached forward and placed a hand on the back of Henry's neck. If Henry made a peep, Martin didn't notice. Most kids probably would have cried. While life in the Ring of Penance wasn't pure torture, it certainly wasn't pleasant.

What it amounted to was this: Henry was to be given a heavy-duty tent, a sleeping bag, some cooking equipment, a flint, a first-aid kit, and a few other odds and ends. He was also allowed to collect some pasta, some rice, some dried fruit. The tent was to be placed in the middle of a circular stone wall that adorned the rocky face of the mountain that overlooked town and was cheekily referred to as Alcatraz. The food was expected to last him about a week. After that, he was on his own.

Henry could serve out his sentence in the Ring, and if his former neighbors were feeling neighborly, they could stop by and slip him some food or blankets from time to time. Or he could do what Kelvin had decided to do, and hit the road. However, hitting the road could mean he might not be accepted back into Xibalba.

That afternoon, Martin watched from Town Square as Henry's green-and-blue nylon tent took up residence on Alcatraz. At that distance, it wasn't much more than a dot of color, but it gave Martin a guilty shiver of excitement.

A few yards away from Martin, the machine was waiting in the snow, its conical tip pointed skyward. There were thirty-seven kids left in town. With their help, it could be ready in a matter of weeks.

— 25 —

The Hole

At one point near the end of Martin's reading frenzy on the island, he had counted the number of books he had finished. Five hundred seventy-eight. He wasn't sure if that was a lot for a single person. He hoped it was at least average.

He hadn't finished a book since he'd arrived in Xibalba. With all that had happened, he'd hardly had a moment to relax, let alone to read. But he was living in the library now. His home had burned along with most of the others, and when they'd divvied up the houses and buildings that remained, Martin had chosen the library. A mattress on a table was his bed. An old wood-burning furnace in the basement gave him heat and a surface for cooking. Since so many of the solar panels had been destroyed, lanterns once again provided light.

As Henry settled into his first cold night in the Ring of Penance, Martin returned to the warmth of the library.

Restless from the day's events, he wandered the stacks and pondered his next move. When he found himself in the science fiction section, he remembered a line from his beloved book, which had burned and sealed Henry's fate.

They piled aboard the vessel, fathers and mothers, and all of the children.

Immediately, he began pulling books from the shelf, checking them for familiar text, and throwing aside the ones that didn't satisfy.

Within twenty minutes he had it.

Amazing Tales from Beyond, Volume III.

That was the title. All these years, he had wondered. He had imagined something elegant and grand—nothing so hackneyed, nothing so rote. Yet there it was. The name of the book that had been so important in his life. His first read, his first love.

This copy was stiff. As he turned the pages, they crackled like gravel underfoot. He wondered how long it had been since someone had read it. Ages, it seemed.

With the book, a pen, and a pad of paper, he sat on his mattress. The stories were just as he remembered them, but they meant something different now. He began to transcribe.

The next morning, Sigrid was on the move. Thirty-six envelopes, addressed to the thirty-six kids, were in her shoulder bag. The letters they held all said the same thing.

> Dear Friends,
>   The machine in Town Square is something I have been building in one form or another for as long as I can remember.

It may not be slick. It may not seem sturdy. It is, however, our future.

I ask you to believe this, because it is something I believe. It is also something Nigel believed. A few days before his death, he gave me a note to share with everyone. The recent tragedies have affected us all, but I hope that we can find inspiration in Nigel's final words. I give them to you here:

I haven't spoken to some of you personally and I hope that you don't take offense to that. I am a stranger in this place and I don't exactly know your language. Yet I do know things. What I know more than anything else is that you have been blessed with a second chance. You wonder what happened to your world, how it became so flooded with fear and confusion. You dream of a place where things will return to what they were, where the water will recede and your lives will bloom again. That hunk of metal, that seemingly unworthy vessel, will bring you there. Heed my words. Step aboard.

With Nigel's message in mind, I will continue work on the machine today at noon. Darla has provided me with the materials necessary to finish it. Henry did not succeed in his plan to thwart its launch. The coordinates are safe in my memory. Those who join me are welcome to step aboard.

In your confidence,
Martin Maple

Less than an hour after the letters had been handed off to Sigrid, Lane arrived at the library. Martin had returned to the book, seeking out other passages he remembered, but as soon as he saw her, he tucked it beneath his mattress.

"'Noah Redux,'" she said, and she lobbed a crumpled piece of paper at him.

"Excuse me?" he said, catching it.

"I'm a sci-fi junkie," Lane explained. "Of course I've read 'Noah Redux.'"

This was not something Martin had foreseen. There was no answer he could think of to explain what he had done. It was better to gauge the degree of his miscalculation. "Has everyone read that story?" he asked.

"Probably not," Lane said. "Plagiarists are pretty safe in this crowd."

"It's the message that's important. Not where it came from," Martin offered.

"You do remember how 'Noah Redux' ends, right?"

"That's not important either."

"They die, Martin. The astronaut who gives that speech, he locks all the aliens in a submarine and sinks it, so he can have their planet to himself. Real sunny story there. I think you missed that it's a metaphor. Missionaries, politicians—"

"They went aboard, didn't they? *That's* the message,"

Martin said firmly. "You're welcome to stay behind if you want."

"Giving out hope can be dangerous, that's all," Lane said. "It has consequences. I know you're dedicated, Martin. But you need to see what being dedicated can mean."

The snow had almost completely melted. The rain and a balmy couple of days had relegated it to an ashen slush. Lane carefully chose the driest path she could, hopping from curbs to tree roots as she led Martin past a row of blackened, gutted homes. The puddles, however, were unavoidable when she and Martin set off down a narrow trail into the forest.

Martin was busy watching his feet, trying to keep them dry. So it wasn't until they reached the hole that he realized he had been on this trail before. It was the same one he had followed Felix down on his first morning in Xibalba. He hadn't thought of it since. There were countless trails in the woods surrounding town, and this one seemed no more special than any other. The only difference was the hole in the side of the ledge.

"You might think we're callous, the way we react to death," Lane said.

The thought had crossed Martin's mind. They hadn't even bothered with a funeral for Felix or Nigel. Even to mention Felix's name made the kids uncomfortable and defensive. Still, Martin had no idea how to react to such a tragedy, and he doubted anyone else did either. He borrowed George's words, hoping they'd provide wisdom. "There are all sorts of people in the world. With all sorts of ways of seeing stuff."

"Maybe," she said. "For us, we've seen death before. Plenty of it." Lane stepped closer to the hole and placed a hand on the rutted and warped wood that formed a frame around it. She didn't look inside. Instead, she pointed to the ground at Martin's feet.

There was another piece of wood there, only this one appeared to be newer. Its grains were fierier and it was cut into a perfectly square block. Martin lifted it from the sludge, brushed it with his sleeve, and saw that it was covered in Felix's unmistakable handwriting.

THE DIGGERS
Allison Swain, Gemma Parsons, Felicia Carmichael, Lee Kim, Kendall Ferris, Amanda Tate, Yusuf Halim, Dave Forbes, Carla Rizetti, Malik Kahn, Eloise Dubois, Mikael Stupinski, and Kelvin Rice.

The Diggers were a group of kids from Xibalba. It was their belief that on the Day, everyone escaped to hidden bunkers beneath the ground. Led by Kelvin Rice, they embarked on a journey into the mine shaft beneath the Popol quarry. Kelvin convinced them they would find a whole civilization down there.

"Felix was pretty upset when we made him remove that page from the Internet," Lane said.

"Why did you?" Martin ran his fingers across the writing, which was beginning to fade due to exposure. There were dents in the wood where the present tense had been changed to the past. The only name he recognized was Kelvin's.

"To forget," Lane said. "It was three days before Kelvin

came back all covered in dirt and soot. Three whole days and we didn't bother to go looking for them. So we took an oath to forget, rather than dwell on what we could've done."

"They went in there?" Martin asked, motioning to the hole. "This is a mine shaft?"

"This is a grave," Lane said. "Twelve kids are buried in there. The mine collapsed on them. Kelvin was lucky to get out alive."

Martin remembered reading references to the Collapse. He recalled the series of letters he'd found written out in tiny stones in the Ring of Penance, the message of *I'M SO SORRY* that accompanied them. The pieces were starting to fit together.

"And Kelvin took all the blame?"

"He did," Lane said in a shaky voice. "During his trial, he told us that Nigel had warned him this would happen. And he had kept those warnings to himself."

"Everyone believed it?" Martin asked.

"Why wouldn't they?" Lane gulped. "Nigel was right every other time. He always gave his prophecies to Kelvin, and Kelvin would deliver them to us. Nigel was right about Tammy Green. He predicted that she'd get sick. And she did. Our first death in Xibalba. Not even Tiberia's pills could save her. Then there was the plague of swallows. Even Felix was amazed by that."

"Did I read about that on the Internet?" Martin asked.

"You might have," Lane said. "But reading it and seeing it are so different. Imagine the sky completely black with little birds. Nigel told Kelvin it would happen and it happened. And when Kelvin began to wear that cloak that everyone thought was so silly, they went away. Like Nigel said they would."

It was almost too much for Martin to process. "Who exactly does everyone think Nigel was?"

Lane forced herself to smile, as if she was embarrassed by what she was about to say. "Think about it. I mean, he killed Felix. Good old Felix. And you know what they're whispering to each other? That it was all part of some cosmic plan. They . . . they think he was God."

"What do you think?" Martin asked.

Lane sniffled. "I think God is dead. And I think you may be in over your head, Martin Maple."

Placing down the block of wood, Martin stepped up to the entrance of the mine shaft and eased his head inside. The air felt delicate and appealingly warm. It was impossible to see anything. He wondered how far they had gotten before the ceiling crashed in on them.

"We go back to work at noon," Martin stated as he pulled his head out. "With or without you. I hope it's with you."

Lane bit her top lip. Then, with regret tinging the words as soon as they came out of her mouth, she said, "It's with me. As long as we're on the same page. Kelvin didn't understand the consequences. You do. There's a difference."

— 26 —

The Trust

They all showed up. Whether it was fear or hope or some combination of both that got them didn't matter to Martin. They were there, and they were ready. He regretted not having enlisted everyone sooner, but circumstances had been different when they'd started. Back then, Martin didn't have such a grip on their trust.

The exterior of the machine was basically complete, but Martin wanted it airtight. His first order of business was to weld all the cracks shut. What would have taken him days with Lane and Chet was accomplished in a matter of hours by a well-organized army of welders following Martin's every command.

Next came the interior, where there were gear trains to align and belts and fans to mount and sync, not to mention the knobs and levers and switches to attach. The work wasn't drudgery, like hauling the machine back on the sleigh, and there was a healthy amount of curiosity among the workers.

"What does this thingy do?" someone might ask.

And Martin would hold up a gyroscope or a pendulum and he'd give them all a quick lesson in mechanics and physics and they would listen intently, as if he were telling the most riveting story imaginable.

For nearly six weeks that was how things went. Outside, the air was cold, and flurries blew strong and sideways. Inside, they were cramped together, but they could move well enough, and the pace of their work kept them warm without requiring extra heaters. With Chet dead and Henry gone, there was little fresh meat and few veggies to go around, but Wendy could bake, and they had an adequate amount of packaged provisions to last them until the launch. They weren't thinking much further than that.

They celebrated Christmas and New Year's in the machine, drinking soda and eating piles of cookies. Instead of carols, they sang a cappella versions of their favorite pop songs, especially the ones they hadn't heard in years because they hadn't located the albums at local music stores. They were a tone-deaf bunch, but music was so new and wonderful to Martin that he encouraged them to sing while they worked as well.

Darla made trips to get more supplies, including a fresh stock of solar panels, which were dedicated to powering tools. Most of the remaining houses and buildings had been without power since the fire. So on especially cold nights, the kids didn't even bother to go home. They would all curl up together on the floor in one big slumber party. Then Martin would wake them in the morning with breakfast and a new set of instructions.

Martin knew he couldn't act as though he was withholding information. Evasiveness breeds suspicion. The enigma that was his father had proved that. So Martin cooked up a variety of replies to allay the kids' concerns, though he was careful not to be so explicit that he could contradict himself or be proved wrong.

When Erica asked him, "Is this thing going to shoot up in the air like a rocket?" Martin explained, "It's going to spin. Only you probably won't feel it spin, 'cause it'll be going so fast. Think of the universe like a spring. You normally travel on the edge of it, along the loop of the coil. The machine is like a big screw. It's going to spin around and shoot right up through the middle. Folds in time, wormholes. It's all very complicated physics."

When Hal asked, "Don't we need, like, space suits or something?" Martin calmed him with a "Not at all. The machine is pressurized and sealed, and at the speed it will travel, we shouldn't feel the effects of atmosphere."

The general questions led to more creative answers.

Gina pressed him one morning. "Are they expecting us?"

"Probably not," Martin responded. "They didn't leave on purpose, you know. They're lost. The machine is very sensitive to vibrations and it can find large groups of people. To be honest, I can't say where it will take us exactly. It's like following a bloodhound. It will pick up the trail. Like we all picked up the trail and ended up here in Xibalba."

And the only time Martin was completely honest was when Damone asked, "Who taught you how to build it?"

"My father," Martin told him. "He was a secretive man. He was never really clear about why he was building the machine. But he taught me how to read using a book about spaceships. And he must have known the Day was coming, and he was preparing me for it. I guess he didn't want to scare me with the details."

He didn't need to lie. All evidence pointed to the fact that his father had been expecting something earth-shattering to happen in their lives. Maybe he had known that Martin was going to be left behind. Maybe this was his legacy for his son, his way to rescue him.

"When is it going to be ready?" was the question that everyone asked.

"Any day now."

— 27 —

The Pilot

It was the night before the launch. Martin's instructions were simple: "Collect only what you can fit in a backpack, because the machine can hold a limited amount of weight. Be there at dawn."

Martin got to the machine first. Cross-legged, he stared at the controls. His father had taught him how to turn it on. They had gone through the procedure at least a hundred times. Move this. Pull that. The dial should read 223 . . .

"I want to make sure you can do this on your own," his father had told him.

Back then, all it did when they turned it on was gently vibrate, hum, and whir.

"When it's finished, will it do more than that?" Martin had asked.

"It better," his father had said with a smile.

Martin was now holding the marble. It was the piece that

would finish the machine, and he realized there was only one place it could go.

He pushed open the interior door, which led to the smaller chamber of the machine, otherwise known as the machine's heart. Glass only reminded them of Chet's death, so instead of glass, they had built the door from sheets of aluminum. It wasn't transparent, but it also wasn't heavy. There was little danger of it injuring anyone.

The smaller chamber was the size of a tiny bedroom. There was a shelf against the back wall, and in the center of the shelf was a giant basin, similar to a sink. Other than that, the room was empty.

He set the marble on the edge of the basin and let it go. It rolled down the incline, then back up until it almost reached the rim. Then down it went again, only on a different path. Up and down, up and down, reaching a lower peak with each circuit. As it zeroed in on the center, it went into a rolling orbit like a planet around a star or, more accurately, like a planet into a black hole. Because the orbit got tighter and faster. And then, right there in the center, the marble stopped dead.

Fear seized Martin all at once.

An hour before sunrise, the first person arrived. It was Trent. The backpack he wore tugged his spine backward with its weight. On anyone else, it would have been a manageable load. As he entered the machine, he took his backpack off and placed it in an empty corner. He sat down on it and set his elbows on his thighs and his forehead in his hands. His fingertips worked their way into his hair and began massaging his scalp.

"What did you bring?" Martin asked in as chipper a tone as he could manage.

Trent looked up and forced a wan smile. "Blanket. And filters and iodine, of course. You know, for the space water."

It was a nice attempt at levity, but Martin could see in the kid's face that he was terrified. He wanted to reassure him, but all Martin could say was, "Thank you again . . . for all your help."

"Oh, it's nothing. Least I could do," Trent said. Then he pointed up at the controls to the machine and asked, "You entered the coordinates yet?"

"Sorry?"

"The ones Henry was trying to steal? You memorized them, right?"

"Yes, right," Martin said. He had forgotten all about that, and the truth was he didn't have any coordinates. It was something he'd made up.

There were, however, the Birthday Dials. A ludicrous name to be sure, but that was what his father called four tiny knobs on the machine's control panel. Martin once asked him what they were for. "Just like the name says, you enter your birthday with them," his father had told him.

With Trent looking on, Martin stepped over to the Birthday Dials and began adjusting them. They weren't marked with dates, but Martin understood the formula. The number of degrees you turned each one represented the position in the sky of certain celestial objects. Together they determined a year, a day, an hour, and a minute.

He had ignored the dials for the most part and had instinctively set them to the day he was born. Now he realized that didn't make much sense. Multiple kids would be piling into the machine, and they didn't all share that birthday. The best Martin could think to do was set them to his eleventh birthday, set them to the Day. After listening to all the Arrival Stories, he had been able to pinpoint the exact minute the kids were left, the exact moment their new world was born.

"All ready," Martin said, backing away from the controls.

"I wanted to be a pilot," Trent told him. "You know, when I grew up. So I've enjoyed watching you build this. It's taught me . . . well, I didn't know anything until you came along."

"Really? Thank you." It was hard for Martin to tell what people really thought of him. Did they all look up to him like Trent did?

"I was wondering. Are we coming back for them?" Trent asked.

"Who?"

"Henry and Kelvin."

Another thing he had forgotten about and another lie he'd have to tell. "Of course," Martin said, "but they made their choices and—"

"Everyone assumes he's dead. Kelvin, I mean. Do you think he's dead?"

The image of Kelvin, emaciated and alone, walking through the forest toward the ocean, had stuck with Martin more than anything he'd seen since he'd left the island. "Yes," Martin said. "He's probably dead."

Trent considered this, and he reached down between his knees and unzipped his backpack. He removed a blue fleece blanket and wrapped it around his shoulders.

195

"When we get there," he said, "and see everyone, what are we going to tell them? About the kids who died?"

It was a good question, and Martin could think of only one appropriate answer.

"I don't know."

— 28 —

The Light

The rest began to arrive a few minutes later. They trickled in, one by one, quietly nodding their hellos. Of course Darla had ignored Martin's request. She left her backpack at home and lugged in a monstrous piece of hard-shelled luggage.

"What do you need that for?" Martin asked.

"Well, let me see," Darla said. "My clothes, my bowling ball, my stuff that survived the fire. I'm a skinny gal. If the tubsters can bring their guts and butts, then I should be able to bring a kitten heel or two."

"It doesn't work like that," Martin said. "What if everyone brought all their stuff?"

"Then they'd be as smart as me." Darla laughed. "Obviously, that's not the case."

There was little use in arguing with her. Martin didn't know whether weight was important. It was better to focus on moving forward. He started by counting them. Thirty-seven, including him.

"We have everyone," he announced.

Thirteen years old. That was Martin. It wasn't much. And none of the other kids could claim much more. Tiberia was the oldest, on the brink of fifteen. Not even a sixth of the way to the end. People had been known to live past a hundred. It seemed impossible, but apparently it was true.

Thirty-seven kids packed together. Two others out there alone, one of them probably dead. Thirteen years of knowledge, some faith, and a machine. This was supposed to return things to the way they were?

What was wrong with forgetting about the past and beginning again the old-fashioned way? Falling in love. Settling down. Starting a family. Martin did the math in his head. It could take dozens of generations, nearly a thousand years, to get the world back to where it was, with a few billion souls kicking around. That was what was wrong with the old-fashioned way. And who was to say it wouldn't happen all over again? Who was to say the slate wouldn't be wiped clean once more?

"Are we going or what?" Tiberia asked.

Martin broke out of his daze and looked around. Their eyes pled and their hands held tight to the loose straps that hung from their packs. They reminded Martin of himself a few months earlier, oars over his shoulder, looking out at the ocean.

"We're all pretty nervous," Riley squeaked.

"One second," Martin told them. "A few more things to prep."

He pushed open the door to the machine's heart and

stepped inside. As soon as the door swung closed behind him, he stumbled forward and caught himself on the edge of the basin. Nausea ruled his body. Convulsions ping-ponged in his chest, and as he stared down at the marble, he wondered what might happen if he bathed it in vomit.

"Magic," his father had said. "It's going to help us start over."

Martin hated him.

Maybe it wasn't the first time he'd felt it, but it was the first time he'd known it. Those kids waiting on the other side of the door, in the other chamber of the machine, they had been part of the world. Martin had been part of nothing, just some vague quest of a madman desperate for hope. Sketches on a piece of paper? Found in the gears of a Ferris wheel? This was what their future depended on?

Yet there was nothing he could do. His fate had grown roots. He couldn't exactly walk out there and call the whole thing off. He could only keep going. Gulping back the panic, he lifted his head to see a reflection of his face, blurred and bloated by the shiny ripples of aluminum on the wall.

Now or never.

Martin instructed them to sit, and they did. He made it abundantly clear that question time was over by turning his back on them, but it didn't stop them from whispering to each other. Humming softly to himself, he tried to block out everything except the procedure.

It started with a crank. Fifteen clockwise rotations until it was too tight to move. He yanked down two levers at the same time. A bloom of air puffed up in the chest of the machine and rattled the looser bits. Then he turned one knob

30 degrees, one 120, one 210, one 300. A pair of pedals, salvaged from an old bakery truck, came next. He worked them like a drummer, stomping out a one-two beat. When they stiffened up, he stopped and moved over to a large plastic handle that stuck out from the console. He drew it toward him in a steady motion, revealing a taut wire, and he paced backward until he was almost touching the crowd. They had quieted down at this point and were following Martin's every move. When he dropped the handle, the wire pulled it back to the console, like the string of a talking doll. And the machine did talk, in its way. The whirring began.

It could be felt down to the guts, and kids instinctively pawed at the floor to stabilize themselves.

"Is it moving?" Wendy asked.

"Just starting" was Martin's response as he flipped a series of switches and tapped his finger on a pink light that was beginning to blink.

"What if you do something wrong?" Sigrid yelped. "What happens to us then?"

"Could we crash?" Ryan asked.

Martin stopped for a second. "Everything is going perfectly," he assured them with more than a little bite to his voice. "I've been practicing this forever. If one of you thinks you can do a better job, then feel free to take over."

This shut them up quick, and he scolded them for their lack of faith with a piercing stare that was plenty harsh but was mostly a bluff. It was natural for them to question him. Though there was little point of it so late in the game.

Turning back, he inched over to a line of buttons and ran his arm across them, making sure to press each one. It didn't have to be precise; it just had to be done. Needles on meters shuddered, then moved. He watched them until he was satisfied they were at full mast. Placing his mouth on the end of a pipe that curled and escaped into the wall, he blew a quick candle-snuffing breath. The whirring intensified.

Two more things to do.

He returned to the crank. Fifteen counterclockwise rotations until it was loose.

The breathing of the kids became synchronized. They might not have realized it, but Martin sure did. They were like one giant organism, clumped together on the floor behind him. He wondered what Lane was thinking. Did she view this as a big contraption, an elaborate entertainment like the ones she peddled? Was she just along for kicks, to see how spectacularly he would fail? He couldn't bear to turn around and look, to catch her shaking her head, mouthing, "I told you so."

And what about Darla? They had hardly spoken since the trial. At times it seemed she wanted nothing more than for Martin to build the machine; at other times, nothing less. Yet there was hardly a moment when she wasn't talking about how wonderful the world and her life were before the Day. Surely she would be the most disappointed if it didn't work.

And Trent, and Sigrid, and Tiberia, and Gabe, and Cameron, and Riley, and Ryan, and Wendy, and, oh God, he didn't know everyone's name. He did, he did. But not off the top of his head, not right then, when he was about to change everything, when he was about to grab the pendulum, when he was about to lift it and send it flying like a metronome on a giant clock.

Tick, tick, tick, tick, tick . . .

It was done. The final step. The pendulum was swinging.

The whir kept whirring. The breathing was steady and constant. And then, the light.

"This must be it," Raul whispered as the first hint of light came from under the door to the machine's heart.

It spread out like liquid on the floor. Before long, it was touching the walls and painting the faces of the kids.

"It's gorgeous," Gina said. "Is it starlight?"

Whirring became whistling, and soon the light shone so brightly that they had to close their eyes. Vibrations coursed through the machine in a series of pulses. The clamor of metal on metal galloped forth, then stopped. Static electricity swept through the room as if blown by a breeze and it grabbed at the tiny hairs on Martin's arms. The whistle mutated back to a whir and the nausea in Martin's stomach retreated. His insides felt downright giddy.

Whether one person started it and the rest caught on or whether it spontaneously happened all at once was hard to say. But the machine was suddenly filled with laughter. Giggles and chuckles and joyful gasps for breath. They echoed and folded into each other and created a symphony of delight. It might have lasted only twenty seconds or so, but it felt like forever.

Then, as the laughter evaporated, everything else retreated. The vibrations, the sounds, the light. Only the pendulum remained, cutting its path back and forth in front of the control panel.

. . . *tick, tick, tick, tick, tick* . . .

It was at least a few minutes before anyone spoke.

"Are we there yet?" Trent asked.

No one laughed. No one responded at all. Martin opened

his eyes. The kids all looked safe, healthy. Whatever the machine had done, it hadn't changed their appearance.

There were no windows, no way of telling where exactly they were. Everyone was still sitting, except for Martin, who was standing at the controls. Clearly, their expectation was that he would make the first move.

He walked over and touched his fingers to the corrugated metal of the machine's wall, but only for a second, like he was testing the heat of an oven. Not sure what to expect, he wasn't helped much by the results. A little warm. He pressed his ear against it and listened for a moment. A gentle wind was complemented by an unmistakable birdcall. Chickadees.

"What *was* that?" Cameron whispered.

Martin rushed to the door. He tossed it open and felt a cool caress of air as he took a step outside.

"Martin? What happened?" Cameron called out from the machine. A soft commotion followed.

"Let him go," Darla demanded. "He must know what he's doing."

Outside, Martin found Xibalba.

It was exactly as they had left it. The buildings and houses were in the same state of ruin. Town Square was neatly plowed. Crusty, gravelly stacks of snow dotted the curbs. Kid Godzilla, scuffed and dented but alive, was parked in the distance, along the street.

A dark cube, about three feet square, was the only difference. It sat on the pavement a few feet from the machine. It hadn't been there when Martin had arrived in the morning.

When he got closer, he realized what it was: the charred remains of the home page to Felix's Internet. It used to tell the story of Xibalba, but all the writing had burned away.

The only mark that remained was a short message gouged deep into the coaly surface. It said:

Welcome to Xibalba,
home of the last people on Earth.
Sorry, but we all killed ourselves.
Hang in there. Or don't.
What do we care?

Martin turned around to see the confetti of disappointed faces bursting forth from the machine. At that moment, there was nothing he wanted more than to go home to his island.

— 29 —

The Lie

"What'd you do to us?" Tiberia asked.

"I don't know what you mean," Martin replied.

"We felt it," she said. "We all felt that machine do something."

"If we go back inside and try again . . . ," Martin said, but Tiberia was having none of it.

"Stand back, everyone! Get away!" she commanded.

They followed her order, scattering from the machine like water bugs from a ripple in a pond.

"But something's changed. This block," Martin said, "it wasn't here last night."

"Because I left it there this morning," Lane said with a sigh. She was standing closer to the machine than anyone else, examining it as if to figure out what went wrong.

"Oh," Martin said. "Well, maybe a few adjustments and we can—"

"Did you know it?" Tiberia asked. "That it would twist

up our insides like that? Make us giggle like a buncha maniacs?"

Martin shook his head. He had felt the same thing, but he had no idea what it meant. His voice began to quake. "It did something good. I know it did."

"How are we to be sure of that?" Sigrid gasped. "How do we know it was safe?"

"No. No. I never would have put us in danger," Martin insisted.

A sideways glance at Lane in search of help was met with a look that was more patronizing than sympathetic. She paced over to him, hooked her hand around, and grabbed his upper back. Then she leaned into his ear.

"Thought it would have at least burnt us to a crisp, Captain," she whispered. "But you didn't have the guts, did you?"

Martin pulled away, searching her for a wink and a nod. A watercolor of sadness was painted in her eyes. How could he have been so clueless?

"Don't say things like that," Martin whispered back.

"Doesn't matter what I say in this pitiful place. Your destiny is mediocrity, Martin. I never should have thought there was anything special about you." She shoved him aside with more malice than he'd ever felt from anyone. Then she bent over, wrapped her arms around the block, and lifted it. She headed into the seams of Xibalba.

"Where are you goin'?" Tiberia asked.

"Home," Lane called back.

"That makes two of us," Tiberia responded.

And that also made the rest of them. The exodus was quick. As all the kids streamed past him, Martin surveyed their faces. Some looked angry, others confused. The majority simply appeared to be on autopilot, denying their disappointment and heading back to their corners of the world.

Only Darla stayed. She sat on her luggage, legs dangling out from a gray pleated skirt. She was fussing with her white frilly blouse and short-cut blazer, trying to pull them straight. Her lips were dabbed—a bit heavily, it seemed—with pink lipstick. When she smiled at Martin, he saw that some of it had found its way onto her braces.

"Hey, you tried, right?" she said. "Can't blame you for trying. It was crazy, of course. But then, it was also crazy that the world disappeared. So there you go."

"They'll never forgive me," Martin said.

"Pffff," Darla said. "They're grumpy 'cause they had to wake up early. They'll get over it. You convinced them once; you can convince them again."

"Convince them? I have no idea what I just did to them."

"Felt good to me," Darla said. "Jeez. If those zeros can't enjoy a laugh, I don't know if they deserve one."

The most honest thing about Darla was her laugh. It skirted annoying, with its stabbing insistence. Yet it never seemed forced. When Darla laughed, there was emotion behind it.

"I haven't been completely truthful," Martin admitted.

Darla waved him off. "Come on, honey. Everybody tells lies to get what they want."

It wasn't exactly a comforting statement, especially coming from Darla, but it confirmed something Martin had begun to suspect: someone has always done worse.

"What lies have you told?" he asked her.

"Today?" Darla joked.

"Whenever."

"Well," Darla said, "I only tell white lies, of course. Fibs. Yes, *fibs* is the word for what I tell."

"Have you ever told me a fib?"

"Besides the marble?" Darla said.

"Wait. What?"

"The marble? That it would make the machine work?" Darla said. "You didn't suspect that was weird? Even a little?"

It was even worse than he'd thought. He curled back, pulling his hands to his chest like she was an infection. "Nigel never said the marble was for the machine?"

"Naw," Darla said lightheartedly. "I made that part up."

"You . . . but . . . why . . ." As the words came out, so too did the previous night's dinner. A purple thrust of vomit met the pavement with a curdy smack.

"Yuck," Darla cried, pulling her feet up. "I was gonna say because you're cute, but I think you changed my opinion pretty quickly there."

"I'm . . . I'm sorry . . . I'm sorry." Martin stumbled sideways and battled dizziness. Stomach acid worked its claws into his throat.

"It's not a big deal," Darla said. "What Nigel did tell me was that I had to give you a push."

"A push?" Martin whimpered as he dabbed his mouth against his sleeve.

"He was worried that 'cause of Chet, you would wimp out or something. He told me to make sure you finished what you started. And I did that." She pointed with her thumb over her shoulder at the machine. "I got that thing here. I got the whole gang to pitch in. And as a bonus, I got a date with you. So you can't call it a lie at all. A fib."

"But the marble . . . ?"

"The marble is just a marble." Darla laughed. "*C'est la*

vie. Forget all that junk and let's get back in the machine. You almost had it, right? A few adjustments? Who needs this gang? Let's leave 'em behind for good."

She didn't get it. The marble was everything. If the marble didn't complete the machine, then what did?

"They'll have a trial for me, won't they?" Martin asked. "And they'll treat me just like I treated Henry?"

"Henry's fine," Darla assured him. "A little uncomfortable maybe, but fine."

"I should go back to the island," he said. "I was never meant to come here."

"Sure you were," Darla said. "Or else you wouldn't be here."

"That's not how everyone else is going to see it."

Darla schemed furiously. There was really no better word for it. Her eyes were the same as they always were— delightfully devious. But it was her fingers that gave her away. Draped over her thigh, they tapped her nervous energy through the fabric of her skirt and into her bones.

"Tell you what," she said. "If you're so worried, lay low for a while. We'll find you somewhere to hide out while stuff blows over. Things will be back to normal in the bat of an eyelash."

She winked.

— 30 —

The Hospital

The hospital on the edge of town was five rectangular stories of yellow brick and rust-edged windows that wept brown tears when it rained. Martin had never been inside, and from what Darla had told him, he knew that hardly anyone else had either. Sigrid used to train in the halls, but those days were over. It was far too spooky in there. Now when foul weather descended, she had other places to run.

Martin could be alone there, and while it wasn't his island, it wasn't all that different. Exploring it, he expected to find a cold, hollow, sterile building. What he actually found was room upon room decorated with photographs and posters and stuffed animals and keepsakes and reminders that, just like the houses on the island, this was a home, if only temporarily. The ravages of nature hadn't touched it. The windows were permanently locked. The doors were heavy. And that was what must have scared Sigrid off. This hospital wasn't a skeleton; it was a warm corpse.

Martin settled into a room on the fourth floor that was stripped bare except for a bed and a dresser. He found a stack of blankets in a closet, and rather than worry about heating the place, he decided that he would drape himself in wool and stay put.

Darla agreed to bring him food and his only other request: books. Because she refused to step inside, they established a system, one that Martin knew well. Every evening, Darla would fill a wooden crate with books, water, and food and leave it by a side door to the hospital. Martin would empty the contents and fill the crate with the books he had finished. They would also leave each other notes.

Are they looking for me? What about Lane?—Martin

Everyone's back to their old jobs and routines, monkeying around like nothing happened. Lane's even worse. No one's seen her in days. Numbskull locked herself in the school. Building a masterpiece of crap, no doubt. —Darla

How's the machine?

Hunky-dory. Sitting where you left it. Everyone stays far away.

Did you really think it would work?

Of course I did, silly! I still do. Like I said, we don't need them. We can try again whenever you want

But Martin didn't want to try. All he wanted to do was read. That was the only thing he truly missed from his days alone on the island—stories, precise and contained, the type that answered your questions, the type that painted the world in simple strokes. Forget the ocean and the forest, the seaweed stink and the cold fog. Under his covers, with a stack of books by his side, he was home.

Blocking the entire world out was harder than that, though. The sound of the wind and the call of the chickadees still made it through the brick and glass. Chickadees rarely flew south in the winter. That was one of their defining characteristics, and Martin thought about that fact all too often. The chickadees were mocking him with their song, saying he was just like them—afraid to leave.

He *was* afraid. Too afraid even to leave the room. With the exception of his daily trip to the wooden crate, he stayed in bed. At night, he would use the dresser to barricade his door, because it locked only from the outside, and he was pretty sure he heard footsteps in the hall. They weren't loud, but they were there, delicate and urgent and terrifying. At first he thought it might be Sigrid, but the steps weren't those of a jogger. They shuffled too much. They were all stops and starts.

He wrote Darla a note.

Is anyone else coming to the hospital? I've been hearing footsteps in the hall.

Don't go all schizoid on me now, Maple. No one's gotten within half a mile of that kook joint. Reading too many horror books, methinks. Going to switch you over to romance.

Sometimes on the island he had wondered if he might end up going crazy. That seemed to happen to hermits in all the books he read. But during those lonesome years, he had never heard voices, or footsteps, or anything that might qualify as a hallucination.

Then again, he had never felt this much shame.

One evening, Martin found that the crate was empty. It had happened before. In the three and a half weeks that Martin spent in the hospital, Darla forgot to load the crate on two other occasions. Her excuses were convoluted and forgettable, and they didn't matter really. Martin had stockpiled enough food and books to last.

This time was different. There was only one book left to get him through the night. The next day would be a dead zone, and he had only three choices. He could while away the hours listening to the wind and chickadees and letting his thoughts take over. He could risk going back into Xibalba, to the library, and loading up a backpack. Or he could try to locate some books right there in the hospital.

The footsteps usually only came at night. After careful consideration, he convinced himself that they were made by a raccoon or a fox that had dug its way into the hospital through the ductwork. So once morning came, he ventured out for some exploration. He started in the rooms closest to his, but the books he found were ones he had already read—fantasy yarns, the Bible, some silly little tale about a seagull.

On the fifth floor, he hoped for better luck. He tore open drawers and thrust his hand under mattresses. He found a few magazines, which he wedged under his arm, but he knew they wouldn't last him long.

By the time he reached room 512, he was almost ready to throw in the towel. The room was a bit odder than others he had seen, but that didn't mean much. There were framed photos of a baby on the dresser, a stack of boxes in the corner, women's dresses in the closet, a crudely formed wooden figurine hanging by a wire from the ceiling, and what looked like a dragon made of clay on the nightstand. Yet the strangest thing was that the bed was made. He had seen tidy beds in other rooms, but none of those rooms had so many decorations. It didn't matter really, though. There weren't any books, and that was all he cared about.

On his way to the door, he stopped to look at a painting on the wall. It was a colorful and absurd scene of armored men storming a beach on horseback while natives in elaborate headdresses rained spears down on them from colossal pyramids rising from a bordering jungle. In the background, there was a moored sailboat. The flag it flew was unmistakable. It was the Jolly Roger.

Martin lifted the painting off the wall to get a closer look. The wood felt flimsy, and the canvas thin, but the entire thing was much heavier than he had expected. He turned it over to see why. Tucked in the frame was a journal.

He'd seen this type of journal before, with a marbled black cover and a white label for writing your name. There was nothing written on this one, but the edges of the pages were puffed up and warped and stained with sooty black fin-gerprints. He set the painting down and walked over to the bed. He sat on the corner, balanced the journal on his knee, and opened it. In messy black ink, the following was written:

The Life and Times of Kelvin Rice
Volume II

— 31 —

The Sequel

The curtains, chunky and powder blue and emblazoned with little cartoon ears of corn, defended the room from the light. Martin yanked them open and felt the early afternoon warmth cling to his face. He scooted back on the bed and got comfortable.

The journal was an absolute mess. Pages were stuck together and warped with water damage. The ink had bled everywhere, creating a gray broth with random fragments of legible text floating here and there. Throughout most of it, Martin could determine where one entry ended and another began, but it was nearly impossible to get a sense of when exactly they were written. They were just a sprinkling of thoughts and observations, completely open to interpretation.

...starting new with a new diary and a new life and a new world! That's right!

Every! Stupid! Person! You turn on the TV and it's static. Radio too. You scream your lungs out and no one can hear a damn thing. Swear. Scream your swears if you want. It happened. Look. Look!

...a pound of peanuts for dinner and drank a beer. Beer is gross, so I won't be doing that again. I went to Marjorie's room to make sure she wasn't there. She wasn't and that's a good thing. It makes me mean I guess but there are so many times when I wished she was dead. This is better than dead. Wherever she is, they're more able to handle her. I've never been able to. Isn't that what loving someone is about, wanting the better thing for them? I could destroy things if I wanted. I could drive a car through the bowling alley. I'm not going to do that because I have been left here for a reason. To protect the world? Probably not. I did go to Tyler's house. I put his clothes on his bed and I peed all over them and I smashed his computer and TV with a hammer. It felt okay to do that, but then, I can do anything I want.

...put a sign up near the highway that said "Zombies keep out, no brains here." Funny stuff, but jokes don't work when there's no one to...

...going out. I didn't think about that. The water too. I guess those things don't run on their own. I bet I could find a generator. You put gas in those and there's lots of gas if you know how to siphon. I'll need heat when the winter comes but that's...

It was stupid for me to think I was the only one. I saw someone today.

...like he's my age. I want to follow him, but he's up to something and I'm not sure it's safe. He collects signs and books and other stuff. He burns them. He stacks them in Town Square and dumps gas on them. It stinks like nothing I've ever...

...a tiger. A tiger!

Since finding that first diary in his basement, Martin had wanted to know everything about Kelvin, but now he thought it might be best to put this book down. It had the potential to reveal things he wasn't prepared to handle. He had operated under certain assumptions, and if those assumptions proved false, then it would be another deafening blow to the voice on his shoulder. But resistance, as they say, was futile. He dove back in.

...to my house with a statue of a lizard in its mouth. "You Have Been Summoned!"

That was written on it. You can't make up that stuff. We met in the church. He was sitting in a puffy chair. A big lizard sat next to him. He told me there was work to be done. He was nice enough about it, polite and all that. His name is Nigel. He wants me to...

Nigel told me there will be others. He said he's seen them out there. It's taken a week or so to destroy everything that "needed to be destroyed" and he said I could name "our new kingdom." Xibalba is what I came up with. He chuckled and he asked me if I knew what it meant. I told him it was the Mayan underworld. He told me it also meant "Place of Fear." He had a bear with him when we were talking about this, so there was that...

...town this morning. He will make his entrance when the timing is right. He took the animals with him. I won't miss him, but I don't hate him. I really don't.

...is Trent and he seems like a good kid. It shocked him to see me, but we sat around in the church and he told me about how he got here. It was pretty wild. He seems wimpy and all, but he swam through a flooded subway tunnel! I told him to stay and he decided to sleep in the McNallys' house. It's yours...

...once or twice a week. Lots of kids on bikes. One girl came in on a monster truck. She's kind of nasty, but she's smart and, you know, she drives a monster truck. I'm not great at being mayor or whatever, but they want to listen to me, so I started giving everyone jobs, based on what they're good at. We should have plenty of fun, but I need to make up more rules. First things first. No one goes in the hospital. This is my place to get away from it all. This is my home away from...

...exactly like he said it would. We were leaving the church after doing the Arrival Stories for this crunchy girl named Gina. There was Nigel, waiting in Town Square with the tiger and the Komodo dragon and he pointed at me all serious and he said, "I will be talking to him and only him." Then he walked up the hill and went inside Dr. Rubio's house. The kids asked if I knew him and I told them I had never seen him in my life.

I kissed four girls today, but not the one I really wanted to kiss. I'd like to bring her here and show her this room and tell her

220

the truth, but there are things you don't tell when you are...

...Felix's wacko plans. His Internet idea seems beyond strange, but Nigel told me to let him go ahead with it because it could prove useful. I call Felix plenty of terrible stuff and I'm not sure why I do it, but the kid bugs me more than...

...Green died right in her own bed. It took about two days and there was blood dripping out of her mouth and it was awful. Tiberia tried, but she couldn't do a thing. Nigel was right on the money. It hurts me to wonder how on Earth he predicted it. He tells me over and over again that "sacrifices need to be made in order to have the world of our dreams." Of our dreams? If he really thinks...

It was almost ten pages until the next set of legible entries. Martin held the smudged and dirty paper up to the light, but he couldn't make out more than a few scattered words. When the entries were readable again, they seemed sloppier. It was as if each one had been written faster than the one before. He could see the anxiety in the ink and he could almost hear Kelvin's voice, exactly as it sounded that night by the fire—wry, exhausted.

...and when I ask him where all this prophecy crap is getting us, he goes full-on jerk and lectures me on leadership and power and how "the weak are here to serve the strong." Kids used to be happy doing what they wanted for so long that I didn't think it would end up like this. Now everyone's getting nervous and arguments are starting. There hasn't been a new Forgotten in almost a year. I think it's finally time to do something. I got the Diggers together and told them about the mine shaft and they're obsessed with it now. There are worse ideas than going down there and looking. For Marjorie's sake, I should at least have a look. What's wrong with...

...her a message in a bottle and she came and we hung out in my basement again and we stayed up for a long time talking about who we were and what we did before the Day. I told her that Xibalba was supposed to be the perfect place, a balsa world, popped out and glued together. Lane told me how much she hated her family and so I pretended to hate Aunt Bonnie just as much, but I really don't. Aunt Bonnie was there and that's all and that's fine. Not that I miss Aunt Bonnie. I miss her laugh, maybe. I miss Marjorie. More now than when I was alone. I don't miss Tyler or school. I miss the feel of being a kid and not making decisions that...

...swallows arrived fast and dark. I'm not sure how Nigel pulled that one off, but there has to be an explanation. Always seems to be. He gave me a bird-shaped clasp for my cloak and when I was leaving he told me that I'll have to "take responsibility for my decisions." What is that about? He can sit in his stinky zoo and blab in riddles and keep them all scared and docile, but he sure can't control my decisions. I'm done with his garbage. I meet with the Diggers tonight and we pack for the...

...begging me not to go. She says she won't be able to handle this place without me. I'm going anyway. I can always come...

I dumped water all over myself to clean off and I must have dumped it all over the journal and it's like it's wiping out my thoughts and erasing my past and telling me I never mattered. I'm worthless. A coward. I am a coward. A coward! They're dead. All of them. I'm in this bed hugging the talisman that I made for Marjorie and I'm telling the demons that I want them out. Out! I want them gone for good because I didn't ask for this. The only thing I ever asked for was to be alone. But Nigel found me. He came to this room and I had to tell him what happened. I explained that I wasn't there. I wasn't even close. I was a hundred yards away, heading out, when it collapsed. Then I went back and there was nothing but rubble. Couldn't even hear their screams anymore. Just like that. Just like that. Nigel didn't seem pleased that he was right again and he didn't judge me. He actually hugged me and he told me that I'll have to wait a few days, to pretend like I was trapped in there, so it doesn't seem like I abandoned them. I'll have to take the blame, but he promised they'll forgive me. As long as I go out into the world and find something to save us all. He said he'll talk to Lane and give her a hopeful prophecy. And he said I should mark my trail to find my way back, because I have to go as far as the ocean. When I find it, I can return, and I'll be welcomed as a hero. I asked him what "it" is. He said when I see "it," I'll know.

And that was all there was. The journal ended there. Martin sat with it open in his lap for a moment. Then he peeled back the pages, prepared to read it all over again. Not all of it made sense, but it gripped him just the same.

A voice came from across the room: "Is it a good book?"

Martin looked up, expecting Darla. A response of "Excuse me?" was perched on his lips, but it didn't come out. It couldn't.

Because standing in the doorway was a woman. Her stringy blond hair was hanging haphazardly over her face. Her feet were sheathed in pink bunny slippers. She wore a floral dress with a puffy white winter coat over it. A large digital watch decorated her left wrist. When she stepped forward, she put a dirty finger to her lips.

"They don't let you read anything that's not approved, you know?" she whispered.

"I . . . I . . ."

The woman was at least twice Martin's age, probably three times. As she got closer, he could see that her lips were chapped and broken, peppered with blood.

"They're coming back, I'm sure," she went on. "And they can't have you in the wrong room. Especially in my room." With each word her voice grew more agitated. Strands of tensed muscle hollowed out valleys in her neck.

"This is no one's room," Martin made the mistake of saying.

"So I'm no one now?" she barked back.

"I didn't say that."

"And is that why you put me in that cage?"

"I . . ."

"You took my kitten," she roared. "What did you do with my kitten?"

Even if he'd had an answer, it was too late. The woman lunged at Martin, and before he could defend himself, she had her hands around his throat. Her thumbs pressed down on his windpipe and sent a jolt into his chest. It was the most terrible feeling he had ever known. He tried to knock her back with his hands, and she thrust her knees forward and pinned his biceps to the bed. In her eyes there was a singular look. He could have been wrong, but he felt they were telling him something: "It's your fault."

As the feeling drained from his face and dizziness worked worms into his skull, Martin decided to let go. He had never given much thought to dying, and he didn't give much more thought to it now. All he knew was that his life had been leading to this moment, to this room, to this woman, whoever she was.

He closed his eyes.

When he felt her hands pull away from his throat, he assumed that his adventure had come to its conclusion. His story had come to an end.

PART IV

"Lane?"

"Yes?"

"We're concerned about you."

"Don't be."

"You lock yourself away for hours. And you build this . . ."

"Art, Mom. It's art."

"Art is painting the ocean. Or maybe a portrait. Have you tried those?"

"Jeez. Could you be more old-fashioned?"

"When you're my age—"

"I'll be all alone, eating cat food and talking to the rosebushes. Is that what you're afraid of?"

"I'm afraid that a twelve-year-old girl knows what she wants, but not what she needs."

"I need you to leave."

— 32 —

The Knife

If it was Henry who greeted souls in the afterlife, then Martin wanted back to the land of the living. Ruddy and sweaty and saddled with a breathy stink, Henry's face looked down on Martin's.

"You alive?" Henry asked.

"Am I?"

"Yeah, you're alive. Dead guys don't say squat," Henry grumbled as he backed away.

"Was I dreaming?" Martin asked, sitting up from the bed. The woman was nowhere to be seen.

"Naw," Henry said. "You were gettin' choked by some woman."

"You saw her too?"

"I pulled her off you, stupid," Henry said, shaking his head.

"Who was she?"

"I dunno, your girlfriend. She took off down the hall. Why you askin' me?"

"Well, 'cause . . ." Martin ran his fingers across his neck. It felt hot.

"I don't know who she is, but I know where she's goin'," Henry told him. "If you care."

Martin stood from the bed. The journal was on the floor, so he picked it up. He looked at the closing passages again. "I care."

Almost all the snow was gone, but the woods were thicker with mud than ever. *They call it mud season around here,* Darla had informed him in one of her recent notes. Henry trudged in front, his hands awkwardly out to his sides, shaking as if they needed to hold on to something. That he didn't seem surprised by the appearance of the woman, presumably the only woman on earth, bothered Martin.

"How do you know where she's going?" Martin asked.

"'Cause I been watchin' her," Henry said.

"From where?"

Henry pointed through the bud-dressed branches to the rock face of Alcatraz, where the Ring of Penance was located. "Cell block six."

"Oh," Martin replied guiltily. He hadn't thought about Henry in weeks. Pity was something he had lavished on himself, not on the boy who spent his nights in a tent above the tree line on a mountain.

"Darla brought me my scope," Henry explained. "I promised to keep an eye on you."

"Has that woman been in the hospital all along?"

"Don't know." Henry picked up a thin dead branch and

began twirling it like a sword. "Noticed her a few days ago. She comes and goes."

"Did you tell Darla?" Martin asked.

"I ain't the mornin' paper," Henry said. "I watch. All I do."

Martin's windpipe ached, but he had to count himself as lucky, and he could thank only one person for that luck. "You save people too. You saved me."

"I came down to see what was doin'," Henry mumbled. "Right place at the right time."

"Thank you just the same."

Henry lifted the branch and pointed straight ahead. "Save your thank-yous. You're the one who's gotta go in there."

Fifty yards in the distance was the ledge and the opening to the mine shaft. Martin had never approached it from this direction, and it puzzled him that of all the places, this was where the woman would come.

"Are you sure that's where she is?" he asked.

"The hospital and the mine," Henry said. "Only places she goes."

"And you want me to go in alone?"

Henry shrugged and flicked the branch to the side. "I don't want you to do nothin'. I'm not goin' in that place is all I'm sayin'."

Even if he was curious about this woman's identity, Henry certainly had done more than his part. It was up to Martin now.

"I don't have a torch," Martin said, staring at the oppressive blackness of the hole.

Henry smiled smugly, dug into his pocket, and removed

a bundle of cloth. He handed it to Martin. "Borrowed it from Felix a while back. He ain't missing it now."

It was one of Felix's headbands, and wrapped inside was a series of his firefly lightbulbs.

"Okay," Martin said, looking them over with suspicion. The lightbulbs weren't glowing at all.

"They may be old, but they still work. All you do is shake 'em and that'll fire 'em up," Henry explained. "Pretty cool, actually." Without giving Martin a chance to do it himself, Henry grasped Martin's wrist and shook it. Within a few seconds, light was sprouting from the cracks between Martin's fingers.

It was foolhardy, dangerous at best. To chase a person who just tried to murder you? Into a mine shaft? For what? For Martin, it was answers. It had been over two and a half years since the Day, and there hadn't been a single adult spotted anywhere. Not by the kids of Xibalba, in any case. Now there was one in the hospital, in the mine shaft. Surely she knew something, and she was willing to strangle to keep her secrets. People strangled for a reason. There were plenty of complicated books dedicated to complicated people strangling for complicated reasons. Martin had read them.

So as he made his way through the darkness, he held in both hands a knife that Henry had loaned him. The firefly lightbulbs worked better than expected. The shell of light surrounded his head and allowed him to see three to four yards in all directions.

Choices were nonexistent. The mine shaft was full of switchbacks, but no forks. It led forward and down, like a long winding ramp into the center of the earth. The walls were flat in most places, but in a few, it seemed as though the

rock had been scooped out with a giant spoon,
patches of smooth craters. Wooden braces framed
nel, but plenty of those had cracked and broken fro
maintenance. At Martin's feet was a railroad trac
rotted from all the puddles.

He didn't feel safe at all, and he thought of tur
and rejoining Henry, who was waiting outside. Th
would have to come out sometime, and he would
her then. It was the smart thing to do, but it wasr
wanted to do. By opening Kelvin's journals, he h
himself to the idea that if the machine wasn't t
maybe something else was. Maybe this mine was

When Martin had met Kelvin, he had thou
come across a boy as different from him as possib
that point on, he had followed in Kelvin's footste
woods, to Kelvin's house, to Nigel's side, where
could be whispered into his ear. From a liar, t
leader of Xibalba, to an outcast—a lost and re
ure. From the hospital room to right here in the
mine. He would stop the cycle now. He would
he had some answers and could return to
something more than empty proclamations. It I
a while to realize that he didn't owe the kids
owed them truth.

Cries reached Martin in echoed flutters. I
close. The air was warmer here than outside,
still, but not stifling. He filled his lungs to the
the next bend, the puddles at his feet turned
black, and Martin saw what Kelvin must have
last frantic moments in the mine. A mound
formed a wall that blocked the tunnel.

"This is a grave," Lane had told him.

But there was light coming from the grave. At the top of the mound was a hole, dug by hand presumably, and through the hole came a soft shaft of light and the sound of the woman crying. Martin kept moving. He placed the knife handle in his mouth and used his hands to pull himself up to the hole. It was just big enough for him to fit through.

Working through it was harder than he'd expected, and in an attempt to wiggle himself forward, he struck his head against a stone and the firefly lightbulbs shattered. Tiny cuts in his forehead let loose with blood. The only available light was coming from the other side. Turning back was hardly an option now.

A cavern was on the other side, a massive room the size of Xibalba's church. As Martin pulled himself from the hole, he tumbled down to the floor. Dirty water splashed into his face and mixed with his blood, and the liquid that wasn't absorbed by his headband ran down his cheeks. He scanned the room for other exits, but there were none. There was only the woman, sitting next to a pile of backpacks, their contents strewn on the floor around her. She held her wrist up to her chin and the light from her digital watch illuminated her face.

"Who's there?" she asked.

"Martin Maple," Martin said as he found his feet. The knife was at the ready.

"Are you the boy from my room?"

Martin hesitated to answer. He thought about what lying might get him. "Yes," he finally said.

"There was someone with you."

Martin took a few steps toward her and saw that clothing and toys and trinkets had been removed from the backpacks. "Henry was with me," he told her. "I'm alone now.

She lifted a T-shirt to her face and wiped away some tears. "Are you here to kill me, Martin Maple?"

"No," Martin said softly. "I'm here to bring you back. If you lead the way out, I'll explain everything."

"Will Kitten be there?"

"I'm sure we can find your kitten," Martin told her. He would have offered her anything if it had meant they could return to the surface.

"Someone brought these bags, but no one showed up," she whimpered. "This was supposed to be the meeting place if we got lost, for me and Daddy and Kitten. All of us, together for once . . ."

As her voice faded out, she closed her eyes. For Martin, it was like watching his father when he would drift off to sleep in his chair next to their wood-burning stove. It was peaceful but undeniably sad, because it was always something of a surrender.

"I showed up," Martin told her, his voice filling the emptiness.

— 33 —

The Theater

Xibalba's two exiles followed the only woman in the world toward town. Henry held the knife now, because as he was quick to point out, "Island boys can only bait hooks." He also squawked questions at the woman.

"So what's your name?"

"Puddin' Tain," she said, giggling. "Ask me again and I'll tell you the same."

"Whatever, lady," Henry said.

It was odd. A few hours before, she was psychotic, and now she was playful—bubbly, even. Her jaunty stride was verging on a skip.

"How do you know where you're going?" Martin asked.

"'Cause I live here," she said.

"How long have you lived here?"

"My whole entire life."

"That's impossible," Henry said. "I woulda seen you before."

236

She stopped and turned around. She pointed an accusatory finger at Henry. "I woulda seen you too. Where you been all this time?"

Henry snorted in response. She shrugged him off, turned back, and surged forward.

"Not too far," Henry commanded.

"Jeez," she said. "Worst field trip ever."

Martin stopped Henry for a moment. "Now, what I'm going to say might sound dumb."

"Shocker."

"Do you think she might be a ghost?" Martin whispered.

"Dumb, all right. Know any ghosts who can choke a person? No, this lady is a psycho. With a capital 'S.' And that's why we gotta knock her out." As Henry said that, he bent over and unearthed a hunk of rock the size of an apple.

Martin grabbed Henry by the wrist. "Are you sure that's a good idea?"

"It's a great idea," Henry snapped back. "I seen it in movies all the time. And trust me, this loony is gonna go all strangle-hands on us at any minute. It's better if we send her to sleepytime."

"It's probably harder to knock someone out than you think." Martin didn't know a lot about anatomy or about concussions, but he did know that Henry was not nearly as strong as he believed himself to be.

"So what's your plan, genius?" Henry asked.

The forest was full of felled trees, each one infested with ferns and fungus. "Well," Martin said, "I've read that certain plants and mushrooms have toxins that if you get them in the bloodstream, then they can knock a person unconscious."

"What about this sucker?" Henry asked as he chucked

the rock to the side and grabbed a red-capped, white-gilled mushroom.

"I think that's an amanita," Martin told him. "It's certainly toxic. But if she ate it, it might take hours to kick in, and even then I'm not sure what it would do to her."

"Gotta get it into the bloodstream, right?" Henry asked, reaching into his pockets.

"Well, yes, but like I said, even if you could get her to eat it—"

Henry interrupted him by whipping out a red-finned dart that had been holstered to his belt. "McNally's Pub. Been using it to kill squirrels."

"Okay," Martin said, "but what does that have to do with anything?"

Henry showed him by dipping the tip of the dart into the stem of the mushroom. "Like an Amazon man. Magic toads and all that voodoo."

"The toxins are actually in the cap of the mushroom," Martin tried to tell him, but Henry wasn't listening.

Instead, he was lining up his shot. "Right for the throat," he said, and in a blink he was letting loose the dart. Martin might have had a chance to stop him, but he hardly thought it was possible that someone, even Henry, would do something so stupid.

The dart flew straight and true and hit the woman in the back of the skull, where it stuck, dead center. Rather than yelping, she turned around and shot them a confused look. Running her hand up the back of her neck, she found it. She tried to pull the dart out with a quick tug, but it didn't come.

"What did you do?" she asked. A shiver of rage raced up her torso and caused her shoulders to convulse.

"How long until she passes out?" Henry asked.

"Never," Martin said. "You weren't listening."

And that was when she came bolting at them.

Martin couldn't really blame her. If someone had thrown a dart into his head, he would have done the same.

Both boys spun off to their sides and began sprinting away, but she didn't follow either of them. She simply kept running.

Martin watched over his shoulder as she sped back toward the mine. She didn't get very far. As she attempted to duck under a branch, her foot caught a root. Her body sailed forward. Her head struck a rock. She lay still.

They approached slowly—Henry from the left, knife held high; Martin from the right, wielding a stick like a club. When they had her flanked, they waited. Only her back moved, and only ever so slightly, as she drew breaths in and let them out. Henry used his foot to flip her onto her side.

"See?" Henry said. "Shoulda done it my way."

An earthy bruise adorned her forehead, and her eyes were mostly whites.

They carried her to the movie theater, Martin holding her shoulders, Henry her ankles. Thanks to its brick exterior, the building had survived the fire. Its marquee had been updated since Martin had last been in town. It had always read CLOSED FOR RENOVATIONS.

Now it read LIFE. STARRING DARLA.

Henry pushed open the doors with his back and led the way inside. The lobby had been redone too. During Martin and Darla's date, it had been decorated with candy advertisements and synthetic plants. It was now arranged as a giant

239

deck, with cushioned lawn chairs, wicker sofas, picnic tables, and gas grills.

They lay the woman facedown on one of the sofas.

"Lookie here. Brand-new BFFs come to visit the only person who still loves them." Darla stood at the top of the stairway to the theater's balcony. She winked, then descended slowly and theatrically, with one hand on the rail and the other swaying behind her back.

"Hello, Darla," Henry said.

"What'd you weirdos bring to my beach club? Mannequin or something?" she asked as she made her way toward the sofa.

"Not exactly," Martin said.

A couple of steps away, she stopped dead in her tracks. "Hold the phone. Are you kidding me?"

Martin shook his head.

"Who is she?" Darla asked. She reached forward to touch the woman's face and then thought better of it. She drew her hand back to her chest.

"She's a woman who lost her kitten," Martin explained.

"And her mind," Henry added.

"And why is she napping on my wicker?" Darla asked.

"We would actually prefer somewhere safer," Martin said. "Do you have a room that can be locked?"

"How about the projection booth?" Darla suggested.

"That should work," Martin said.

Darla squinted, and her face twisted up in confusion. "Guys," she said. "There's a dart in her head."

A line of lanterns revealed the aisles, and Darla ushered all the kids into the theater with the promise of a surprise. In front of the screen, behind the drawn velvet curtains, Martin and Henry sat on spools of film. "We'll give you a dramatic entrance," Darla had assured them. Through the crack between the two curtains, they could see that almost everyone was there. Only Lane was absent.

"Good evening, gang," Darla said as she stood on a seat in the front row. "I'm guessing most of you thought I was gonna announce that I got the projector running again and we were gonna have the long-promised movie night. Sad to say, but it ain't so."

A volley of good-natured boos were lobbed her way.

"Fair enough, fair enough," she went on. "What I do have, however, is far more exciting. Two of Xibalba's finest, back with intriguing news. Fellas."

That was their cue. Together, they stood, pushed open the curtains, and stepped forward. Strange as it was, having Henry there with him made it much easier for Martin. Pariahs couldn't be pariahs if they came in a pair.

The boos burst forth again, and there was nothing good-natured about them now. Martin could accept that. He had earned it. He wasn't sure about Henry, though. Henry resorted to giving the crowd a meager wave, and they responded with hisses.

"Hear them out," Darla said. "You'll be very interested. Trust me."

When the racket finally lowered to a mild clamor, Martin coughed away his anxiety and got right to it. "There's a woman," he said. "An adult. Still left in the world."

"Sure there is," Tiberia said, her voice soaked in snark. "Teaches home ec at the school, right? Bakes brownies and directs the school play. Can you believe this moron?"

"He's not messin' with ya," Henry said. "I seen her too."

"Where is she, then?" Tiberia asked.

"She's locked away at the moment," Martin offered. "For safety reasons."

"Is that right?" Sigrid responded. "To make sure everything is clear, let me go through it, then, yeah? Martin Maple, the boy who builds giant, dangerous toys. Henry Dodd, the boy who plays with guns and fire. They come to tell us there is a woman, only they have locked her away from us. For our safety."

"Yes," Darla said. "That's the gist of it."

"Prove it," Tiberia said.

A violent thumping sound filled the theater. Everyone turned around. The face of the woman was pressed against the glass of the projection booth. She pounded at it with her fists. It was supposed to be soundproof, but it barely muffled her scream.

"Where! Is! Kitten!"

— 34 —

The Kitten

A bonfire was ruled out. Too many bad memories. They opted for tiki torches, planting them in a circle in Town Square. The chairs and table were configured as they had been during the trials, but it was yet to be decided whether they would hold a trial for Martin. A more pressing matter was at hand. This meeting was about making a decision about the woman, away from the woman.

"Who is she?" Gabe asked.

"We think she was living in the hospital," Martin said. "She believes she's been here her whole life."

"I never saw her in the hospital," Sigrid said. "It does not mean she was not there. I never felt . . . correct in that place."

"What's her name?" Trent asked.

"Pudding something, I think," Martin said without a hint of sarcasm.

"So stupid," Henry grumbled. "She was jokin'. An old person's idea of a joke."

Stupid perhaps, but Martin couldn't help it. He was hardly comfortable with kids his own age. Now he had an adult to decipher. And apparently, this one was insane.

Insane or not, the woman was surely someone, from somewhere, and the kids decided the only way to know her identity was the obvious one: ask her. If her answers were incomprehensible or illogical, then they'd lock her back up and go on with their lives. Martin didn't necessarily think this was the best course of action, but his opinion was hardly valued anymore.

Tiberia was sent to fetch her. While they were waiting, the kids said very little. No one seemed to care what Martin or Henry had been doing during their weeks away. If anything, they were annoyed by the boys' return and the introduction of this new problem.

The woman arrived with a bandage wrapped around her head and her arms tied behind her back. She appeared calm, pacing deliberately as Tiberia guided her to the table and sat her down at the end. Tiberia untied her wrists, whispered something in her ear, and backed away.

"The nurse said that if I answer your questions, then you'll bring me Kitten," the woman said firmly.

They had a kitten. They had six, actually. On the night of the fire, a litter of newborns had been nursing in an aluminum shed behind Nigel's house. They were some of the only animals to survive. A boy named Vernon had taken them in, and the potpourri of tabbies were now waiting in large aquariums in the front window of the Smash Factory. If all went as planned, the woman would spot one that looked like her kitten and cease with her wild accusations. It didn't matter really, though, because they would get answers first. Kittens were just bargaining chips.

"You got it," Darla told her. "Answer our questions and we'll bring you to your kitten. Easy peasy." Darla had appointed herself lead inquisitor, and there had been no objections. History had told the kids that leadership came with few benefits.

"What do you want to know?" the woman said in a perfectly pleasant voice.

"Who are you?" Darla asked.

"Marjorie," she said plainly.

"Where are you from, Marjorie?"

"I'm from here."

"From Xibalba?"

"I don't know what that word means."

"You're in it, lady," Darla said. "But we haven't ever met you. So what have you been doing since the Day?"

"Which day?"

"The day everyone left us."

"The day they emptied the rooms, you mean?" The woman's eyes narrowed on Darla, then moved to the crowd.

"Yes," Darla said. "That day."

"There are only children here," Marjorie said suspiciously.

"Nice of you to notice," Darla said. "Many of us would actually be considered adults in certain cultures, but yes, compared to you, we're a bunch of toddlers."

"It's odd," Marjorie said. "They empty the rooms and leave children in charge. But not even a place for my kitten, so smart and kind."

"I'm sure your kitten is a prodigy," Darla said, "and you

can hear his clever purr once you tell us what you've been doing since that day they 'emptied the rooms.' 'Cause, you know, that's all we really care about here. It was ages ago, Marjorie. Over two years."

"More like a few weeks," Marjorie said with a contemptuous snort. "Children have no concept of time."

Martin didn't like the tone of Marjorie's voice. It was confident. When she had attacked him, her voice was a muddle of confusion and fear. Now it was sharp, sure. She truly believed what she was saying.

"Where were you a few weeks ago," Martin asked, "when they left?"

Marjorie turned her gaze to Martin and she placed her fists on the table. He feared she might make a move for him, and he cocked his chin at Tiberia, who nodded in acknowledgment and stepped closer. But Marjorie didn't budge. She simply said, "Martin Maple. You are one persistent boy. Do you know things that I don't?"

"I believe it's the other way around," Martin said, fighting through the fear that was choking him almost as savagely as her hands had.

"On the day they all left, I woke up in a cage," she said. Then she raised one fist, extended a finger, and pointed through the flicker of the tiki torches to the machine. "That cage."

The machine, poised in the same spot as it had been on the day of its failed launch, did indeed look like a rocket ship, but it also resembled a metal-shelled birdcage.

"No one ever put you in there," Martin said defiantly.

"You lie," she shot back, her voice crackling with menace. "Did you lie to my kitten? When you took him from me? And

I woke up in that cage? And are you going to lie again? Say you didn't taunt me?"

"I never taunted you," Martin said.

"You left Kitten's birthday present in there," she said. "The present I gave him."

Darla seized the reins again, yelling, "What in the half-baked heck are you talking about, lady? We've done nothing to you!"

Marjorie opened her other fist. It held a marble.

"You left Kitten's birthday present sitting in a sink in that cage," she said. "I took it and I waited until I couldn't hear your voices anymore and I escaped from in there. I went back to the hospital, where they're supposed to look after me. But they were all gone. The doctors, the nurses, all of them. They emptied out the rooms. But when they come back someday, I'll tell them what you did to me."

From a distance, in the darkness, Martin couldn't be sure she was holding the same marble that had been in the machine. Marjorie let out an exhausted breath. The marble fell from her hand and rolled across the table. As if guided by instinct, it rolled directly to Martin. He made a wall with his arm, stopping it.

It was the same one.

He began to put the pieces together.

"What is your name?" he asked her carefully.

"I told you. Marjorie," she sighed.

"Your full name," he said.

"Marjorie," she said again. "Marjorie Rice. There. I've answered your questions. Where is Kitten?"

"*Who* is Kitten?" Martin asked.

"Kitten is my son."

— 35 —

The Soap

There had been one morning on the skiff when Martin was watching the men in the lobster trawlers and he asked his father, "What do they think when they see us?"

His father considered the question as he reeled in his line. "They envy us," he said.

"Why?" Martin asked.

"Because we're together," his father said. "They're out working. Their kids are at school. While you and I get to be together."

"Did you get to be together with your father when you were a kid?"

"Not much," he said. "My father ran a circus, which is like a story, but it's real, and it has animals and rides, and it travels. So we were always on the road and that made me angry. One day, I decided to leave my father, and I haven't seen him since."

"What about your mom?"

"I didn't really know her."

"Kinda like I don't know mine?"

"Yes. Kinda like you don't know yours."

"Did that make you sad?"

"It did," his father said with uncharacteristic tenderness. "I'm sure you can relate to that. But I found ways to deal with it."

"You have to."

"True," his father said with a nod. "But my ways were . . . Well, you might think this is a bit strange, but my dad had this metal cigar tin that he carried with him wherever we went. It had a bar of soap in it. He never took it out of the tin. He never used it. Which didn't make sense to me for a long time."

"Maybe it was special to him," Martin offered.

"You're exactly right," his father said. "Because one night I decided to spy on him, and I figured out why. I watched him open that tin and talk to that soap. He was talking to it like it was my mother. I realized that the soap used to be hers."

Martin did indeed find this strange, but he didn't tell his father that. Instead, he asked, "Did he miss her?"

"Most definitely," his father said. "I think the soap was all he had to remember her by. He was obsessed with it. I became obsessed with it too. And whenever my father was working, I would search through his things until I found that tin and that soap. But talking to it wasn't enough for me. I would take an eyedropper and I'd put a few drops of water on it until bubbles formed. I would blow those bubbles off the soap. I'd watch them float and catch the light and become streaked with a rainbow of color. Then they'd pop and melt into the air."

"You told me once that *my* mother was like a bubble," Martin said.

"Did I?"

Of course he did, Martin thought. It was the only thing he'd ever been willing to say about her. Martin mimicked his father's gesture, spreading his fingers out to show a bubble bursting in the sky.

This made his father wag a finger in recognition. "Well, things have a way of coming full circle, don't they?"

"Why would you blow the bubbles away?" Martin asked.

"I felt like my mother was trapped in the soap, and I was letting her out into the world. It helped me deal with things somehow."

"Did your father ever know?" Martin asked.

"He must have, because the soap kept getting smaller, day by day. Yet he didn't say anything. When the soap got to be nothing but a sliver, I was so ashamed of what I'd taken from him that I decided it was time for me to leave. I found a job fixing tractors for farmers and I lived in a room above a barn until I had enough money to buy a farmhouse nearby. I lived there until after you were born. It burned. So we came to the island."

It was the autumn after Martin had met George. Guilt about the secret friendship still plagued Martin, and he wondered if, by telling him this story, his father was trying to hint at something.

"Are you angry with me?" Martin asked. "Have I done something wrong?"

"Quite the opposite," his father said. "You've shown me

patience and you've shown me trust. In ways I never did with my father. So I hope you can understand that sometimes something as small as a sliver of soap can mean the entire world."

None of the other kids wanted to join him, so Martin went alone. Stepping into the machine, he was flooded with the same feelings he had felt when he'd last left it. Empty. Useless. Still, once inside, he pressed on. He pushed open the door to the machine's heart. Almost nothing had changed in there either. The only difference was the marble was no longer in the basin. It was now in his hand.

He set his lantern down next to the basin and examined the marble in the firelight. It didn't appear different or special. In its simple way, it was pretty, but it was nothing more than that. He examined the basin. Empty. Useless.

His father's story about the soap returned to his head. As if piecing together one of the countless mysteries Martin had read, he went through all the clues. Timelines and quotes. Objects and objectives.

The thought came to him in a rush. It was clear. It was right. He was sure.

— 36 —

The Scope

"Does anyone here have an object? Something your parents might have given you?" Martin asked the kids as he approached them.

Heads shook in response.

"It all burned," Cameron said. "My guitar strap, my songbook, all of it."

"Or we left it back where we came from," Trent added. "You couldn't carry much to Xibalba."

Martin thought of his own situation. His father had given him two things—his book and his alarm clock. Both were gone.

"I have something," Henry said. "But whatcha need it for?"

"To test a hypothesis," Martin explained.

"That like a science experiment?" Henry asked. "No thank you. Don't want it melted and covered in chemicals."

"It won't melt," Martin assured him.

"You're gonna need to show me what you're gonna do first."

"That's fair," Martin said. "Come inside with me." He turned to head back to the machine.

"What are we supposed to do with . . . ?" Darla motioned to Marjorie, who was still sitting in her chair but not paying attention to the conversation. Through the torchlight, Marjorie was surveying the burnt remains of Xibalba, as if examining a person's face she only barely recognized.

"Tiberia could bring her to the hospital," Martin suggested. "Room 512. There's a journal there. Show it to her. Tell her it's Kitten's."

"And why should I listen to you?" Tiberia asked.

"You don't have to," Martin said. "Henry and I are going in the machine. We're going to turn it on again. The rest of you can do what you want."

He could have told them his plan, but showing was so much better than telling. He didn't even wait to see their response. He trekked back to the machine and went inside.

Henry joined him a few minutes later.

"Anyone else coming?" Martin asked.

"Naw." Henry walked over to the controls and reached his hands out like he was going to adjust a dial.

"Don't touch. It's already set," Martin scolded.

Henry shrugged and pulled his hands back. "Whatever. If you turn it on, is it gonna make us feel all gooey again?"

"Did Darla tell you that?" Martin checked the controls to make sure Henry hadn't changed anything. He hadn't.

"No," Henry said. "I felt it myself."

"Wait . . . what?"

"Man, you're dumb. I was in Darla's luggage on the day of the launch, you stain. I'm supposta think you got a good hypothe-whatever, and you can't even sniff out a stowaway?"

There was no denying one advantage Henry's short stature afforded him. He could fit in things. It was funny, really, and Martin might even have laughed at the thought of Henry stuffed in a piece of luggage. But he had an important question to ask.

"So you felt it then? And you were okay with it?"

"I ain't afraid of nothin'," Henry said. "If Darla was okay with it, then so am I. It felt kinda good, right?"

"It's because it did something good," Martin said. "It brought Marjorie to us."

Of this, he was sure. The last time he'd turned on the machine, he had been operating on faith. Now he was operating on logic. Logic told him that the machine was never designed to take them anywhere.

"Rice," Henry remarked. "Marjorie has the same last name as Kelvin, you know?"

"I know," Martin said. "It's because she's his mother."

"Who told you that?"

Martin didn't bother explaining the obvious. Rather, he put out his hand. "What do you have for me? Your object?" he asked.

"Oh. Right." Henry reached down beneath the collar of his shirt. A leather cord was strung around his neck, and he pulled at it until a black metallic cylinder emerged.

"Your scope?"

"From my rifle," Henry said. "Dad gave it to me for my first huntin' season. Never needed it for huntin', though. I'm better than that. So I never screwed it on. Only used it for watching."

"Can I take it?" Martin asked.

"Depends what you do with it."

"I'll show you."

He led Henry through the interior door to the second chamber and to the wall next to the basin. "Your father taught you how to hunt," Martin said. "Mine taught me how to build. He told me this part of the machine was its heart. I didn't fully understand why until now."

"Sounds like you're writing a friggin' valentine," Henry said with a snort.

"Not exactly," Martin replied. "Put the scope in the basin."

"Why?"

"You haven't figured it out?"

"Figured what out?"

"It's probably better if you see it."

Martin had the pendulum in his hand and was about to let it go when he realized that he should give Henry the honor. There had never been an apology, from either of them. Sure, Henry had broken into his personal page, but Henry hadn't started the fire. Martin's book probably would have burned anyway. What Martin had done to Henry was much worse. It was deceitful and vindictive, and it had put Henry's life in danger.

Letting Henry drop the pendulum was a small gesture that would echo through the rest of their lives. That was Martin's hope, at least.

"Let it go," Martin said, handing Henry the pendulum. "That's all you have to do."

Henry didn't hesitate. He dropped the pendulum, and the sequence was complete once again. It swung back and forth and ticked out its steady rhythm. Martin pointed to the crack beneath the door to the heart. Light, strong and warm and pure, came rushing at them.

"It's happening," he said.

They couldn't resist. Energy enveloped them, and they began to laugh, and they laughed for as long as the machine held them under its spell, and for the first time since meeting him, Martin saw joy in Henry's face. He liked that side of him. Henry looked like a kid, a true kid.

Then it all went away—the sounds, the light, the feeling in their guts.

Henry spoke first. "So what'd it do?"

"Go back to the basin and you'll see," Martin said.

"It melted my scope, didn't it?"

"Just go back to the basin."

Henry couldn't have known what lay beyond the door to the machine's heart, because he threw it open as he would any door. To him, it was just an obstacle in his way from one place to another. It wasn't a gateway; it wasn't a turning point—at least, not until he stepped through it.

His scope rested in the basin, and in front of the basin, on the floor, sat a man. His legs were splayed out to the sides, and he rubbed his eyes with the heels of his palms. Henry stopped, and Martin watched as he fixed his stare on the man's muddy boots.

The man grumbled and moaned, as if woken from a deep sleep. His eyes remained closed as he pulled his hands away and placed them on his paint-splattered jeans. A wispy goatee of red and gray hairs sprouted from his chin, and when he opened his mouth, he yawned and he ran his tongue along his bottom lip, moistening it with spit.

Henry dropped to his knees.

"Who's that?" the man asked.

When it looked like Henry might topple over, Martin placed his hands on his shoulders. Quick breaths sent tremors through Henry's body, and Martin instinctively tried to calm him by patting his back. It seemed to work. At the very least, Henry didn't slap his hand away.

"Is someone there?" the man asked. He began rubbing his brow in an attempt to break the seal that was holding his eyelids shut.

"It's me," the boy whispered. "Henry."

"Henry?" the man said. "What's going on?"

"We found you, Daddy."

His eyelids peeled back, and Martin saw the amber irises of Henry's father. They were identical to those of his son. Henry crawled toward him.

"Henry?" his father said, recoiling.

"It's okay," Henry said.

"What happened to you? Your face looks different."

"It's been so long since I seen you," Henry said. "Daddy, I'm so glad you're back."

"Where are we, boy?" his father asked. "Who done that to your face, Henry? Where's Mom at?"

This wasn't the time for explanations. When Henry's crawl brought him to his father's side, he collapsed on the man. He wrapped his arms around his chest and nuzzled his face into his armpit. He began to cry.

"I missed you so much, Daddy. So much."

Henry's father didn't look up to see Martin standing in the doorway. He closed his eyes and bowed his head and petted his son on the back. "Whatever it is, it's gonna be fine," he whispered. "Come on now, Hanky. Tell me what's goin' on."

Martin backed away and let them have their moment alone. When he exited the machine, he discovered that Tiberia was gone, and Marjorie with her, but the rest of the kids were still there. Darla approached him first.

"What's the matter?" Darla asked.

"What do you mean?" Martin said.

"You're crying."

"I am?" He brought his hand up to his cheek.

"What happened to Henry?"

Martin smiled. "Leave him alone for a while. He'll be out eventually."

— 37 —

The Wristband

They came out at dawn. Henry led his father past the kids and away from town. His father eyed them suspiciously, and they were all poised to ask him questions, but Henry delivered a stern shake of his head. "Not yet," he told Martin.

Henry's father's name was Keith. At least, that was what Darla seemed to think. She remembered Henry bragging that he was an expert in martial arts. "Keith Dodd," he had told her. "More belts than a . . . a belt store."

Other than his tent, Henry didn't have a place to live, so he took his father to the river, and they sat on an old barge that was docked in a marina. Martin retrieved Henry's scope from the basin, and Darla used it to watch them from the bough of a nearby tree. She reported her findings to the group.

"He brought his dad a beer. And a pear. Can't hear a word, though."

Late in the afternoon, Henry came back to town alone and was confronted with a stampede of queries.

"Where was he?"

"How did he get there?"

"Did he see my parents?"

Henry could offer only one response. "He don't remember a thing about the last two and a half years."

This was hard for the kids to accept, but for Keith, it was nearly impossible. He could see that his son had aged, but for him those two and a half years had gone by in a blip. And to find out that the entire world was gone, that the boys and girls of Xibalba were all that was left? It was almost too much for him to bear.

Martin tried to attribute it to the theory of relativity. If he understood it correctly, the theory stated that people could travel at or near the speed of light away from the Earth, and when those people returned, they might have been traveling for only a few hours or minutes, while years would have passed on solid ground.

It was difficult for everyone to grasp, and there were, of course, problems with the concept.

"But he don't remember traveling into space," Henry said.

"Neither does Marjorie," Tiberia added. Tiberia had brought Marjorie back to the hospital and had sat with her and spoken with her and tried to understand her story. She had also shown her Kelvin's diary. When she had closed and locked Marjorie in her room, the woman had been poring over the pages, whispering, "When could this have happened?"

Martin couldn't explain the inconsistencies. Sure, some alien force might have stolen their memories, or they might have been lying to cover up some vast conspiracy, but there was no evidence to support any of that. Xibalba was now in possession of two confused adults and plenty of confused kids and one big machine.

"How'd you do it? How'd you bring 'em back?" was the one question Martin could answer.

"The machine did it," he told them. "I had something wrong the first time around. It doesn't bring us to them. It brings them to us. We need something they're connected to, though. Maybe a gift they've given us. Like the marble. Marjorie gave that to Kelvin. And the scope. Keith gave that to Henry."

"Does it only work with parents?" Sigrid asked.

"I'm not sure," Martin admitted.

"Because Christianna, my sister, she gave this to me." Sigrid held her arm up and showed them an orange rubber wristband.

That night, Henry and Keith went back to the barge to be alone. Tiberia agreed to bring Marjorie food and sit with her and try to explain what was happening. Trent went to the school to track down Lane and tell her the news. No one had seen Lane in weeks.

The rest of them met in the machine.

The wristband was set in the basin and Sigrid gave it a kiss for good luck. Then Martin went through the sequence again. The cranks and dials and levers and the pendulum. The light came, followed by the laughs, and soon Sigrid was at the door to the machine's heart, waiting for a signal to go through.

When she opened it, she found Christianna on the other side. As Christianna struggled to open her eyes, everyone pushed together in the doorway to get a closer look. Conjured out of thin air was this girl, like a younger version of Sigrid—blond and fit and angular.

"She's your kid sister?" Ryan whispered.

"She is my older sister," Sigrid whispered back. With her hand out, she stepped forward and said something in Norwegian. Christianna answered her in a soft but worried tone. Sigrid began to cry.

Right away, the kids were running wild through Xibalba, digging through the remains of their former homes, trying to find anything to put in the machine. A bit of cloth from a T-shirt that Riley was sure her grandmother had once touched. The twenty-dollar bill Gabe kept in his pocket as a guilty reminder that he had swiped it from his mother's desk on the eve of the Day. Even some melted and balled-up wire that was the braces Vincent had removed from his teeth nearly three years before. His father had paid for them, so it seemed they might do the trick.

None of these things worked. The kids tested the machine over and over, all through the night, but Martin's hunch appeared to be correct. The objects needed to be gifts, things one person had given to another, physical expressions of generosity, not objects passed on by necessity or reciprocity. When they were too exhausted to keep at it, the kids retreated to their beds with a common goal: Rest up. Try again in the morning.

Martin was the last to leave. The sun was teasing the horizon, and the grass was standing a little higher, encouraged by the dew. Mornings of frost were most likely behind them now. Martin's body ached, but it was a good ache, a *finally* ache. Sleep would have to wait, though. Someone was standing at the door to the library. It was Henry's father. It was Keith.

"Are you their leader?" Keith asked.

"I don't know about that," Martin said.

"You're their leader a'right," he said firmly. "Henry told me you boss folks around. Make big decisions."

"I do what I think is right," Martin answered.

"So do I." Keith was not a tall man. He stood only an inch or two higher than Martin. Yet his voice, raspy and ragged, had height. It had a frightening power.

"Is everything okay?" Martin asked. "Do you want me to get you anything?"

"I'm takin' him," Keith said. "We're leavin'."

"Oh."

"Henry tells me there ain't no one else in the world. You kids are the last of the Mohicans. That sounds like a load of bull to me. Somethin' that someone makes up to keep folks from goin' out and findin' the real truth."

"I can see how you might think that," Martin said.

"You can't see nothin' in me," Keith snarled. "You built somethin' powerful there. More powerful than you know. I'm taking my kid away from you. We're gonna find his brother, his momma."

Martin understood what he needed, but he also knew what such a quest would require. "Your wife," he asked, "has she ever given you any gifts? Just out of the blue, 'cause she cared about you?"

"What kinda question is that?" Keith snapped. "My wife is a fine woman. And we're gonna find her. We're goin' home."

"Now?"

"Tomorrow. Henry, he's a bit attached to you folks. We're goin' huntin' this morning. Gonna bag us a few turkeys. He'd like us to have a goodbye dinner."

263

— 38 —

The Kazoo

Thanksgiving had come and gone when the machine was
still living at Impossible Island. No one really cared then.
They would make up for it now, preparing the grandest of
feasts to send Henry off. There were, of course, the turkeys.
They also had some potatoes and squash left over from
Chet's greenhouse. Wendy baked bread, and there were
mushrooms to gather for stuffing. Gnarly crab apples and
canned pumpkin were good enough for pie.

They cooked it all on giant charcoal grills they lugged
into Town Square. Everyone pitched in, and by the afternoon they had a line of tables set with china and crystal.
They giddily filled their plates, picked their seats, and toasted
new beginnings.

Forgiving Martin and Henry wasn't an issue at this point.
The world had opened up and all the kids could talk about
was how they were going to bring their friends and families

back. As they gorged themselves, they made gift lists, annotated with addresses. The plan was they would fuel up Kid Godzilla, and Darla would drive to their old homes and bring back the magical loot. On her way, she would drop Henry and Keith wherever they wanted to go.

Keith hardly said a word during the meal. He passed the food and passed judgment with disapproving sneers and squints. The only time he spoke was when he chided Darla for trying to open up some champagne.

"You're a little girl," he said, grabbing the bottle from her.

"A little girl who's driving you home," she said, angling over to grab it back.

Keith tucked it safely under his arm. "Not so sure about that, sweetie."

"You ever driven a monster truck before, mister?" she asked.

"I've driven pickups."

"Totally different, old man," she said. "Pickup ain't gonna do squat on those crowded roads. And driving the Kid requires skill. You know how to take a hill without flipping? How about the difference between rolling over a minivan and an SUV? 'Cause there's a difference, you know?"

"So where'd you learn how to drive it?" Keith asked.

"My dad."

"Wait a sec," Henry said. "You told us you taught yourself how to drive it."

"That was a lil' fib, Henry," Darla said. "Made for a better story."

"I'll let you drive, 'cause my son says you can handle it," Keith said. "But if I get to feelin' you're nancy-footin' the pedals, then I'm takin' the wheel."

At the other end of the table sat Christianna. Sigrid did her best to introduce her sister to all the kids, but Christianna would hardly raise her head to look at anyone, let alone to say hello. The entire scene must have been terrifying for the girl, and Martin couldn't help studying her, searching her face for an explanation for why she was who she was.

What worried him most was that she hadn't aged at all. She had gone from being Sigrid's older sister to being her younger one. Christianna told Sigrid that she had no memory of traveling into space or anywhere else. So again, if the theory of relativity wasn't the answer, then what was? Martin could imagine all sorts of scenarios, but all were drawn from science fiction and fantasy books. Suspended animation. Cryogenics. Fountains of youth.

The answer couldn't be as complicated as all that. On the island, Martin had taken apart the machine multiple times. He had examined every gear and bolt, every pedal, every piston. He understood the basic mechanics. What he had never questioned, however, was the procedure. The procedure was gospel. He and his father had practiced it so many times that it had never occurred to him to ask, "Why do we turn the crank? Why do we drop the pendulum?" And most of all, "Why do we set the Birthday Dials?" They hadn't been moved since that morning Trent had pointed them out and Martin had set them to the Day.

Martin looked into the sky to see the first star of the evening revealing its face. The stars were the calendar of ancient man. The stars were their map. He did calculations in his head.

"No moon tonight," Trent told him.

"What's that?" Martin was so wrapped up in thought that he had forgotten where he was. Tiberia had been sitting next

266

to him, but she had left to bring food to Marjorie, and in the meantime, Trent had snagged her seat.

"You pay attention to the moon and stars, so you probably already know," Trent said as he handed him a bowl of stuffing.

"Thank you," Martin said. "Don't you want some first?"

"I don't eat stuffing," Trent explained. "Too gooey."

"Know what you mean," Martin said as he took another spoonful. "But I like that about it. I like that there's always new foods for me to try."

Trent nodded at this, then slipped in a confession. "Don't be mad at me, but you probably already figured out that I didn't have any luck with Lane."

"I'm not mad," Martin said, "but I'm sorry to hear it." Martin had really wanted Lane to see the machine in action, if only to prove to her that all their sacrifices were finally paying off.

"I went to the school," Trent explained. "She's still there. She's locked herself behind a door. Room seventeen. I talked to her, and I told her that we could bring her parents back. She said she didn't care."

"We can't force her to do anything, I suppose," Martin said.

"*I* care," Trent said bluntly. "And when I was talking to her, I realized that I have something. For the machine, I mean."

"You do?"

"My kazoo. It's a silly thing, but it was metal and it wasn't completely destroyed in the fire. I forgot, but Mom gave it to me when I was just a kid. Can we try it after dinner?" Trent asked.

"Darla wants to continue the party over at the movie

theater. Besides, it's getting dark and it's probably best to wait for morning."

"It's my mom," Trent said. "I'd rather see her now. She's a doctor, you know? She might be able to help Marjorie. I can probably run the machine myself if you're too busy. I've seen you do it."

It would be cruel to make Trent wait, and Martin realized his mistake. "Not necessary," he said. "Let's meet at the machine around eleven. I should at least say goodbye to Henry first."

— 39 —

The Luau

As soon as dinner was over, Keith declined the invitation to Darla's after-party, opting to catch up on sleep in the bowling alley instead. His son was his only concern, and as he left him outside the theater, Keith whispered into Henry's ear. Henry didn't whisper back, but he hugged his father and then they shook hands, like they were entering into an agreement.

Envy found a harbor in Martin's chest as he watched from a distance, but he couldn't begrudge them their reunion. Was this the way the men on the lobster trawlers had once looked at Martin and his father? Possibly.

When Martin walked through the door to the theater, he was handed a floral-print shirt and a pastel polyester lei. Darla must have raided a party supply store at some point and stockpiled for a luau. Ukulele music filled the room as Cameron strummed cheerfully, and kids gathered around inflatable palm trees and buttoned up their new shirts to get in the mood.

For the next few hours, the party seized the energy from the dinner and amplified it. Chatting evolved into flirting, and flirting gave way to dancing. No one was particularly good, but it offered them a chance to put their hands on hips and lock eyes and see things they had failed to see in their more than two and a half years together as neighbors.

The boys seemed broader in the shoulders and quicker with compliments than ever. The girls' faces were starting to sprout cheekbones that evened out their dimples. They didn't seem the least bit afraid to ask a guy to dance. But Martin turned down their offers and just sat on a wicker sofa and watched. It was the right choice. The food had been so rich at dinner that he could feel it swirling and bubbling as it descended into his intestines. Punishment for indulgence, he figured.

"You can build other machines, can't you?" Henry asked as he flopped down into the seat next to Martin. "Ya know, types that do the same junk as this one?"

"I suppose so, given time," Martin said. "I guess we'll want more, eventually."

"That's cool," Henry said, but he didn't look at Martin when he said it. He couldn't take his eyes off Darla, who was dancing in a circle of girls in the middle of the room. "What are you havin' Darla bring back for you? To put in the machine, I mean."

"Nothing," Martin admitted. "I don't have anything that would work." It was true. The only gifts his father had given him were gone. And really, what else was there?

"You got this now," Henry said. Flicking with his thumb

and finger, Henry sailed a folded piece of paper into Martin's lap.

Martin opened it over his thigh and flattened the creases out with his hands. It was the paper with his father's address on it.

"How did you . . . ?"

"I took it from that stupid book that burned, and I've been holding on to it for, I don't know, angry reasons," Henry explained with a shrug.

Martin was speechless. Of course he'd memorized the address, but he'd been certain that the paper had been relegated to ash. It was the paper that meant something. Its potential was huge, and Martin felt the itch to get right up and head straight to the machine. But first—

"I'm sorry, Henry," he said. "I treated you badly."

"People do bad things," Henry said. "I done plenty of bad things."

"No you haven't. You acted far better than I did."

Henry's eyes were still on Darla when he said, "I used to steal things for Nigel sometimes. Felix thought I was stealin' something the night of the fire. But I wasn't. Not that night. That night I was just lookin'. I wanted to learn. Thought maybe there was somethin' in your personal page that would teach me. That's why I broke into it."

"What did you want to learn?" Martin asked.

"You know about her. You know what she's into and all that. Or you know somethin' about what it takes to make her love . . . to make her like a guy."

Hopping in place and letting her head rock back and forth, Darla might have heard them, but she paid the two boys no mind. She continued to shake and whoo and whinny. It was only ukulele music, but to her it was bliss.

"Darla likes whatever Darla likes," Martin said. "That's all I know."

"I'm gonna miss her."

"I'm thinking you'll miss everybody," Martin said.

"Maybe," Henry grunted. "I guess it don't matter much. I'm taking off in a few minutes, anyway. Promised my dad I wouldn't stay long."

"It was . . . good. Very good to know you, Henry," Martin said.

"Yeah, well, same to you."

Without another word, Henry got up from the sofa. He maneuvered through the crowd unnoticed and stopped by a table of snacks, where he munched alone, facing the wall. This probably wasn't the way Henry had imagined the evening would play out, and Martin decided to flag down Darla, to suggest she shift the focus of the party back to its guest of honor. But as he rose from his seat, he felt the flood and the tension, the twist and the fear.

He needed a toilet.

Plumbing had always been an issue in Xibalba. Rather than figure out a way to make the porcelain toilets work, a boy named Rex had cut holes in the center of armchairs and retrofitted the bottoms with removable buckets. Each kid was responsible for the maintenance and cleaning of his or her own "throne." After the fire, almost everyone was in need of a new model, and at the suggestion of more than one kid, wheels were added. This meant the toilets were mobile.

Martin kept his toilet in a gazebo behind the library. It

was for the view, but also for the fresh air and the privacy. No one could see him back there and he could look into the woods and up into the mountains, and even in the dead of winter, he could feel completely at peace.

Peace was far off now. Martin couldn't possibly make it to the library. The best he could do was grab an empty popcorn tub from a closet and hurry up the back stairs of the theater to a hanging iron ladder that led to the roof. On the roof, he hid behind a ventilation duct, set the tub on the tar floor, and thrust his pants to his ankles.

Hovering over the tub, head in hands, Martin surrendered to the convulsions of pain that pillaged his body. The sound and smell were utterly repulsive and allowed nausea to join in. Soon he was vomiting too. It had all come on much faster than he had feared. He was scheduled to meet Trent in thirty minutes, but he couldn't see that happening now. The only future he could imagine was one in bed.

False finishes kept tricking him. Every moment he thought he was ready to stand, he was forced back down with the rush of sick. Maintaining his balance was near impossible, so he decided to lie on his side and close his eyes. He hummed to himself, hoping the vibrations would soothe his body. All they did was muffle screams from inside the theater and a hoarse voice calling out from the direction of Town Square.

"Martin Maple. Come quick. He's tying it up. Martin Maple. Martin Maple."

A strange buzz was in the air, like the desperate call of a dying goose. And tangled in with it all was the rattle of chains. Dizziness made hallucination the main suspect, and Martin hummed even louder to force it all away.

Only after a bout of dry heaves did he have the confidence to think his body was empty and it was safe to get up. Aching, he found his feet, pulled his pants to his waist, and dragged himself—rigid, crustacean-like—to the ladder.

Weak knees were merely the beginning. Climbing down, he lost his ability to grip and fell hard onto the concrete landing below. It injured his ankle enough that he didn't bother standing up, but even crawling his way down the stairs took every bit of concentration. He could focus on one movement at a time. Right hand forward. Right hand down. Right knee forward. Right knee down. It was two flights of stairs, but it might as well have been twenty.

The screams were dissipating, but odors had muscled into their place. Downstairs, it was a nightmare of the rancid, and as Martin reached the hallway to the lobby, he began to understand why.

Sigrid and Christianna were bent double on the floor, their hands on each other's cheeks. They were pale-skinned to begin with, but their faces were as white as dead coral now. When he came to their sides, he could see that Sigrid wasn't moving. Christianna was whispering into her sister's ear, then mumbling in Norwegian.

"What's going on?" Martin asked her.

She looked up at him with red eyes. "Sick . . . dying," she said. "All of us. Back door is locked. And you cannot get your way past him."

Under other circumstances, Martin would have stayed with them, but moans from the lobby compelled him to keep moving. If the hall was an omen, it was a subtle one. For in the lobby, Martin found a horror show.

Kids were draped over the wicker furniture or spread out

on the floor like slaughtered animals. Most weren't moving. The ones who were appeared pained by it, and they didn't move much. They shifted their weight so they were in more comfortable positions and then they stopped completely.

Henry was the only one who appeared unaffected. He was standing in front of the table of snacks, which had been moved to block the front door. One of the floral-print shirts was wrapped around his mouth and nose like a mask, undoubtedly to block out the foul smells. With one hand, he wielded his knife. With the other, he scooped cups of water from an orange plastic cooler. Martin watched as Henry hurried through the room, setting cups next to the ailing and then returning to his guard post at the door.

Tiberia attempted to get up, and Henry raced over and pushed her back to the ground. Violence wasn't needed. She was so weak that all he had to do was nudge her, and down she went.

On hands and knees, Martin struggled his way to Darla. She was sitting in a wicker chair, completely upright. In both her hands were cups of water. She held them on her thighs as if they were columns from some ancient temple.

"Are we . . . ? What are we . . . ?" Martin coughed the words out as he grabbed the arm of the chair and pulled his head up to the height of her armpit.

Darla's face trembled, but she wouldn't turn to look at him. "I can't move," she whispered. "I can't feel a thing."

It was then that Henry spotted him. "There you are," he said, pointing the knife at Martin.

"Henry," Martin pleaded. "Please help us."

"I *am* helpin' you," Henry said. "Keepin' you all hydrated. I just need to know where that other kid is."

"Which other kid?"

"You know, the . . . little . . . the . . ." Henry tapped the wall with the back of the knife and the sound made Martin feel like he was jabbing the knife into his chest.

"Henry stole the . . . keys to . . . ," Darla said, but her voice trailed off.

"Probably asleep somewhere," Henry finally said. "Like you'll all be in a few. Doesn't matter anyway. He can't stop us alone."

"What do you mean?" Martin asked. "What have you done, Henry?" Nearly everyone in the room was now unconscious, and those who weren't remained frozen in place, their eyes staring in blank terror.

"Mushrooms," Henry said. "Just like you told me. Put 'em in the stuffin' and let everyone chow down. In a few hours, it's nap time."

"Mushrooms?" Martin asked. "Which type?"

"All types," Henry said. "Whatever we could find. It's called playin' the odds, dummy. Don't worry, you'll all wake up tomorrow and you'll start building another machine."

"I don't think you understand," Martin mumbled. "You have to know what . . . each mushroom . . . does. Some could . . . could . . . kill a . . ." It felt like there were fingers over his mouth and the heel of a hand pushing up against his chin, trying to hold it shut.

Henry brushed him off and faced the crowd. In a voice that sounded more innocent than it should have, he said, "Sorry, guys, but this is the way I gotta say goodbye. That's my dad out there. My dad. You understand that, right?"

Holding a hand to the side of his face in obvious embarrassment, he shielded his view of Darla, shoved the table to the side, and went out into the nighttime air, not even bothering to close the door behind him. Martin could hear him for longer than he could see him. The jangle of keys in Henry's pocket indicated he had taken to a sprint.

Giving up wasn't an option. Even though his muscles were clenching up and his ankle was swollen, Martin got on his belly and used his elbows to propel himself through the field of fallen bodies. Hacking as he went, he snaked his way through the inflatable palm trees toward the door. Each time he came upon someone, he checked to make sure the kid was still breathing. They all were. He placed his head to their chests and listened to their hearts. The hollow spaces between beats told Martin he didn't have much time.

It might have taken an hour to reach the exit, or maybe only a few minutes. Martin's brain was mud, and his eyes worked only well enough for him to see a blur of the door, so that was what he focused on. Prying it open with his elbow, he created enough space to slither through.

Outside, the glossy glaze retreated. Martin was given a single moment of clarity to watch the world's fate unfold before him. There, in the middle of Town Square, was Kid Godzilla, coughing and spitting and ready to roll. It was sporting a tail made of thick chains, which were braided and attached to the base of the machine. Martin couldn't see a trailer or even a set of skis below the machine. Still, the truck jolted and the pavement screeched as the machine was dragged behind it. A holler came from the driver's seat.

"Make sure it's moving back there, Hanky! This thing weighs more than a busload of nose tackles!"

Henry's head hatched from the passenger-side window.

"Keep it going, Daddy. It's working. It's not too far to the barge. We can make it."

Sparks fanned out from the bottom of the machine as the convoy surged forward. Martin couldn't move a muscle, let alone catch up. Stomach down, head tilted sideways, he could only watch as salvation screeched its way out of town.

Still, hope remained. Only he couldn't hear it. Had Kid Godzilla not been running full bore, had the pavement been icy and slick, allowing the machine to glide soundlessly along, then he would have known that inside there had been a hum and a whir and a whistle. Now there was laughing.

Martin's heart roared when he saw the evidence. The cracks and tiny holes in the shell of the machine had been filled and welded with due diligence, yet light still found its way through. Stiff threads of white sprouted from the base and moved up to the nose, until the entire thing twinkled like a galaxy. Gravity got its hands in and held the machine in place. It didn't shake or spin or do anything but stay put and shine.

The chain tightened up as Kid Godzilla's engine gave its all.

"Move, you hunka junk! Move!"

Like a mouth releasing rings of smoke, the machine shot a series of glowing billows into the air. There was goodness for a moment, happiness in Martin, even though he was nearly fifty yards away and his body had folded its cards. To see his creation persevere made him proud like a father might be proud. He didn't care if he survived, as long as the machine made it. But as it released a final belch of light, the world went dark and the moment was gone.

The front wheels of the truck rose off the road; then it rocketed forward, yanking its massive captive by the chain.

The machine skipped along the surface a couple of bounces; then it crashed into the ground with a mighty wallop.

Howls rose from the fishtailing truck.

Martin tried to scream them down, but nothing came, not a sound.

The curtain fell on his eyes.

— 40 —

The Dream

Bubbles of light carbonated the sky. An umbrella of stars. The sea was flat, and the rowboat sliced it and turned the water over with the sound of pages flipped through by thumb.

When the sun came up, there was no fog. On the mainland, seagulls hot-stepped the roofs of cars and houses and lobster trawlers left to rot. Above the door to the Barnacled Butcher, Christmas lights were strung. Martin climbed from the rowboat and hurried down the dock. Inside the butcher shop, the kids of Xibalba were hung up by hooks, their stiff bodies encased in floral shirts. Their eyelids were drawn and they didn't say a word. There was a scorching stink inside, so Martin escaped to the street.

Down the street, at the library, lived every book Martin had ever read, shelved in the order he had read them. He pulled *Amazing Tales from Beyond, Volume III* down and turned to "Noah Redux." He read the passage he had once plagiarized, and then he read the final line of the story: *Fifty years later, the astronaut found the periscope in a tide pool, where it had become home to a dose of crabs.*

A tiger emerged from the shadows of the stacks. There was a lobster in its mouth. It dropped the lobster and lunged at Martin, who dodged and slammed into the shelves. The books were launched into the air. When the books landed, they landed on their spines, stacked up, and built the walls of an intricate maze. The lobster led the way through the maze until the walls of books were walls of trees, and Martin was approaching a campfire.

Kelvin Rice sat by the campfire, a dollhouse in his lap. As he placed a bottle inside, he turned to Martin and said, "Oh God, don't tell me you're like him."

"Like who?"

"Never mind," he said. Then Kelvin pushed the dollhouse into the fire and Martin watched it crumble into embers.

When he looked up from the flames, Martin was no longer in the woods. He was by a campfire in the Ring of Penance. Keith and Henry were there too, poking at the burning logs with the muzzle of a rifle and the blade of a knife. At Martin's feet, he found a series of letters written out in pebbles. They were the first initials of the names of all the kids from Xibalba. Without realizing what he was doing, Martin arranged burnt bits of wood into a message.

I'M SO SORRY.

"You built somethin' powerful there. More powerful than you know," Keith said, and he pointed down the mountain to the river, where the machine was sitting on a barge, shooting rings of light into the sky.

Martin sprung to his feet and sprinted down the mountain. In no time, he was in Chet's backyard, then in his house, where he found a framed copy of the Declaration of Independence and a scene both gruesome and surreal—Chet crushed beneath a giant peanut in the living room.

Through the living room window, Martin spied a marching band that had taken to the street to play a rouser of a tune. Trumpets and snares and fiddles ablaze. The band consisted entirely of the zombified kids of Xibalba. They looked exactly the same as they had in the butcher shop—floral-shirted, eyelids drawn. Only they were moving now, parading toward town.

Martin left the house and joined them in their march, but they halted when they reached a sign that read ZOMBIES KEEP OUT, NO BRAINS HERE. They would go no farther. Still, Martin soldiered on, and Trent, Tiny Trent, provided him with a sound track in the form of a buzzing kazoo.

Alone in Xibalba, Martin visited the church and the bowling alley and the movie theater. Nothing had burned, but nothing was occupied. Xibalba was a ghost town, no different than the ones he'd encountered when he'd first left his island. It frightened him beyond words, so he decided to find solace in the forest. He proceeded to a trail. He followed it to the mine shaft.

Guarding the mine's entrance was Felix, clothed in a glimmering jacket made from firefly lightbulbs. "Use the string," he told Martin. In the middle of Felix's forehead was a perfectly round hole, and out of the hole came a string. The string was taut and it led straight into the mine. Martin

held the cotton between his thumb and forefinger and he followed it, zigzagging through the tunnel of puddles and stone.

Ahead of him he heard the voice of Darla: "Everyone was gone and if it had been a dream, then I would have known it was a dream and pinched myself awake 'cause it was all so crazy. But I was awake and afraid and alone."

And he heard the voice of Marjorie: "This was supposed to be the meeting place if we got lost, for me and Daddy and Kitten. All of us, together for once."

And he heard the voice of Lane: "Thought it would have at least burnt us to a crisp, Captain. But you didn't have the guts, did you?"

He didn't see any of them. The string only led him to a glowing door. On the door, there was a message, written in fire:

Greetings, Martin! Come in.
Have a seat in the living room.
You will find the red chair to be lovely.

In Nigel's living room, Martin sat in the red chair and waited. The dogs and cats and goats and pigs swirled through the room in organic chaos and then dropped to their bellies one by one. When they all were lying down, someone entered the room.

It wasn't Nigel. It was Martin's father. He was accompanied by a deer, a live deer. He approached his son cautiously.

"What happened on the Day?" Martin asked him.

"I think you know that," his father said to him as he stroked the back of the deer.

"I don't think I do. Why don't you tell me?"

"You used your machine," he said matter-of-factly.

"No I didn't," Martin said just as the tears started coming. "I was on the island, waiting for you. It was my eleventh birthday, and you were supposed to be home. But you left, just like the rest of them."

"I left because you used your machine," his father said again. "Not the one we built. The one you built. And you will keep using it and they will keep coming. There will be more and more of them, until the place becomes a theme park."

"I don't understand. I never understand anything you say. Why me? Why us? Why were we left behind? Why were we the only ones?"

"Because it couldn't have happened any other way," his father said. Then he leaned in and hugged his son and his chest covered Martin's eyes and splashed darkness over his world.

Bubbles of light carbonated the sky. An umbrella of stars. The sea was flat, and the rowboat sliced it and turned the water over with the sound of pages flipped through by thumb. . . .

— 41 —

The Bottle

On a nightstand, by his bed, Martin saw little bits of
metal—copper handles and thumbtacks and bolts.
There was also a line of tiny bottles, nine in all, warped and
blistered brown. Next to the nightstand, a series of medical
machines beeped. Or they clicked. A couple flickered.

"He's awake," Darla squealed.

The rumble of a generator filled the room and tickled
Martin's muscles through the mattress. He couldn't sit up.
He could only lift his head to see Darla bouncing excitedly on
her knees in a chair at the foot of the bed.

"Yeehaw!" she hooted. "Martin Maple. Back from the
dead!" Wild and loose-limbed, she came at him and kissed
him all over the face.

The sheets were tight, and he wished that he could push
or kick them loose, but he was far too weak. He turned his
head and gave her a cheek to assault. On the floor, he saw

extension cords and wrinkled balloons. Outside was a leafy flutter, but he couldn't feel any breeze, because the windows were closed.

"Am I . . . ?" he whispered.

"Hospital, room 112," Darla said, backing away and catching her breath. "Your home for almost three months. Man, is it good to hear your voice. Or to hear it outside of your crazy dream world. You wouldn't wake up, but you kept mumbling those same questions, over and over again. Hope you found your answers."

For now, Martin needed only one answer. "How?"

"You got here like we all did," Darla said. "Trent and his mom. Thank God that kid doesn't like stuffing. But I mean, really, what kind of weirdo doesn't like stuffing?"

Martin rubbed his face and pulled together his last waking memories. "That night. He was . . . ?"

"In the machine, bringing his mom back," Darla replied. "Flipping switches and cranking cranks, like he's doing right now. Kid pays attention."

"But Henry and . . . ?"

"They couldn't even get past the bowling alley, the amateurs," Darla said, laughing. "Once Trent summoned his mom, Tweedle Dum and Tweedle Dumber got all freaked out and ran into the woods. We haven't seen them since."

"They're still . . . out there?"

"Lots of people are out there," Darla said. "'Cause lots of them can't handle it. Not our concern. We summon them. Hopefully they learn to deal."

"Y-you . . . ?" Martin stuttered. "I'm . . . I'm sorry, but what . . . what . . . has been happening?"

"Tons," Darla said. "Dr. Bethany was lucky enough to

get the combination to Tiberia's safe before the big girl went all comatose. Then the doc got us all on medicine, got us healthy, and most were up and at 'em in a week or two, saving the world. You, Martin Maple, were a heckuva lot more stubborn."

"Three months?" Martin shook his head. "But . . . everyone's okay?"

"Well," Darla sighed, "when you're feeling up to it, I'll show you around."

For the next two days, Martin worked hard at recovery, to prove that he was feeling up to it. Dr. Bethany, a small and stern woman, visited him every couple of hours to take his vital signs and ask him questions. She was shocked to find that Martin could stay awake for long stretches and that he had a big enough appetite to eat three full meals a day, considering he'd been fed by a tube and a syringe for the past three months. His body was weak, but his motivation made up for it. He shunned all visitors for fear that they would only encourage him to rest. He needed to get up and see for himself what had happened out there.

Three days after he woke, Martin pleaded with Dr. Bethany to release him for a quick tour of town. She relented but wanted him back in bed in a few hours.

"Not everything at once," Dr. Bethany advised Darla as the two hoisted Martin into a wheelchair. Darla flashed her the OK, then swept an arm across the nightstand, knocking the little bottles and bits of metal into a shoe box.

"What are those for?" Martin asked.

"Had a scavenger hunt at your old place," Darla said as she slipped the box onto a shelf beneath the seat of the wheelchair. "Thought we'd dig up something you could use. Hope you don't mind, but we also picked your pockets. Found a piece of paper with an address on it. Sorry, but I haven't had a chance to get to that place yet. You tell me what's there, and when I'm out that way, I'll fetch it."

"Oh," Martin said. "I don't really know."

"One thing at a time, right?" Darla said, and she patted him on the shoulder.

The wheels chirped as she pushed the chair from the room, down the hall, to the back exit where they used to exchange books and notes. Outside, there was a freshly blazed, firmly packed dirt trail, and it was a short trip along the trail to a hilly clearing, where pieces of limestone stuck up from the ground. There were names painted on the stones.

Martin saw Felix's name, and Chet's. Also Sigrid's, and Ryan's, and Cameron's, and Wendy's.

"We moved Chet and Felix here from the regular graveyard," Darla explained. "But it's all temporary. Until we get their parents back, and they decide what to do with them."

"What's that?" Martin pointed to a shovel that was sticking up from the ground like a tree. Its handle was buried in the dirt and its spoon was pointed into the sky.

"Monument to the Diggers," Darla said. "We went in the mine, you know? Marjorie insisted that we check it out. No bodies in there, just the stuff they brought with them. Weird, huh?"

Martin nodded. He had thought about that fact a lot, and perhaps he had been thinking about it for the past three months as he dreamt the same dream over and over again. Because he was pretty sure he knew what had happened to them.

"Is Lane still around?" he asked.

"One thing that hasn't changed," Darla explained. "She hasn't left the school since you last saw her. People say they see her sneaking around town at night. Hard to believe, though. She'd block out the moon!"

"You haven't changed either, have you, Darla?"

Darla winked and turned the wheelchair toward another trail, which led to town. "Sweetie," she said. "I don't have time to change. Making movies and driving and looking after your sleepy butt can keep a girl plenty busy."

Xibalba was a flurry of activity. People of all shapes and sizes shuffled between the remaining buildings. Some were in groups, led by kids Martin recognized, like Riley and Gabe, who pointed to landmarks and spoke in amplified voices. A man in a ruffled suit wandered aimlessly and shouted to no one in particular, "Don't believe them! It's damnation, people. We're in Hades!"

Before the man could say much more, Tiberia appeared from a nearby building, accompanied by a group of stone-faced boys. She approached the man and spoke to him calmly, though Martin couldn't hear what she was saying. Whatever it was appeared to appease him. He smiled, and she put an arm around him and led him away.

As Darla pushed Martin through town, his eyes jumped from new face to new face, and he pondered the countless stories the faces guarded, but he didn't have the courage to introduce himself to anyone.

"It's kind of a transfer station," Darla explained as she waved toward where all the torched houses had once been. Demolition had left vacant lots, and nothing was being built in their place.

"How long do people stay?" Martin asked.

"Depends," Darla said. "There's a bit of a system. They're greeted by someone they know, then they watch the movie, then they . . . Well, every case is different. There have been some difficulties, obviously. Violence."

"They watch the movie I watched?" Martin asked.

"Not exactly," she said, pointing the chair toward the movie theater.

The lobby of the theater had been redesigned once again. It was airy and clean and empty except for a single desk. Christianna sat behind the desk, poised with a pen, a leatherbound book open below her hand. A line had formed in front of the desk, and people were approaching in twos. They would say a few words; she would write in the book; and they would proceed into the theater.

When it was Darla and Martin's turn, Christianna hardly looked up. "Hello, Darla. So you have finally brought someone, yeah? Name?"

"Martin Maple," Darla said proudly.

Christianna pulled her pen back and leaned forward to peer over the desk at the wheelchair. "My goodness," she said. "He *is* awake. Well, this is very good news, is it not?"

"Very good news," Darla said firmly.

"Hello, Christianna," Martin said.

"Please, please, go on in," Christianna said.

"No," Darla said. "Let's get the whole dog and pony show. I'm sure he'd like to see how it's done."

"Okay, then," Christianna said, wielding the pen. "What is your full name?"

"Martin Maple."

"What is your age?"

"I'm . . ." Martin had to think about this one. His birthday hadn't come, had it? "Still thirteen," he said with a fair bit of confidence.

"Where are you from, Martin Maple?"

This one would require even more thought, or perhaps introspection. "Here, I suppose," Martin said. "Xibalba."

"We call it Ararat now," Christianna said. "Like where Noah finished his trip. I wanted to name it Asgard, but no one cares about Norse mythology around here." She shrugged and smiled and she wrote in the book.

It was dark inside—not pitch-black, but dark. Lanterns were scattered along the aisles, and cigarette lighters flicked to life among the seats as people huddled together and whispered. Martin's wheelchair fit in a nook in the back, and Darla sat next to him and used her hand to rock the chair gently on its wheels. Martin might have stopped her if it weren't so soothing.

After a few minutes, Christianna entered and paced through the room, dimming all the lanterns. When she dimmed the last one, she closed the door and stood next to it. "Please. Quiet," she announced. "Our film is about to begin."

The chatter trickled away, revealing the rumble of a generator. Then the screen was struck with a punch of white light, which expanded and swirled and then dissolved into a soup of color. When the color became crisp, when it sharpened into focus, there was the image of Darla, sitting cross-legged in an armchair.

"Greetings," she said. "My name is Darla Barnes. If you're watching this, then it means you made it back from wherever the heck you were. You know what? It's mighty fine to see you."

The image on the screen shifted to shots of the town— the crumbled houses being cleared away, the muddy trails and budding trees, the remaining fortresses of brick that were the library and hospital and bowling alley.

"This is Ararat," Darla's voice narrated. "Not exactly paradise, but it's the place we've called home for almost three years. We used to call it Xibalba, and it was cuter than this, trust us. But we've had some problems. There were incidents."

The screen went black. The sound of Kid Godzilla's engine dominated the sound track. When the light returned, the audience was looking at a highway and a flat, endless landscape pocked with immobile cars. The shot was taken through the windshield of the monster truck. It bobbed up and down as the truck lumbered forward.

"These are your roads," Darla narrated. "Talk about gridlock! Work is under way to clear them, but for now Kid Godzilla is king. It's taken its fair share of licks, but the Kid can still roar. And every three weeks I drive it loaded with your lists and I come back with your loot. We have a pamphlet to explain, but for now, know this. We'll reunite you with your friends and family as soon as we can."

The screen went black again and music swelled, a swooning mix of strings and piano. Martin recognized the tune as one Darla had piped into the bowling alley on the night of their date. When the images came back, they were of cities, colonized by weeds. Cars everywhere. Buses on their sides. Shattered windows and tiny tornados of paper. Deer and wild dogs strolling carefree over the concrete and glass.

"Just so we're clear: these are your cities," Darla narrated.

Next the images were of small towns, of main streets abandoned, of front porches broken and covered in leaves, of ransacked general stores, of cornfields and orchards left untended.

"And these are your villages."

Now the images were of Xibalba again, of Ararat, but they were taken from the roof of a building. The camera zoomed in on Town Square, on a crowd of kids circling the machine, cheering as it shot light into the air and pulled another rabbit out of its hat, as it belched forth another bleary-eyed person.

"This is us. You left us. We don't know where you went. We don't know why you went. But we brought you back. And this is the world. Welcome."

Black.

There would be one last stop. The sun had set, and Martin was due back at the hospital, but he needed to see the machine. It was in Town Square, dented and scratched, though otherwise intact. Leading up to it, a series of metal gates formed a trail of switchbacks. Martin had seen a similar setup at Impossible Island; crowd control was the purpose.

Darla lifted a chain that hung over the entrance, and pushed Martin inside. "You should see this place during the day," she said. "Line around the block and getting longer by the minute. Can't have people here at night, though. Too dangerous for Trent. At sundown, they move the line out to the tent city in the fields behind Chet's old house. We call it Nylon Vegas, and what happens in Nylon Vegas . . . well, let's just say that funny business doesn't fly near the machine."

As they weaved their way along, Martin read a series of signs that decorated the path.

From this point, your wait will be three hours.

**We regret to inform you that we can summon
only one person at a time.**

**Two objects per person per day, please.
No exceptions!**

Two boys stood at the entrance to the machine. Martin didn't recognize them, but their faces lit up when they saw him.

"Holy cow, is this really him?" the shorter boy said.

"Martin Maple, in the flesh," Darla replied.

"Pleased to meet you, sir," the other boy said, putting out his hand. His shirt rose and Martin saw a sliver of steel peek out from the waistband of his jeans.

"The same," Martin said with a grimace. The bones in his palm had been temporarily rearranged by the boy's enthusiasm.

"Is he awake?" Darla asked.

"Getting ready for bed," the first boy said. "Long day today."

"Mr. Maple would like to see him," Darla explained.

The two looked at each other. The taller one nodded. "I think we can make an exception for that," the shorter one said.

Inside the machine, they found Trent stomping method-ically on a plastic set of bellows to pump up a rubber air mattress. Hearing the door, he stopped and turned around. His eyes were watery and bloodshot and it took him more than a moment to recognize who was sitting in the wheelchair. According to Darla, he saw dozens of new people every day.

"Martin?" he asked.

"Hello, Trent," Martin said. "I hear you've been hard at work."

"I've . . ." A combination of guilt and pride colored Trent's face.

"I'm impressed," Martin said. "You've done a fantastic job."

"Thank you," Trent said.

"He's here twenty-four seven, guarded by his cousins," Darla explained. "No one gets to see him work, but, boy, does he work wonders."

"I don't do anything except what Martin did," Trent said humbly. "I'm like a substitute teacher."

"You do more than that, I suspect. How do you . . . ? What happens here exactly?" Martin asked.

"Well, it's pretty simple, actually." Trent explained, "Every morning, people line up outside. I place their objects in the basin, run through the procedure, and summon their loved ones. No one else is allowed inside, so no one else knows how I do it. I summoned my cousins first. Now they take shifts guarding the machine and watching the line and making sure everyone is orderly. Most of the time, people are."

"What if someone gets out of control?" Martin asked.

"We don't like it, but we have guns," Trent sighed. "We've been lucky so far, but they're demanding new machines in new places. It can't go on like this forever."

"No. I guess it can't," Martin said. His arms were just strong enough to push him from his chair onto his feet. Standing for the first time in months, Martin felt as if his chest and shoulders weighed a thousand pounds.

"Martin," Darla chided. "Dr. Bethany doesn't think it's time."

"I think it's time that Trent went home," Martin said as he toddled forward. He placed a hand against the wall to brace himself. "It's my responsibility now."

"Oh no, Martin," Trent said. "It's an honor to run the machine for you, and if my mom wants you to rest, then I think you should rest."

"I'm sure your mother also wants to spend time with her son," Martin said with a smile. "Go . . . just as soon as you finish pumping up that bed. I'm sleeping here tonight."

They let him. After all, this had been the plan. The night of the disastrous dinner, Trent had run the machine out of necessity. Things had gained momentum from there, but it was never supposed to be his calling. It had always been Martin's mission. Trent was happy to hand back the reins.

"You remember how to do it?" Trent asked as he left.

"It would be impossible for me to forget," Martin said.

Yes, the procedure was written in Martin's bones. He didn't doubt that he could do it in his sleep, and once he was alone, he thought maybe that was what it would come to. He hardly had the strength to keep his eyes open. Yet through those three months of suffering the same dream, there had been an idea rattling in Martin's mind, something impossible to shake. It gave him the strength to put his wobbly hands on the controls.

Martin turned the Birthday Dials. He set them to the morning after he arrived on the mainland, after he had outrun the bears, after the campfire and the conversation with Kelvin. He set them to the moment when Kelvin had left him alone in the woods. Then he crawled back to the wheelchair and he retrieved the shoe box of metal bits and bottles that Darla had placed on the shelf beneath the seat.

The bottles had been cleaned, but they were still brown and warped, hardly the glittery little jewels that had once sat in that strange dollhouse. Martin took all nine and he struggled his way through the interior door, to the machine's heart. He placed the first one in the basin.

It wasn't until the fourth one that it worked. And thank God it did. Martin was at the point of collapse when he dropped the pendulum that fourth time and was greeted with a *tick, tick, tick* and a whir. But also the light. Also the laugh.

In the heart of the machine, next to the basin, Kelvin Rice had emerged. The boy tried to pry open his eyelids, and Martin spoke to him.

"Are you okay?"

"That you, Martin?" Kelvin asked. "You been following me?"

"When did you last see me?" Martin asked.

"Weird question, buddy. I saw you like two minutes ago, when we traded goodbyes," Kelvin said as he finally got his eyes open. He took in his surroundings with a suspicious squint. "Though I'm drawing a blank as to how we got here."

"This is the machine."

"Is this what I was supposed to be looking for?" Kelvin asked. "Nigel said I'd know it when I saw it. For a little while I thought he might be talking about you. But I gotta say, this thing is a lot more impressive than you, Marty."

"You're done looking," Martin said. "There's only one other thing for you to do now."

"What's that?"

"You're going to lift me into that wheelchair, and you're going to push me to the school."

"School?" Kelvin asked. "Which school?"

"You'll know once we get outside. There's someone you need to see."

As Kelvin helped Martin get situated in the chair, Martin reached over to the Birthday Dials. He adjusted them until they were once again set on the Day.

As soon as Lane heard Kelvin's voice, she turned the lock and opened the door to room 17. Martin pushed off with his toes, scooting his chair back along the linoleum floor, and let the two of them look at each other.

They couldn't have been more different in appearance—Kelvin pale, tattered, and gaunt; Lane dark, sleek, and curved. She held her tears back, a battle that quivered through her cheeks. She reached forward and touched him lightly on the ribs.

"Hey, kid," Kelvin said.

"Hey, kid," Lane said back.

"I'm not sure how I got here. I can't say I understand what's going on," Kelvin said.

"I can't say I do either," she said. "But you're here. Standing right in front of me."

"I am."

"I got some peanuts inside," she told him.

As Kelvin followed Lane into the room, Martin hovered in the doorway.

"Hello, Martin," Lane said. "I'm glad to see you're still around. Crazy world you dug up out there."

"I'm . . . ," Martin started, but what he saw beyond the door derailed his train of thought.

It was a scanty low-ceilinged room, the antithesis of Lane's previous abode. The walls were brick, and the floor was concrete. Candles in glass vases decorated ledges, and trunks, and wooden crates. A Ping-Pong table, with a stack of boxes on it, was pushed into the corner. The boxes held kits for model cars and boats and trains. Lane pulled a woven wool blanket off a grimy plaid sofa and draped it over her shoulders. She patted one of the seat cushions.

"I can't believe it," Kelvin said as he spun in circles, marveling at every object in the room. "It looks just like my basement."

"We had a fire," Lane told him. "Your house didn't make it. It took some looking. It took some lugging. But I found stuff that matches pretty closely."

"It's perfect," Kelvin said. "You did this for me?"

"No, not really," Lane admitted as she picked up a wooden bowl full of peanuts. She gave it a shake in front of Kelvin's chest, and the peanuts scuffed and scraped the wood. "I did it for myself. Those nights hanging out in your basement were some of the best times I've ever had."

"They were?" Kelvin said, reaching for some peanuts.

"Of course."

"They were for me too."

"I missed you, more than I've missed anything." With a hunter's stare she watched him chew the peanuts. "Thank you, Martin," she said, not turning her head.

One of Trent's cousins met Martin outside the school. He pushed Martin back through town and helped him into the machine.

"We'll be outside for you, Mr. Maple," the boy told him. "Just let us know if you need anything."

"Thank you," Martin said. "Sleep is what I need."

The boy nodded and left him alone, and Martin lowered himself onto the inflatable bed. He pulled the covers up to his neck, and he let his mind linger on a thought. He remembered that night months back, when he was alone on the ocean, rowing the boat away from his island. He remembered thinking that on the mainland there was a world where all the books he had read were born. The books told stories, and the endings to the stories that still stuck with him weren't always the ones filled with happiness. They were the ones that could end only one way.

"Mr. Maple?"

"Yes."

"She's not here."

"What?"

"She's gone."

"But where?"

"We don't know. She went to the bathroom. Then . . . we lost track of her. The doctors, the nurses, we've all been looking."

"She just . . . disappeared? But is he . . . ?"

"He's in the nursery. He's beautiful."

The Summer People

MARTIN MAPLE lived in the town of Ararat, in a sturdy brick library a short walk from a machine his father taught him how to build. The machine hummed and whirred every day, and it brought forth laughs and people. When they arrived, the people were shown a movie in the local movie theater and they were told that the world was new.

Not far from Ararat, up and down the river and east and west into the mountains, were other towns waiting to be sparked back into existence. It wasn't as easy as some had hoped. Even adults, capable and confident ones, knew little about what starting from scratch really meant.

Clearing roads was a priority, and the monster truck named Kid Godzilla was nearing retirement. It still traversed the country with Darla Barnes at the helm, and it came back every three weeks, packed to the scales with objects. Once families had been reunited, they called forth friends, and neighbors, and coworkers, and teachers. They brought back anyone who had left pieces of themselves behind in the form of gifts. They brought them back one at a time, but occasionally two people would appear in the machine. Babies, and toddlers, and kids who were just too young to have had a chance to make their mark would materialize alongside someone they loved and trusted.

"Innocence is their gift," was Trent Bethany's explanation for the anomaly.

Martin had a slightly more pragmatic answer. "Until someone is ready to survive alone, they're inevitably bound to someone else."

When other doctors volunteered to work at the hospital, Dr. Bethany, her son Trent, and their family went on their way. This left Martin as the only person in Ararat permitted to run the machine. It was one of the rules. There were many rules.

At night, Martin would remove a few essential pieces from the machine, rendering it useless. He would sleep with the pieces hidden beneath his pillow while a series of trustworthy guards patrolled the town and protected the machine and its master. In the mornings, Martin would return the pieces to their designated places and cater to the swirling line of eager folks who waited with their trinkets and their WELCOME BACK signs.

Darla brought her parents back on a brilliant summer afternoon, when the clouds were hearty but white, and the soggy ground had firmed up from a spat of blazing days. She used a jump rope and a necklace.

"Don't laugh," she told Martin.

"Why?" he asked.

"Because they're regular," she sighed.

Martin didn't know if they were regular, but the Barnes were a quiet couple, in sweatshirts and nylon pants, and when their daughter saw them, her impious smile disappeared and she became a mush of sniffles and giggles. Martin couldn't join them in the theater, but he assumed that Darla sat next to her parents and watched them as they took in her movie. When they left the theater, Darla held both their hands and showed them Kid Godzilla, and they listened intently as she chattered nonstop. Martin heard there was something close to awe in Darla's father's eyes. Finally, she brought them to the bowling alley to eat lunch.

They would leave a few days later. Ararat couldn't hold everyone, nor should it have. With the roads opening and nearby communities coming to life, Ararat was merely a gateway, and Martin a gatekeeper.

"Come with us," Darla pleaded to Martin.

He wanted to, more than anything, but the rules paralyzed him. Until he allowed someone else to operate the machine, he was committed to it. "I can't," he told her.

She understood why, and she didn't argue, but Darla being Darla, she made a proclamation. "I'm going to come back for you, Martin Maple. And I won't let you say no again."

Then she kissed him on the lips and he didn't have time to think about it. He could only experience it. It was a fragile and lovely thing, like ocean fog at dawn. It bloomed and it held and it was gone.

Tiberia Davis still lived in Ararat, but with the influx of adults, her strength was less in demand and her knowledge of medicine and vitamins was no longer unique. This didn't bother her, however, because through her experiences with Marjorie Rice, she learned that she possessed a hidden talent. She could talk to people, set them at ease. Almost everyone needed someone to talk to these days. So she convinced her family to stay in Ararat with her, where she could do the world some good. At least for the time being.

Every once in a while, Tiberia would visit Marjorie in the hospital, but doctors and Marjorie's son, Kelvin, and his girlfriend, Lane Ruez, provided the primary care. Marjorie was medicated now. Her mood swings and delusions were kept mostly at bay, but her survival would always depend on the help of others. It consumed much of Kelvin's and Lane's free time, so they rarely stopped by to see Martin. Neither of them had much interest in the machine.

A few people posed an obvious question: how exactly had Kelvin come back if he had never disappeared on the Day? Martin didn't get into details. He didn't talk about the Birthday Dials. He simply said that the machine brought Kelvin, and he left it at that.

"Can it bring back dead people too?" was often the next question. And they trucked in gifts from the deceased. No matter what they tried, it never worked. The dead were gone, and gone for good.

Martin sometimes found himself thinking about the boy named Nigel Moon and wondering about the night of the fire, when he had sprinted back into his burning house. They had never found Nigel's body. Had he burned away in there or had he escaped into the woods? Was he still alive?

The question mattered less and less as the summer went on, until it didn't matter at all. Nigel was both dead and alive. He was both a con man and a prophet. He was a nurturer

306

and he was a murderer. He was almost anything you wanted him to be. But he had never been one of them. Gifts, the kids' links to people from the past, were more than simple objects. They were symbols of connections. Nigel never had any real connections, at least not with humans. There were probably no gifts in Nigel's past, given or received.

The only gift Martin had was the one he thought he'd never see again. It was that piece of paper with his father's address.

A few nights after Darla left, Martin decided not to return to the library after his long day of work. He stayed in the machine instead, and when he was sure the line of lonely souls had been led away, he finally did something for himself. He placed the piece of paper in the basin. He summoned George Hupper.

Martin was nearing his fourteenth birthday, but George was still a ten-year-old, fresh off his summer visit to the island and as confused as everyone else who had been funneled into the future by the machine. Rather than showing him Darla's movie, Martin walked the scared boy down the trail past the mine shaft and up a hill to a clearing, where the moon held them in its snug light. There he told George the story of his last three years.

Over the next few weeks, a fleet of trucks went into service and set out on reconnaissance missions, including one that would stop in George's hometown. Meanwhile, George remained in Ararat, and every night, he and Martin met in that clearing on the hill, and Martin told him everything he could about their new world. The Internet might have been ash, but it still lived in Martin's mind. So he enlightened George about Chet and Felix and Sigrid and the greenhouse and Impossible Island and the Arrival Stories and the marble and the Diggers.

"You ever think about why no one found the Diggers' bodies in the mine?" George asked one night.

"Sure I do," Martin admitted. "It's because they never died in there. I'm going to bring them back someday."

"How you gonna do that?"

"We know the date and time the mine caved in. Ask Kelvin. He can give you the exact moment. The Diggers left things behind, and some of those things are probably gifts. Those gifts will help summon people, and those people will provide us with gifts that will help summon the Diggers."

"But the Diggers didn't disappear on the Day, right?"

"Neither did Kelvin," Martin said. "Let me show you something."

Martin led George down from the clearing and to the trail. They walked past the entrance to the mine shaft and back into town. Martin's guards patrolled the empty streets, but there was an anxiousness in the air. As dedicated as these kids were, they were still just kids. You could see it in their tentative steps. You could hear it in their stutters. They wouldn't be able to handle their duties for much longer.

They accompanied Martin and George to the machine and opened the door to let them in. Once inside and alone, Martin showed George the control panel.

"The machine has levers and switches and all sorts of things to make it work. But it also has a calendar, a way to set a date." But Martin didn't reveal what that calendar was. He didn't show George the Birthday Dials. As much as he trusted his friend, he knew that it was best if only one person knew how to set the machine's date.

"Why would you set a date?" George asked.

"Because you have to pinpoint the exact moment in time from which you want to summon someone. When my father and I built the machine on the island, the date was supposed to be set to when I was born. And I'm pretty sure it was only supposed to summon one person."

"So what's different about this machine?"

"Well, first of all, it's summoned a lot of people. And second, I've set it to other dates. I've set it to the Day."

"You never told me what caused the Day."

"I'm telling you right now," Martin said in a calm but somber tone. "I caused it. This machine caused it. It started when I summoned Marjorie. Then Henry's father, Keith. Then Christianna. And it kept going while Trent was at the helm. And it will keep going, well into the future, whether I'm running this machine or thousands of other people are running thousands of other identical machines. We'll keep bringing people back, one person at a time, until everyone is here again."

George walked over to the interior door. He opened the machine's heart, looked inside, and said, "I don't know if I get it. So where did they all go on the Day?"

"No one escaped into space, or underground, or to an alternate universe," Martin explained. "They came to the future. Some of them have made it here already. A whole lot more will be coming later. That's why people don't age between the Day and when they emerge next to that basin. Not a second has passed in their lives, while here . . . well, years have passed."

"So they all disappeared at the same moment, but they end up in different times?"

Martin nodded. He understood that it might be a bit confusing. "It helps if you think of people like they're a school of fish. On the Day, every fish in the school bit a hook and was pulled out of the water. But each hook brought each fish to a different moment in the future. The machine's calendar is set to the Day. So every time we use the machine, we drop one of those hooks to that exact moment in the past, and we hook one of those fishes and bring them to the present."

It was hard to say whether George fully understood what Martin was telling him. While they used to be peers, Martin was now the elder, someone for George to look up to. George closed the door to the machine's heart and sat down next to the control panel. He sat cross-legged and stared at the jumble of knobs and levers and buttons in front of him.

"Why don't you stop using the machine, then?" he asked politely.

Martin had thought of that, of course, but he knew it couldn't happen. "I've read a lot," he told George. "The thing is, you can read a book a bunch of times, and while the story may seem different, the words are always the same. Once the words are on the page, they don't change. The Day happened. There's no changing that. This will go on, for years and years, for as long as it takes, because everyone disappeared, which means everyone will be brought back. That's the way the story was written."

"But you're talking about the future?"

"The future is written too, and it affects the past," Martin said plainly. "People like me will think about old friends like you, and we'll put objects like that piece of paper in machines like the one I built, and we'll drop all those hooks, and we'll hook all those fishes. It's inevitable. We'll keep causing the Day. We'll keep making them all disappear."

George was starting to grasp how monumental this was. He turned his attention to his own hand and traced the lines in his palm with an index finger. In a whisper, he asked, "Are you the only person who knows this?"

Martin shrugged. "For now. But then again, everyone just wants to be reunited with the people they love. That's all that matters to them. And when they figure out what I'm telling you, they'll also figure out that there's only one way to see those loved ones again."

Martin motioned with his head to the controls of the machine.

"There's something that doesn't fit, though," George said, lifting his chin and finally looking Martin in the eyes.

"There is?"

"You didn't disappear. Why were you and those other kids the only ones who were left?"

For a brief moment, a breeze of memory swept over Martin and his mind sailed back to his first lonely summer on the island, to those days sitting on the rock outcropping and waiting for the summer people to arrive. He remembered worrying that George, the only person besides his father he'd ever known, had simply forgotten about him. That worry had lived with Martin for a long time.

"Lane told me once it was because we're awful," Martin said. "I don't think that exactly. I think it's because we chose to live alone, secluded from the rest of the world. As the years go on, and more and more people are remembered and summoned, no one's ever going to think to summon us. We're the only ones who were forgotten. So in the long run, we're the only ones who *will* be forgotten."

Martin could tell from George's squint that he wasn't buying it. "They're gonna make movies about you guys.

311

Write songs. Books. They'll write more books than even you can read, Martin! They'll keep on telling the story about how you kids got the world working again."

"Really? You think so?"

George stood up and placed his hand on Martin's shoulder. "You didn't live alone. You were a bunch of amazing kids who created this crazy machine and put the world back together. People won't think to summon you because they'll know they won't have to. Everyone will know that you were here all along. You're the only ones who'll always be remembered."

It was true. The logic could go either way, but Martin had never considered that before. "It's possible," he said. "It's a nice way of thinking of things, I guess."

It was late. They were tired. So they left the machine and walked back to the library, and on the way George mused about all the stories that might be written about Martin and the other kids. Perhaps someone would tell the tale of Henry and his dad and their cowardly escape on the night of the luau. Maybe they would imagine the conversation between Darla and Nigel on the afternoon of Chet's funeral. Felix's arrival in Xibalba could surely be fodder for a chapter of a book. His strange sparks of genius deserved at least that much. And while Lane was unlikely ever to tell anyone besides Kelvin what past pain had given birth to her cynicism, plenty of wordsmiths were sure to speculate.

Of course, they'd all want to write about Martin's father, about what kicked off this chain of events in the first place. Because everyone loved an origin story.

"Heck," George said as the two paused outside the library. "I was never much of a reader, but I'd read all that stuff."

"So what will my story be?" Martin asked.

"Yours? Yours will be a hero's story," George said.

"Hardly," Martin said, guilt flavoring his voice. "I'm just a kid who convinced myself I knew what I was doing. When I didn't. But that doesn't matter, does it? 'Cause I'm also just a victim of inevitability."

George wrinkled up his nose. "Do you know the future? I mean, you say that everyone is gonna be brought back, but do you know exactly how that's gonna happen?"

"No," Martin admitted.

"Have you ever known exactly how anything is gonna happen?"

"No."

"Then who cares about inevita-whatever?" George said, his smile flattening out the nose wrinkles. "You just go out and try to make the best of things. And that's what you've done, right? That's all you can do, right?"

Now Martin's thoughts drifted to the kids of Xibalba and how they'd always seemed so self-absorbed, so different from George. But were they really all that different? What if the entire world had been pulled out from under George's feet? How would he have found comfort? How would he have survived? How would he have made the best of things?

Martin remembered the kids holding the lanterns and welcoming him into their odd little community. Not even a year had passed since then, but those kids weren't kids anymore. They were out there in the world, beyond the lights of Ararat and the campfires and high beams Martin could see dotting the banks upriver and the roads through the mountains. He couldn't speak for everyone, but he was pretty sure that despite all their mistakes and all the forces of fate they were bound to find themselves up against, his former neighbors would always try to make the best of things.

Martin gave George a simple nod of agreement.

"I should make the best of things too," George replied. "When I see my parents again, I'm gonna have 'em bring me to your father's old address. See what I find."

"There's nothing for me there," Martin replied. "Just a place my father and I once lived. It burned a long time back. Besides, I don't even remember it."

"But you wanted me to go. I haven't forgotten that."

The autumn came in, furious and orange. Wind and rain whipped Ararat, but the machine ran nonstop. Keeping busy put a mask on Martin's loneliness, but it was still loneliness. George left soon after his family was summoned, and Martin was without a best friend once more. Other people swept through his life with barely a hello. He would summon them, and he would usher them to the door, and he would never see them after that. Then he'd do it all over again. The only difference was the weather when his guards walked him home every night.

It didn't sit well with many adults that a boy could have so much power. People arrived confused and compliant, but men and women who had lingered in the vicinity of Ararat for months were beginning to band together and call for Martin's removal.

The Council for a Blessed Kingdom, as one collection of overly zealous citizens named themselves, invited Martin to a secret meeting nearly a month after his fourteenth birthday and the third anniversary of the Day. It was a torrent outside, one of the nastiest storms in memory. With his cabal of guards accompanying him, Martin arrived, cautious and drenched. He sat on a cold, hard wooden chair, below a stuffed moose head, in a hunting lodge a few miles up the river.

A man named Crawford Dixon presided over the meeting, and he was a no-nonsense type, even though his features were soft and small and his voice wasn't much more than a gravelly whisper.

"We could have you . . . removed . . . if we wanted," he told Martin, his patronizing gaze gliding over Martin's guards.

"I'm sure you could," Martin admitted.

"You are, however, a hard worker and a genius of some sort," Crawford said. "So here is how we will proceed. The Council has chosen five people who will be your apprentices. You will teach them how to build the machine, and how to run the machine, and they will each teach five more. And things will go on like this until these machines are like post offices. Every town will have one."

"I assumed that this would have to happen," Martin said.

"So you comply?"

"Do I have a choice?" Martin asked.

Crawford answered the question by jotting down a quick note, looking up, and saying, "We start tomorrow."

On the way back to Ararat, Martin made a decision, if it could be called that. He knew that his days running the machine were numbered, so he would do as instructed. He would teach them how to build new machines, but he would make one small change to the blueprints. All the Birthday Dials would be permanently set to the Day. Because if anyone other than Martin had the ability to conjure people from times other than the Day, then there was too much potential for chaos. The future could become a place where the vindictive or the heartsick or the just plain curious could snatch people up with the push of a button, the flip of a switch, the simple turn of a dial. Martin wouldn't let that happen.

When he finally arrived home at the library, the rain was so heavy that he didn't notice the Jolly Roger flying on the flagpole. He bid his guards good night, and he ducked inside, already plotting out the revised blueprints in his head.

From his seat on the edge of the circulation desk, a smiling and soaked George greeted Martin with a wave.

"My goodness," Martin said in shock. "Are you okay?"

"Never been this far north this time of year," George replied as he wrung water from his sleeve.

"It can be dicey," Martin told him.

George held an envelope in his hand. Somehow, he had kept it dry. "It used to be a farm," he said with a smile. "It's only a field now, down a dirt road, far away from anywhere. I think there was a house. There was concrete that my dad said was probably the foundation."

"You really went?" Martin asked.

"Of course I did."

"I appreciate it."

George pushed the envelope at him. "There was a tree. A maple. It wasn't too big. On the ground next to it, there was a plaque. You know, like for a statue or something. I did a rubbing, using a broken pencil."

He pushed the envelope at Martin again. Martin took it and picked lightly at the corner until he had made a small hole. Running his pinkie finger along the seam, he opened it. Inside, there was a message written in chalky, chunky gray.

TO MY DEAR HUSBAND, GLEN.

WE ARE HAVING A BOY!

MAY HE AND THIS TREE

GROW HEALTHY AND HAPPY TOGETHER.

ALL MY LOVE,

HOPE

Taped to the bottom of the page was a small maple leaf, no bigger than a boy's hand.

The alarm clock Martin's father had given him on his eighth birthday had told him he was born sometime shortly before 12:21 a.m. The exact moment of his birth wasn't as important as the moment his father received the call about it. He turned the Birthday Dials. He set them accordingly.

He went through the rest of the procedure. When the sounds and the light and the laughs were finished, Martin opened the door to the machine's heart.

Behind the door, the maple leaf sat in the basin. A woman lifted herself to her feet. Her eyelids wouldn't open immediately, so Martin decided to wait. He wouldn't speak until he saw her eyes.

The woman wasn't much older than Martin. Eight years. Maybe ten. Her auburn hair was thick, but tangled. She pulled it away from her eyes with damp hands. Her face was similar to his, but it wasn't like looking in a mirror for Martin. It was like opening a book he'd never read but somehow knew the story to by heart.

"Is this the bathroom?" she said, squinting.

"No. But you're safe," Martin told her.

317

"Are you an orderly?" she asked.

"My name is Martin," he said. "Your name is Hope, right?"

She smiled as she ran her hands down the long, papery gown she wore. "It is. And my son's name is Martin as well. But I haven't met him yet. They had to put me under when he was born. He's in the nursery now."

"You'll meet him," Martin assured her. There was a shimmer to her, and even in the darkness, he could see what his father had meant when he'd equated her with a bubble. She was gorgeous, but she seemed destined to disappear in a blink.

"I have to get back to my room," she said. "The doctor will be expecting me. And I don't want to worry my husband. He'll be on his way. Martin came a month early. He was a surprise."

"Stay," Martin pleaded. "I have some things I need to tell you."

"You don't understand," she said. "My husband is out of town on business. They're calling and waking him and he'll be on his way. I didn't tell the nurses I was going to the bathroom. Nobody knows where I am."

Back on the island, there was the smaller version of the machine, the one Martin had built with his father. Martin assumed it still sat in that empty room in that gray-shingled cabin, where they had lived and worked and waited. That version of the machine had a glass door, which opened into its heart. In the heart, there was a small basin at the back of a tall hollow chamber.

Looking at Hope now, Martin imagined an alternate past. He imagined an alternate eleventh birthday, where his father's skiff was arriving safely on the island. He imagined his father stepping out from the boat, with that tree branch resting over his shoulder and the alarm clock tucked under his arm. He imagined the two of them climbing the ladder and going to the cabin and pulling the machine out into the yard. He imagined placing that branch in the basin and running through the procedure and laughing with his father and looking through the glass door into the machine's heart and seeing Hope standing in there, looking back at them. She had the type of eyes that memories held on to, the type you yearn to see again.

But that moment never happened, because it was never meant to happen. This was the moment life was giving Martin, and he didn't care whether he had any choice in the matter. He was taking it.

"Don't worry," Martin told her. "Your husband figured out a way to find you. And together, we can figure out a way to find him."

ACKNOWLEDGMENTS

JAMIE WYETH. I don't know him, but his painting planted a seed.

ELISABETH WEED AND STEPHANIE SUN. They cast a light on a strange little sapling.

REBECCA SHORT AND MICHELLE POPLOFF. With patience and brilliance, they pruned and watered and trusted.

JENNIFER BLACK. Her clear eyes and magical pencil set things straight.

LISA ERICSON AND VIKKI SHEATSLEY. Give them an object and they'll summon art.

CATE STARMER. She encouraged. She believed. She loved. None of this could have happened without her.

ABOUT THE AUTHOR

Aaron Starmer is the author of *DWEEB*. He lives with his wife in Hoboken, New Jersey.